REPENTANCE

REPENTANCE

ANDREW LAM

TinyFox
PRESS

A Tiny Fox Press Book

Cover design by Damonza

Author Photo by Todd Lajoie

Library of Congress Catalog Card Number: 2018959663

ISBN: 978-1-94-650112-7

Tiny Fox Press and the book fox logo are all registered trademarks of Tiny Fox Press LLC.

Tiny Fox Press LLC
North Port, FL

PRAISE FOR *REPENTANCE*

"Andrew Lam has penned a gorgeous, emotional book that fans of *The Nightingale* and *Hotel on the Corner of Bitter and Sweet* will devour, tissues in hand. Focusing on a Japanese American family, and moving fluidly between WWII France and late 90s California, *Repentance* is a story of honor and sacrifice, of loss and reconciliation, but most of all, of love. An important, and timely, American story."

—Karin Tanabe, author of
The Diplomat's Daughter and *The Gilded Years*

"*Repentance* is the story of a man who grapples with the mystery of his parents' past, not knowing if it is heroic or tragic, discovering that it is both, and coming to terms with it. At the same time, it's the wider story of what Japanese Americans suffered at home and abroad during WWII, where they shone bright on the battlefield. Suspenseful, touching, and beautifully written."

—Margaret George, *New York Times* best-selling
author of *Elizabeth I* and *Helen of Troy*

"Gripping, engrossing, and poignant. *Repentance* reveals the nature of combat and its affect on men long after the guns fall silent."

—Susumu Ito, 442nd Regimental Combat Team veteran and
recipient of the Bronze Star and Congressional Gold Medal

"In *Repentance*, Andrew Lam poignantly explores one man's search into his father's past during WWII, only to discover just as much about himself along the way. What follows is an intimate, revealing, wide-reaching story of family secrets, sacrifice, love and honor during a turbulent time in Japanese American history. Lam has written a thoughtful, compelling story that sheds light on a long respected group of Japanese Americans whose sacrifice and struggle lingered long after the war ended."

—Gail Tsukiyama, author of *The Samurai's Garden* and
The Street of a Thousand Blossoms

"Readers will be moved by Daniel's plight as he desperately tries to understand a father for whom he still harbors profound resentment. A poignant, nuanced tale of familial pain and renewal."

—Kirkus Reviews

For Christina

AUTHOR'S NOTE

On February 19, 1942, President Franklin D. Roosevelt signed Executive Order 9066, authorizing the War Department to forcibly relocate approximately 110,000 persons of Japanese ancestry from California, Oregon, Washington, and Arizona to ten isolated inland "internment" camps. Many evacuees were given less than a week's notice and, as a result, lost their jobs, homes, and any property they could not carry with them. More than two-thirds of the evacuees were American citizens.

In 1943, the 442nd Regimental Combat Team was formed as a segregated unit comprised of Japanese American soldiers. These volunteers from Hawaii and the relocation camps distinguished themselves again and again in difficult campaigns in Italy and France. They became well known for bravery, initiative, and self-sacrifice. The 442nd was ultimately awarded an unprecedented seven Presidential Unit citations and twenty-one Medals of Honor. It is considered the most decorated unit in U.S. military history.

ONE

PHILADELPHIA, PENNSYLVANIA
Hospital of the University of Pennsylvania
September 1998

An unbroken line of blood ran across the white-tiled floor, smeared at one point by a wheel track. It came from the patient waiting area, a sinuous cherry red stripe, a painter's brushstroke too perfectly haphazard to be anything but frighteningly real. Dr. Daniel Tokunaga scrutinized the scarlet streak, momentarily mesmerized until a pair of EMTs brushed past him, disappearing through the Emergency Room's swinging, frosted-glass doors.

Daniel followed and suddenly found himself thrust into bedlam. Shouting voices. Running bodies. He jumped—a cascade of supplies tumbling off a nearby shelf. A nurse cursed, dropped to her knees, frantically searching for something crucial. Across the room, a police officer struggled to restrain a prisoner—or was it a patient? From their beds, two drunks, an asthmatic, and a boy with a broken leg stared at the unfolding melee.

1

"Crash cart, now!"

"O-negative blood!"

"Page trauma and CT surgery, stat!"

An overhead speaker blared: "Code Blue, Emergency Department, Code Blue."

"Dr. Tokunaga?" A shrill female voice. Daniel turned and recognized the charge nurse. "How'd you know about this? I haven't even paged your service yet."

"Just cutting through on my way home. What is this?"

"Gunshot. Kid dumped out of a car. Driver yelled 'innocent bystander!' before zooming off—the damn thugs."

Daniel's face tightened. Gang bangers. Known to speed by and slow down just long enough to open the door and roll out their wounded friends.

He peered across the ER toward the trauma room, already overflowing. They would need either him or the cardiothoracic surgery fellow on call. Daniel wasn't assigned to back up the CT fellow, but he knew none of the surgeons driving in from home would arrive in time to make any difference.

"CT surgery to the ER stat!" an announcement rang out.

Daniel looked at his watch and swore under his breath. The twins would be disappointed. Beth would be furious. Already, he regretted staying late to attend a meeting for the hospital's department heads.

But as he found himself moving toward the trauma room, he felt a burst of adrenaline. He came to the swinging doors and slipped inside.

A dozen people filled the room. Near the head of the gurney, an ER resident bent low to assess an airway. At one arm, a nurse struggled to insert an IV—at the other, another tried to draw blood. A couple of medical students stood against the far wall, petrified.

Daniel recognized the ER attending, Sam Griffin, a rotund and affable man just a couple of years removed from his residency, an average clinician by all accounts. Griffin's face was pale. Beads of sweat

2

glistened on his brow as he shouted orders.

"Type and cross six units now!"

"Get O-neg now!"

"Watch his neck! Watch his neck!"

Daniel caught a glimpse of the gurney.

My God, he's just a kid.

The patient was a thin Hispanic boy no older than fifteen. The resident was cutting off his T-shirt, a dripping, bright red rag. The boy's eyes were closed. He made ragged little breaths. When he coughed, droplets of blood mixed with spittle ran down his chin.

"Vitals?" Griffin asked.

The wheeze of a deflating blood pressure cuff made Daniel look toward the monitor: BP 60/30. Way too low.

A nurse fumbled with the boy's arm. "Very thin. I can barely feel a pulse."

The resident who'd cut off the shirt carefully rolled the boy over. "One exit wound in the back," he reported.

The shrill alarm of a telemetry monitor rang out. Daniel looked— the blinking numbers had turned from green to red. Dangerous tachycardia—the heart was racing at 180 beats a minute. Yet the pressure was low and there was barely a pulse . . .

Daniel knew: the boy would be dead in minutes.

"No pulse!" the nurse cried out, wrestling the boy's limp arm. "Now I can't get a pulse!"

The resident leaned in close to the patient's face, checking for a breath. A moment later, he looked at Griffin and shook his head.

Griffin's mouth opened but no words came out. Seconds passed. The boy's face began to pale. The resident started chest compressions.

"What's going on here?" Daniel said.

All eyes turned to him. Sam Griffin's face flushed with relief.

"Dr. Tokunaga! Thank God. Gunshot wound, left chest."

Daniel took off his Armani suit jacket and began to roll up his sleeves. "Gown, gloves, mask," he commanded.

"If you're not actively participating in this code, then leave the room. Nobody speaks unless they are directly addressing me about the care of this patient. First," Daniel pointed to Griffin, "intubate. And you," he pointed to the resident, "get a femoral line. You—" he pointed at one of the medical students, "Get over here and restart compressions once the endotracheal tube is in."

Daniel leaned in close. Entry wound in the chest, just left of midline. It was small—just a dark black gouge the size of a dime. Blood oozed out of it.

Griffin crouched over the head of the bed, laryngoscope in hand, squinting as he tried to insert a long plastic tube past the vocal cords and into the trachea.

"You okay, Sam?"

"Almost . . . got . . . it . . ."

"Go for a right main stem intubation. Push that tube in as far as you can."

"What?"

"Right side only. I want the left lung collapsed."

"Dr. Tokunaga?" a new voice interrupted. Daniel spun. It was the ER charge nurse. "X-ray is here."

"No time for that."

"We're in!" Griffin proclaimed. He briefly listened for breath sounds on both sides of the chest. "Right side only. Start bagging."

"Restart CPR," Daniel said. He noticed Niraj, his cardiothoracic surgery fellow, had just arrived. "Niraj, get a thoracotomy kit."

Niraj hesitated. "No echo or chest tube? What about a pericardio-centesis?"

"No time. Move it!"

Ten seconds later, Daniel had a scalpel in his hand. A nurse swabbed betadine quickly across the chest. Daniel felt the position of the sternum and made a deep, curving incision from the midline across the chest laterally to just under the left armpit. His hands glided effortlessly, maneuvers he had performed thousands of times. Above the fifth rib, he dissected through the pectoralis muscle and used the tips of blunt scissors to go deeper. He felt a pop as he entered the pleural cavity and a foot-high fountain of blood shot up, nearly hitting him in the face. A nurse gasped.

"Block it!" Daniel said.

The nurse deflected the blood with her hand. Daniel leaned in to enlarge the opening. When he did, the stream of blood began to flow across the chest and onto the gurney. It puddled on the floor.

"Chest full of blood," Daniel muttered. "Rib spreader."

Niraj handed him a large metal retractor, shaped like a C-clamp. Daniel placed the blades between the ribs and turned the crank to draw them apart.

"Suction."

Niraj placed a plastic handpiece into the chest cavity. As the space between the ribs widened, Daniel pushed the collapsed left lung aside to expose the pericardium.

It was bulging, tense, and dark.

"Scissors."

Sam Griffin stared, wide-eyed.

"It's tamponade," Daniel explained. He cut a small hole in the pericardium. There was a gush of blood.

Daniel felt the heart pulsing beneath his hand. On the monitor, the EKG line jumped jaggedly.

"More suction." He enlarged the opening in the pericardium and began to inspect the heart. Blood flowed more briskly now.

Where was it coming from?

He used his fingers to gently feel the front and back of the heart. Then—he saw it and felt it at the same time.

There was a small hole at the edge of the right ventricle.

Was part of the bullet inside the heart or had it passed all the way through? Daniel stuck his finger through the hole and felt inside the pulsing chamber.

Nothing.

He gently lifted the heart and turned it slightly.

"More suction."

No exit wound in the back.

He returned the heart to its normal position. It was a tangential wound. The bullet had grazed the heart then gone out the patient's back.

"We've got to plug this hole to stop the bleeding."

"Can you suture it?" Griffin asked, incredulous.

Daniel ignored him. "Get a foley."

"What?" the nurse said.

"A foley, dammit! You know, foley catheter—you stick it in so people can pee. Hurry up."

She ran into the hall and returned moments later with a thin rubber tube. The foley catheter had a double lumen—when inflated, the outer space at the tip of the catheter became a small balloon that normally kept the tube inside a patient's bladder and prevented it from sliding out.

Daniel threaded the catheter through the hole in the heart. "Inflate it," he said. Niraj gently depressed the plunger of a small syringe to fill the balloon inside the heart with saline. Through the heart wall, Daniel felt the tip of the tubing inflate.

"Stop."

Now the small balloon in the right ventricle was the size of a marble. Blood flow inside the heart pushed the balloon against the hole, plugging it.

Daniel watched the monitor. The EKG line jerked up and down irregularly.

"Ventricular fibrillation. Give me the internal paddles and charge to 20 joules."

A nurse handed him two small metal paddles, which Daniel placed on the front and back of the heart.

"Clear." Daniel shocked the heart, which froze momentarily, then began to beat regularly.

The EKG returned to normal sinus rhythm.

"There's a pulse!" the nurse called out. The next blood pressure reading came on the screen: 90/45. Better.

A little cheer went up among the others in the room.

Daniel looked at Niraj. "We've bought him some time. Keep a close eye on the foley. If you need to, just keep a little tension on it like this," Daniel demonstrated, "to make sure the balloon stays against the hole. Continue wide open fluids. Start transfusing; as soon as the first unit is hung I want the second unit spiked and ready to infuse. And get him up to the OR. I'll see you there in fifteen minutes."

"You got it," Niraj said, awestruck. His boss had just brought a kid back from the dead. "But Dr. Tokunaga, I know you're not on call. Do you want me to call Dr. Feinberg? I just finished a case with him and I think he only left about twenty minutes ago."

"No, don't bother him. I can see this through."

Daniel was glad to see the color returning to the boy's face. He turned away, stripped off his blood-soaked gown and gloves, and walked out. There was blood on his leather shoes, and also on his pants near the ankles.

In the hallway, he stopped one of the nurses.

"What's the story with the kid? Do you know?"

"A policeman just told us. There was a shooting at 49th and Spruce. Probably gang-related. This kid was just walking home from school after basketball practice. Wrong place, wrong time."

Daniel felt a hand on his shoulder. It was Sam Griffin.

"You were amazing in there, Dr. Tokunaga. Thank you so much."

"You do what you have to do. That's all."

"Will it be a tough case? To close that hole in his heart?"

Daniel shrugged. "I'll do my best." He cleared his throat and shifted his gaze to the cell phone in his hand. "Would you please excuse me?"

He needed to call Beth and explain why he'd miss dinner and the special night with the twins. Heaving a sigh, he dialed.

"Hello?"

"I'm really sorry, honey. Something's come up in the ER just now—"

"—you're not coming?" Beth said.

"I'll be there. Later."

"Later?"

"Probably after dinner," Daniel said. He felt his voice tighten. "Pretty late, actually. A kid got shot in the chest. He's stable right now but I've got to take him to the OR."

"But you promised the kids. It's James' last night."

"Yes, I know—"

"You're not even supposed to be on call. I asked you last week, when we planned this. Isn't Steve on call?"

"He is."

"Then why can't *he* do whatever this is tonight?"

"Well, because I've already started with this case and I have to see it through. I can't walk off now . . ."

"Can't or *won't*?"

Daniel didn't answer.

"Julia's going to be *so* disappointed. She baked her brother a beautiful cake with a big, ugly Yale bulldog on it. You've got to see it, Daniel."

"I'm really sorry."

"So . . . you won't make it before ten, is that right?"

"I don't think so."

Daniel heard Beth exhale in annoyance. An orderly pushing a gurney came around the corner and Daniel flattened himself against the wall to avoid being bumped.

"You know what?" Beth's words were hard and carefully spaced. "It's fine. We'll take a picture of the cake. I'll tell the kids we'll see you when we see you. Simple as that."

"I'm sorry, Beth—"

He heard a click, followed by silence. She'd hung up.

He closed his eyes and rubbed them. The tension was rising in his chest—twenty years of marriage, and the same thing over and over.

The cell phone rang. Niraj.

"Yes?"

"We're about to get started up here."

"Okay, good. Open the chest properly and I'll be there in a second."

Daniel snapped his phone shut and drew a deep breath. He really did regret missing this evening with the kids. They'd both grown up so fast. And now it was James' last night before heading off to college in the morning.

For a moment, Daniel couldn't keep his thoughts from drifting to his own college days, and the words that his father had spoken to him. Beth would appreciate the irony, he thought. With effort, he managed to purge the memory. It did no good to remember a past that no one could change.

TWO

D aniel slowed his black Lexus to a stop in the driveway of his Swarthmore home, a large, grey stone colonial on two manicured acres. He went inside and up the stairs. A glance at the wall clock: one a.m. Quietly, almost secretively, he opened the door to his bedroom. In the darkness, Beth was an inert mound, a range of seemingly distant hills obscured by the covers. Then her body suddenly shifted.

Was she awake?

Daniel froze, then drew closer and, by the light in the hallway, watched her face in repose. Her blonde hair and light freckles gave her a girlish look that made her look younger than her actual age. But her taut lips, closed eyes, and furrowed brow made him wonder if she was having a bad dream.

He stood there, half in darkness, half in light, thinking.

For a few months now, Beth had seemed different. Her moods often changed from day to day, or even within the same day.

10

Sometimes talkative and energetic. Other times reticent, tired, and off to bed before nine.

Menopause?

Or because both kids were leaving home at the same time?

After years of controlled chaos, the house was going to be that proverbial empty nest. He could already hear the echoes of children, grown and gone—and the kids were still here—what an odd thing that was, the way things played out in the mind with past, present, and future all jumbled.

Daniel left Beth to her dream and brushed his teeth. Then he got into bed, but before stretching out he leaned close and kissed Beth's forehead. There was a time when he'd kiss her in her sleep and she'd always stir a little, and sometimes even smile.

This time, she didn't stir.

Daniel awoke to Julia's shrill voice coming from downstairs.

"What the hell? No way are you taking that!"

"Why not? I use it more than you do!"

Daniel rubbed his eyes. Sunlight glittered at the edge of the still-drawn curtains. He glanced at the alarm clock and sat up abruptly.

"Mom! James is *not* taking the new Powerbook! I need it to run the videos for my design projects."

"You mean you want to use it to watch weird movies in your dorm," James countered.

"You have no idea what I do or don't do. You're an idiot."

"Look, all my stuff's already on this one. You can take the other one."

Daniel staggered out of his bedroom and steadied himself at the rail near the top of the stairs. Looking down, he saw James at the front door with a large black suitcase at his side and a tennis bag, large enough for six rackets, slung over his shoulder. Julia faced him, her hands on the contested Macintosh laptop held tightly in James' grip.

11

Beth came into the foyer.

"What's this about? We've got to hurry or James is going to miss his train."

"We have two laptops," Julia explained. "One's two years old. This one's new." She made a face. "James didn't even ask me before I saw him packing it up."

"Does it *really* make a difference?" Beth asked impatiently.

"This one has 32 megabytes of RAM. It's a lot faster," James said.

"That's why *I* need it," Julia insisted.

"You don't even know what RAM *is*."

Beth crossed her arms. "You two are just going to have to work this out—" she glanced at her watch, "—in the next fifteen minutes— because we've gotta go."

Daniel cleared his throat. "Why don't we just buy another one?" he said.

All three of them looked up. Beth frowned.

"We shouldn't *just* buy a new one," she said. "We have another perfectly good one already."

Daniel shrugged. "Trying to help, that's all." He looked at Beth defensively. "Sorry, I guess I overslept. Can I still bring James to the station?"

Beth's shoulders sagged—a sign of weariness that, to Daniel, seemed exaggerated and meant to emphasize that she'd been single-handedly managing everything in his absence. "If you want to," she replied. "You've got to hurry or he'll miss it." To James—"Everything ready? Did you forget anything? How about your rain boots? It rains a lot in New Haven."

"Oh, right. I forgot. Thanks, Mom."

"And I bet you forgot your umbrella too. How are you ever going to take care of yourself up there? Make sure you eat at least one piece of fruit a day, by the way, and—"

"—Okay, Mom, okay." James wrested the laptop from Julia's hands and said, "Dad will get you a new one, Sis."

Daniel headed to the shower. He hated when the twins argued. When he was home, he liked it quiet. Serene. Everyone getting along. He would just buy them another computer. How much could it cost? Twenty-five hundred? Totally worth it to have some peace in the house. And besides, it's always best to treat the kids equally, he'd always said. But it didn't surprise him that Beth didn't like his quick solution. She wanted the kids to learn frugality. Like the way she was raised in Minnesota, in her family of rigid, rugged Scandinavians.

Ten minutes later, Daniel was dressed and ready to go. He came down the stairs and found James rearranging the contents of his tennis bag. His son was lean and darkly tanned. Naturally, most girls liked his looks—that bronzed, chiseled face that some called exotic because it wasn't easy to place, until they learned he was half-Asian. James straightened up. He was a head taller than Daniel.

"Looks like your stuff's all tennis-related," Daniel said, giving his son an amused grin.

James flashed his own self-effacing, yet winning smile before a look of concern overcame him, like a cloud quickly covering the sun. "You think I can make the team?"

"Of course you can. Come on, let's get the car packed." He took the handle of James' suitcase and opened the front door.

"I heard last year all but one spot was taken by a recruit," James said.

Daniel popped open the car trunk. "This is Yale, so you shouldn't think about recruiting in the same way. Kids aren't getting scholarships to play tennis. Some just got a letter of likely admission."

"Well, I didn't get one of those," James muttered.

"They don't have a big recruiting net. Not like regular Division One schools. Don't worry about it. Go to tryouts; see what happens. Hope for the best and don't expect the worst; leave the rest to . . . well, at least you know you got in for smarts, not just your serve. That's something to be proud of, James."

"I guess."

How did they grow up so fast? Daniel wondered as he watched his son loading the car. It seemed absurd. He could still hear them fighting over crayons, not computers, and now James was leaving for New Haven, Julia flying to Stanford in a couple days. It seemed like only yesterday that he and Beth were standing in the driveway of their old bungalow home in west Philly watching Julia wobbling on her bike while James wept over a skinned knee.

They were good kids and he was proud of them. The credit for raising them belonged to Beth, of course, but just having a positive relationship with the twins was something Daniel had always worried he might fail at . . . especially when his thoughts turned dark and he thought of his own father.

The car trunk full, Daniel realized he'd forgotten his wallet inside the house. "I'll be right back," he said. "And I'll tell your mom and sister to come say goodbye."

He found the wallet on a dresser in his bedroom. Then he heard a sound. It was like a little squeak. He listened closely. There it was again. What was that?

Daniel went into the hallway and listened again. The sound came from Julia's room. He went to the door and knocked lightly.

"Julia?"

There was a muffled sob. He opened the door. Beth was sitting with Julia on the bed, and to Daniel's surprise, it was Beth who was crying, not Julia. Beth quickly wiped the tears away from her eyes. Her mascara was running. Julia dabbed at her mother's cheeks with a Kleenex.

"What's wrong?" Daniel asked. His voice sounded hollow even to himself.

"Nothing," Beth said. She stood up and smoothed her light green blouse.

"I'm about to get going with James."

"Okay. We'll be right down."

Daniel's uneasiness with emotion often made him feel unequal to the task of dealing with his wife and daughter, especially at the same time. There followed an awkward silence. Julia broke it—"You look like crap, Dad. Maybe you should go back to bed."

Daniel shrugged. He was the outsider, as usual. "Very funny," he mumbled. "Anyway, come say goodbye to your brother. You won't see him till Christmas and—"

"—Good thing!" Julia said.

Beth smiled.

"But surely you're going to miss him," Daniel chided. "You'll see. You'll be on the plane and think about the last time he stole your homework, and then you'll feel so sad he's not around."

"There's a reason I'm going to school on the opposite coast, remember?"

Daniel chuckled, shrugged again.

The phone rang.

"That'll be Maddie," Julia said. "I'll take it downstairs."

When they were alone, Daniel glanced uncertainly at Beth.

"Honey, I'm sorry about last night," he said.

"It's okay."

"Is there anything you'd like to do today?" he asked. "I mean, when I get back from taking James to the station."

"Don't you have to go in to check on your patient?"

"I asked Steve to do that. He's on call."

Beth looked out the window. Two children, a boy and a girl, were riding bikes in the street. A little Maltese dog was barking at them.

"I promised I'd take Julia to the L.L. Bean store over in Jersey. Then lunch in the city, you know that restaurant near Rittenhouse Square."

"Maybe I could join you there . . ."

Beth thought for a moment. "Well, sure. That would be nice."

"Dad!" Julia shouted from the bottom of the stairs.

"Now what?" Daniel said. He walked out of the bedroom.

"Uh, Dad. This call is for you."

"Is it the hospital?"

"No, it's, um, Grandpa. Calling from California."

Daniel felt ice in the pit in his stomach.

He went downstairs. "Hello?"

A gravelly voice on the other end. "Danny?"

"Yes Dad, I'm here."

Several seconds of silence followed. In those strange seconds, Daniel tried to recall the last time he'd spoken to his father—more than ten years at least.

"What's wrong?" Daniel said.

"You sound strange. Are you sick?"

"No, I'm not sick. Dad, why are you calling?"

"It's Keiko."

"What's wrong with Mom?"

A pause, then, "There's been an accident."

Daniel felt the ice spread in his stomach.

"Is she—."

"—A car accident," his father said.

"Oh my God . . ."

"She's in the hospital."

"What? Is she okay?"

"Of course she's not okay. She's in the *hospital*. Are you listening to me?"

"I'm listening, Dad. Just tell me what happened."

"Last night . . . driving home from church. She crashed into a telephone pole. Of course I wasn't there. The EMTs say she passed out. They told me it might be a stroke . . ."

"I need to call the hospital, Dad—"

"—Keiko wanted me to call you. Thought you might want to talk to her doctors."

"Of course I want to talk to her doctors!" Beth frowned and shot Daniel a disapproving look. He paused, then deliberately lowered his voice and spoke with the soft, certain cadence he reserved for

16

emergencies. "What hospital is she at? Do you know if she's in the ICU? Have they scanned her and what did it show?"

Beth and Julia studied Daniel's face for a sign of the answers to these questions.

Daniel raised his voice one octave. "Dad, are you there?"

"I am here," came a whispery reply.

"Dad, please just tell me what hospital she's at and I'll give them a call. And I'll be on the next flight I can get to LA . . ."

THREE

LOS ANGELES, CALIFORNIA 1998

A t LAX the air was crisp and held the fragrant aroma of hydrangeas. Recent rain had swept the day's pollution and smog out to sea. A specialty car service brought Daniel a brand new silver-grey Lexus LS curbside, and within minutes he was on his way to the Kaiser Permanente where his mother was hospitalized.

A stroke.

Or a pulmonary embolism.

Or a seizure.

These were at the top of the differential according to his mother's doctor, whom Daniel had reached by telephone. Keiko had no recollection of driving into a telephone pole. Now she seemed fine. They were running tests and treating her with anticoagulants as a precaution.

He weaved through late evening traffic and remembered the last time he'd been back to LA. Ten years—when he'd come for the funeral of his mother's sister. He'd seen his father from afar at the service, but they hadn't spoken. His father never accompanied Keiko on her annual Christmas visits to Philadelphia, and he'd only seen James and Julia a couple of times when they were babies. Daniel knew his estrangement from his father was inexplicable and baffling to Beth and the kids. They all had suspicions about what might have happened between father and son, but none of them could truly guess which man was at fault. To James and Julia, their grandfather was like a historical figure—someone real and to be respected, but too distant from reality to warrant any thought or affection. They received birthday cards with checks signed by him every year, but never a personal message or phone call.

Daniel arrived at the hospital and located his mother's room. It was designed for two, but he was glad to see she had no roommate. Was she asleep? Her body appeared small and almost child-like beneath the thin blanket. Though her eyes were closed and her face at peace, she seemed to have aged ten years since he'd seen her last Christmas. There was plastic tubing strung across her face with nasal prongs to deliver oxygen; beneath her thin gown he saw EKG leads affixed to her bird-like chest. She looked just like any number of the thousands of patients Daniel had treated in his career. But he felt a thickness in his throat and a surge of affection for this woman who had raised him and for many years had been the only person in the world he knew would always love and support him.

Daniel put his bag down and moved close to the monitor to inspect his mother's vital signs and telemetry.

"Danny, is that you?" his mother's soft voice asked.

"Yes, Mom. I'm here."

"Thank you for coming. I know you are so busy."

"Never mind that. How are you feeling?"

"Tired."

Daniel sat down on a chair next to the bed. "It looks like you're doing okay. Heart rate's steady. Blood pressure's good. They're running plenty of fluids into you."

Keiko made a face. "I hate this IV. When can they take it out?"

"Probably not for a while, sorry. Are they treating you well?"

"Food's terrible. But they somehow know all about *you*. So now I'm the mother of the *world famous* heart surgeon."

"Yeah, well, that's a good thing."

There was a knock at the door. A young-looking Asian American doctor entered the room.

"Dr. Tokunaga?"

Daniel stood up. "Yes?"

"I'm Aaron Hsu, your mother's cardiologist. I understand you're the chief of cardiothoracic surgery at Penn?"

"I am."

"It's an honor to meet you."

They shook hands.

"Tell me how she's doing."

"Quite well, actually. Her head CT was negative, so we don't think it was a stroke. Her cardiac enzymes were normal, so it wasn't a heart attack. Her pulmonary function tests were a little low so we got a V/Q scan and I just saw the results. I believe she had a mild pulmonary embolism, then may have passed out, which led to the car crash."

"That sounds like a pretty complete work-up," Daniel said, impressed. "But Mom, do you remember having trouble breathing before the accident?"

Keiko sat up a little higher on the cluster of pillows behind her back. "Maybe. I think I felt some pain in my chest. But then I got very dizzy and lightheaded."

"Luckily the car crash didn't appear to cause any significant injuries," Dr. Hsu added. "Her neck got cleared in the ER last night. And no broken bones."

"Just broken pride," Keiko muttered. Then she coughed hard, and grimaced.

"Please Mom, take it easy."

"We want to monitor her for another day or two, of course. We have her anti-coagulated on heparin right now, and we'll switch to coumadin when she goes home."

"That sounds fine," Daniel said. "Thanks a lot for taking care of her."

The doctor spent a few minutes examining Keiko and reviewing her lab results.

After he left, Daniel said, "In a way, you were lucky, Mom."

"Yes, lucky I only hit a telephone pole and did not run over a kid."

"That's true. But sometimes a clot that forms in your legs can travel up to your lungs and kill you. I see it all the time."

"Well, it's going to take more than this to get rid of me. You saw your father at the house?"

Daniel exhaled. "No, I came right here from the airport."

Keiko's face fell. "Oh no. I hope he is okay. I tried to call home twice already but there was no answer."

"You mean he hasn't been here to see you?"

"Well, no. He doesn't drive. You know that. Besides, I crashed our car. They towed it to the shop."

"Couldn't a friend drive him?"

"You know he doesn't have any friends. It's strange that he didn't answer the phone. He never leaves the house."

Daniel suddenly felt angry. His father was impossible. How could he not drop everything and come to the hospital?

"What if he's had another heart attack? Or a stroke . . . what if he's fallen and broken his hip?"

"Mom, you're imagining things. I talked to him on the phone this morning. He's fine."

An unsettled silence fell between them. Keiko looked drained from the effort of conversation. Her face was pale, and the last thing Daniel wanted to do was upset her. After a few minutes, Keiko raised a paper cup to her face and frowned. "Danny?"

21

"Yes."

"I'm out of ice. Could you get me more from the machine down the hall? I like to chew on the ice chips. Then you come back and tell me all about the kids and Beth."

"Sure, Mom. I'll be right back."

He stepped out of the room. Though it was a relief to see her stable, he knew she'd had a major medical event and more than anything just needed to rest. He located the ice machine and began to fill up his mother's plastic container. Still, he thought, if the doctor's diagnosis was right and there were no more tests to perform, there was a chance that Keiko could be discharged tomorrow. In that case, he might be able to fly home in a couple of days and be back at work a day earlier than he'd planned. His unexpected departure had thrown his clinic and OR schedules into chaos.

"Daniel? Is that you?"

It was a soft female voice. He stood up straighter and removed the bucket from the ice machine. He knew that voice.

He turned. "Anne? Anne Mikado?"

They were close enough for him to see the gentle creases at the corners of her eyes. There were strands of grey intertwined with her jet-black hair. He felt the urge to smooth out the wrinkles in his dark suit and pat down his tousled hair, but his hands were glued to the ice bucket, and his eyes were glued to Anne.

Her face brightened into a wide smile. "I saw your mother's name on the census and thought: could it really be your family? So I came up to take a look."

"You were right." Daniel's gaze traveled down to her neat gray business suit that appeared to fit her body well. A hospital ID hung from a lanyard around her neck, but he couldn't quite make out what her position was.

"What happened? Is she okay?" Anne asked.

"They think she had a PE, then fainted, and then ran her car into a telephone pole. Other than that, she's great. Telephone pole, not so much."

Anne smiled at his deadpan joke. "Thank goodness it was nothing serious. Your mom was always so kind to me."

"What are you doing here, Anne? And what's it been? Thirty-some years?"

She brushed her hair out of her eyes. It was a gesture he remembered. "Yes, it's been about that long, I think."

"What do you do here?" he asked.

"I'm a social worker. I've worked here for fifteen years."

"A social worker . . ." Daniel repeated softly.

"And I already know you're a famous heart surgeon," Anne said, teasing gently. "I always knew you'd do something amazing, be someone amazing."

"You're embarrassing me. How did you know what I was doing? I haven't been back here in years."

"Word gets around. You know how it is."

Daniel did know. In the Japanese American community, word could travel fast, especially among gossipy mothers and aunts. He couldn't stop looking at Anne's face. It was remarkable how much she was just as he remembered her. She was grinning a little foolishly at him, and he realized he was doing the same.

"Listen, is there a place we could go talk?" He held up the ice bucket. "I just need to drop this off with my mom. I'd really like to catch up with you."

"Definitely. We should. But . . ." she looked at her watch. It was almost six p.m. "I've got to run to the airport to pick up my parents right now. They're visiting from Japan. What about tomorrow evening? Will you still be here?"

"Yes, I'm sure I can do that. Your parents moved back to Japan?"

Anne smiled at his ignorance. "They've lived there for more than thirty years now. We have a lot to catch up on. But what's your cell phone number? We'll talk tomorrow."

"Okay. For sure." They exchanged numbers.

Anne took a step back. "Well, I'm happy to see you, Daniel."

23

"Same here, Anne."

"See you tomorrow."

"You bet."

Daniel watched her walk down the hallway. At the very end, she turned around and looked back at him. Both caught staring, they each grinned again. Then she turned the corner and went out of sight.

Daniel stood there, momentarily stunned. Anne Mikado. To see her here, decades later, seemed unreal. He realized he should have asked if she was married, or had kids. Was she wearing a ring? He hadn't thought to look.

He couldn't wait to talk to her again, to learn about everything that had happened in the years since they'd last seen each other. And to finally understand why she'd left, and never come back.

Daniel returned to his mother's room and set the ice chips on the bedside table. Keiko was on the phone but not speaking. After a few moments she hung up.

"Your father is *still* not answering."

"Strange," Daniel said.

"I just don't know where he could be."

"Does he ever go out to do anything?"

"No, he rarely leaves the house . . . Danny, you need to go find him. Something's wrong. I can feel it."

Daniel sighed and shifted in the cold metal, straight-backed hospital chair.

"Why should I do that?"

She shook her head. "What if something terrible *has* happened to him?"

I wouldn't really care, Daniel thought. "Isn't there someone we can call?"

Again, she shook her head, and it was her turn to sigh. "You know how he is around people. He's a stranger to almost everyone, and you haven't seen him in a very long time. He's much worse than he used to be."

Daniel shrugged.

His mother said, "You don't understand. I'm going to need him when I get out of here. Please find him for me."

"He's not going to take care of you, Mom. He can't even take care of himself. Can't cook, wash dishes, clean house. Nor would he want to. I'm sorry, but the man's useless."

"Oh Danny, don't say that. Couldn't you try to be nice? It's been so long . . ."

His face hardened. "Nothing's changed, Mom. I feel the same way I always have. And so does he. And that's why he's not here. Because he knows I'm here."

"That's not true. Don't say that . . ." Daniel saw that his mother was on the verge of tears. "Please just go find him. Make sure he's okay, Danny. That's all I ask."

For a long time the two of them just looked at each other.

Finally, Daniel rubbed his eyes and took a deep breath. Then he asked in a neutral voice, "So how would I go about finding him?"

"Just go to the house and see. Make sure he hasn't fallen down or hurt himself, or worse. It's only been a year since he had his heart attack."

Daniel hung his head—and nodded.

"Thank you, Danny. Good boy."

FOUR

LOS ANGELES 1998

It didn't take long to reach the old neighborhood in Monterey Park. Even at night, it looked similar to how he remembered it. Rows of 1940's California bungalows. The Longo's old house. The Foster's. But he had no idea who might be living in these homes now. The street-lamps were new, and the lawns looked nicer, but he still recognized the familiar spot where he and his brother and friends would play stickball until sundown, and the neighbor's fence they'd hop every morning to take a shortcut to elementary school.

He saw the house. The rhododendrons had grown huge. The dented mailbox was the same. He pulled into the narrow driveway and stopped in front of a detached garage with peeling grey paint and a rusting basketball hoop attached above the door.

Daniel got out of the car and surveyed the tiny backyard. The house was quiet. He walked to the front door and rang the bell.

No answer.

He went to the rear and banged on the back door.

Nothing but a sea wash of cicada and cricket sound. Then a sudden silence. Then the ratcheting of cicadas again. Far off, the mournful howl of a pent-up dog.

Now what? Daniel wondered, frustrated. He began to truly worry that his father might be incapacitated inside. He banged the door again, harder this time, and listened to the silence.

Then he remembered his parents used to keep a house key taped underneath the outdoor electrical outlet. Pushing aside knee-high weeds, he located it. The duct tape was difficult to get off; the key felt sticky. It hadn't been touched in years.

It took a little jiggling with the key, but Daniel felt the back door lock click and the door swung open. He flicked a wall switch and was momentarily blinded. Slowly, his eyes accepted the fierce bright, and adjusted. He saw the linoleum floor, worn down and darker in front of the sink, its edges curled underneath the dishwasher. A glimpse at the rest of the kitchen was just as he remembered it: yellow rice cooker on the counter, a pile of chopsticks in the drying rack, the same chipped, white and blue rice bowls. He breathed in and caught the old burnt-out smell of ancient cigarette smoke, the cloying aroma that he always connected with his father.

"Dad?"

Daniel's echo came and went, quickly, fading like a ghost.

He walked through the first floor: the small dining room with the table piled high with crisp old newspapers, faded magazines, and crumpled bills; and the living room, a maroon La-Z-Boy positioned in front of an out-of-date Hitachi TV in the corner. He peeked in the bathroom; no one.

Daniel took the stairs two at a time, searched the second floor bedrooms, the bathroom.

"Dad?"

The house sucked up his voice, offered no return.

He sat down on his father's bed, tried to think. It was a relief not to find him passed out or dead. But where the hell was he?

His dad wasn't one for walking, and he didn't have a car. He wondered if someone could have taken him somewhere.

But who would do that? His father didn't have any friends. He was reclusive and a pain to be around. Daniel couldn't think of anyone who'd want to spend any time with him, except for Keiko, who was used to his grumpy mood.

Daniel stood up and walked down the stairs, passing photos of himself graduating from high school, graduating from Columbia, and Harvard Medical School. Downstairs, his old cello trophies stood sucking up dust on a knotty-pine shelf.

The house was a time capsule. A grave, he thought. Even a clock's tick would have been welcome music. The dead room gave Daniel the creeps. Inside, the distant pulsation of the cicadas felt far away. Inside, time had died—life gone elsewhere. Even the past had passed on.

A single photograph on a table in the living room stopped Daniel in his tracks. It was a black and white he hadn't seen in twenty years. The subject had a young Japanese face, smiling, wearing a U.S. Army dress uniform with his cap at a rakish angle.

Kenny.

Daniel picked up the wood frame and touched the glass over his younger brother's face. A wave of emotion welled up inside him and he didn't know whether to laugh or cry.

Sudden, probing headlights climbed across the darkened living room wall. A car pulled into the driveway. Daniel heard it creak to a stop behind his rental car.

Going out the back door, Daniel saw the second car was an old Buick Regal. The driver's side door was a different shade of blue than the body. A little trail of smoke emanated from the exhaust.

The passenger door opened. Daniel's father got out.

He was seventy-three, but he looked much older. Wizened and gaunt, he walked with a noticeable stoop. Even in the dim light, Daniel could see he was angry: face drawn, eyes narrowed. With his wrinkled, untucked shirt and wild grey hair blowing every which way in the breeze, he had the look of an old soldier who had lost his way.

"Dad?"

Mr. Tokunaga's head jerked up. He stared oddly at Daniel, as if he couldn't really see him. Then, suddenly, a spark of recognition. The old man's eyebrows lifted in surprise. "So you came. Did you see your mother?"

Daniel nodded. "She's doing okay."

"That's good."

"Where have you been all day?" Daniel asked.

Before his father could answer, the driver's side door of the Buick opened and a man got out. He was Japanese and maybe the same age as Daniel's father. He wore a navy blue baseball cap with "WWII Veteran" blazoned across the front.

"You must be Daniel," the man said. "I'm Joe Fukuda, your dad's old war buddy."

War buddy? Daniel looked at the man. Then he glanced at his father, whose face was full of irritation. Daniel knew that face well.

Joe ignored it. He held out his hand to Daniel. "Nice to meet you after all this time."

Without warning, Daniel's father pushed past his son. He turned his back completely on Joe, and disappeared inside.

The door slammed.

Daniel didn't know what to do. He shook Joe's hand.

"Sorry about this," Joe said. "We had a little disagreement in the car, I guess he's still upset about it."

"You said you were war buddies? Didn't think my dad had any friends from his old Army days. Were you in the 442nd, like him?"

Joe smiled. "Sure was. Your dad, he had plenty of friends back then, not just me."

"Really? How come I never met any of them?"

Joe rubbed his chin. "Well, I suppose sometimes things happen that way. Your dad . . . well, to be honest, he changed quite a bit after the war. Plus, he and I haven't always seen eye to eye." Joe touched the side of his face with his open right hand, then shook his head. "But there's so few of us now . . . I guess we've got to let bygones be bygones, right?"

Daniel had no idea what to say to that. "Where did you take my dad today?" he asked.

"We took a drive up into the central valley, that's all."

"All day?"

"We had a lot to talk about."

"But don't you realize my mom's in the hospital?" Daniel snapped. "He should have been there with her today."

"What? What's happened to Keiko?"

"You know my mom?"

Joe nodded. "A long time ago. What happened?"

"She was in a car accident," Daniel answered, not wanting to go into details. "But she'll be okay."

"Thank God. I'm sorry. Your dad never mentioned it. Otherwise we wouldn't have gone."

"And what was so important that you had to tell him today of all days?"

Joe scratched the side of his neck. "I had to warn him about some calls I've been getting. You know, from the government."

"The government?"

"Department of Defense. They've been calling my house, leaving odd messages. They say they're reviewing some medals they gave out—want to open old war records, interview vets like me, and even eyewitnesses if they can find 'em. I haven't called back." Joe smirked. "What do they want to do? Take 'em back?"

"War medals, you said. Why would my dad care about that?"

Joe wrinkled his brow, squinted. "What do you mean?"

"I know my dad spent a little time in the war, and that the 442nd was famous for bravery, but he didn't get any medals himself."

Joe looked surprised. "Yes, he did. He never told you?"

"Told me what?"

30

"That he won the Distinguished Service Cross for heroism in France."

"That can't be true."

Joe chuckled. "You ask him." Then he opened his car door and fished his keys out of his pocket. "It's getting late," he said. "I can see you weren't expecting me, so I'll be on my way. But hey, if you want my advice, you ought to talk to your dad about this. It's no small deal, you know."

Daniel watched Joe back out and nearly hit the mailbox as he swung onto the street. He stood there for a long moment, shaking his head.

Of all the crazy, unexpected things . . . The war. Medals. Friends. None of it made any sense.

FIVE

"Come on Hiro, let's go back. We're not gonna find it."

"Not yet, those Hawaiian Buddhaheads from the 100th said it's close to here, I'm sure of it."

Ray stumbled over a root trying to keep up with his friend Hiro. The forest's dense canopy blocked most of the light on even the sunniest days. Today, a thick, low-hanging fog made it tough to see even ten feet away. A ground-hugging animal darted to the right, startling Ray. It skittered across the moss-carpeted earth and dove into the ferny undergrowth. Ray was beginning to regret this excursion.

"Do you think they could've purposely given you the wrong directions? They don't like you, you know, being a *mainlander*."

Hiro laughed. "Could be. Those pranksters would. You sure you're from Hawaii, like them? Sometimes I ain't so sure, you're way too serious."

Ray did not find this funny. It was a sore spot whenever anyone pointed out he was from Hawaii but wasn't in the 442nd's 100th Battalion; he was not one of those islanders who'd jumped at the chance to join the 442nd earlier in the war—these men had already distinguished themselves in combat in Italy. Ray had enlisted much later, and come into his battalion as a replacement.

Hiro shrugged, then added, "Can't be helped now, and we didn't come all this way to fail. Haven't showered for almost two weeks." He made an exaggerated show of sniffing under his armpits. "We stink, and if there's a swimming hole within ten miles, we're gonna find it. I don't think I can stand sleeping in the same tent with you another night."

Ray smirked. He had to admit, it would be nice to get clean. There'd been no time to rig running water and field showers at the regiment's makeshift base. The boys from the 100th said the swimming hole was only a mile from camp, but Ray and Hiro had already hiked for almost an hour. Before much longer they'd be on report for being AWOL. More worrisome—the omnipresent chance of running into a German patrol. The Vosges Mountains were so wooded that the lines between the 442nd and the enemy were anything but clear. There'd been stories of men discovering Jerries to their rear, or not realizing they'd accidentally ventured deep into German-held territory.

"Don't you think we should have taken the lower trail, instead of the upper?" Ray asked.

"What trail? You see any trails? I don't." Hiro turned around, facing the way they'd come. "You know, come to think of it, I'm not sure we're going to be able to find our way back. Maybe we should've brought breadcrumbs."

Ray glanced all around, feeling uneasy. The forest looked the same in every direction. *We should have memorized landmarks*, he scolded himself.

Hiro was grinning at him. A joke. He was making a joke.

"Come on," Hiro quipped. "Don't look back. Only ahead."

The two men pushed on in silence.

Through a gap in the trees Ray saw a patch of grey sky. A hawk flew into view, visible for only a second, and he checked to see if it had a red tail or reddish shoulders, but the raptor was too swift for him. Wish I had your eyes today, he thought.

"Found it!" Hiro shouted, ten yards ahead of Ray.

"Shh!" Ray hissed. "Not so loud."

Hiro waved his hand dismissively. He was standing on a ledge of some sort. Ray came up behind him and the sky opened up quite suddenly. No trees. He looked down.

Oh my God.

They were standing on a rock outcrop, thirty feet above a crystalline pool of water that looked very small to Ray's eyes. Around its rim, the circle of water was translucent green; towards the center, the color changed to deep cerulean blue. A few boulders sticking out of the water made Ray think there might be more under the surface. The pool was ringed by ferns and a narrow circlet of yellow pebbles. Ray took a step back.

"We found it!" Hiro repeated, and it was as if he'd found the Holy Grail.

"We should have taken the lower path," Ray said, annoyed. "Now we'll have to go back around."

"No way. If we go back, we might never find it again. Plus, I bet you're worried that we don't have much time, right?" Hiro unbuckled his belt.

"You're not thinking of jumping, are you?" Ray peered over the ledge. "You've no idea how deep that water is."

Hiro, sitting down in the ferns, unlaced his boots and stripped off his shirt and pants. "True, it's far, and true, we don't know how deep it is. But we're here. We found the pool. We're gonna get clean . . . at least I know I am!" Hiro stood up, naked.

"You're crazy."

Hiro grinned. "That's why we're friends." Ray watched him tie up

34

his clothes with his bootlaces and then toss the bundle over the ledge. It landed with a thump on the narrow strand of pebbled sand.

Hiro laughed. Placing his hands on his hips, he threw back his head and said, as if to the sky itself—"Now I have no choice."

Ray was speechless.

Then he muttered, "What about me?"

"You can just watch me," Hiro taunted. "Or maybe you'll back me up, eh?"

Ray looked at the circlet of blue down below. It was a long way down. The bundle of clothes appeared small. The height made Ray's stomach clench and he felt a strange ticklish feeling in his testicles as a wave of fear rose all the way up into his chest.

Hiro rolled his eyes. "Okay. How bout I make it easy for you?" With one last look over the ledge, Hiro centered himself, and leapt off. Ray rushed to the edge, watched his friend plummet through space . . . down, down, and then a huge white plume of water. Dead center. Hiro disappeared, then shot to the surface in a boil of bubbles that exploded all around him.

"Woo hoo!" Hiro cried. His voice echoed along the chill walls of stone and limp hanging vine. "Plenty deep, feels great! Come on down!"

Ray felt the tightness in his balls. He stepped back into the ferns, sat down, head in hands. Every instinct told him not to jump. But . . . what choice do I have? Hiro always does rash and foolish things. Act first, think later, that's his philosophy.

And, when he was truly honest about it, Ray grudgingly admitted to himself that he wished that he could be more like his friend.

"Come on!" Hiro called, his voice spiraling an echo round the gorge.

Ray willed himself to stand up. He took a deep breath, and slowly, ever so slowly, he began to unbutton his shirt.

Six

LOS ANGELES 1998

Daniel went inside the house after watching Joe Fukuda drive off. "Dad?"

"In here." He found his father reclining in his La-Z-Boy, smoking a cigarette. His face was drawn and pale. He wore khaki shorts that had faded almost white, and there was a dark grease stain on the chest of his wilted blue polo shirt. Daniel watched him kick off his dark green flip-flops and frowned at the plume of blue smoke beginning to collect above the old man's head.

"You got here fast," his father said. "I just talked to you on the phone this morning."

They're called airplanes, Daniel said to himself. "Why didn't you visit Mom today?"

"Wasn't it obvious? This guy came by and said he needed to talk to me."

"Okay, but why were you gone all day?"

"I had no idea the fool would drive that slow."

"Where did he take you?" Daniel said, still trying to understand.

"Manzanar."

"You mean . . . that detainment camp where Mom and her family were during the war?"

"That's right."

"But why? I thought it was completely abandoned."

"They made it into a national park or something like that. Forget about it. Now, why don't you tell me about your mother?" his father groused, like it was Daniel who was holding back information.

Only a few sentences exchanged and already Daniel found himself annoyed by his father's crummy manners. His shabby clothes. His rude, ignorant comments. The way he slouched and smoked and cast off his flip-flops like a child.

Daniel tried to hide his irritation. "She had a pulmonary embolus—a clot from her leg went to her chest and cut off the blood supply to part of her lung. But the good news is, I think she's going to be okay."

The old man furrowed his brow. The long-embered cigarette dangled between his lips. He sucked at it and smoke came out of his nose. Daniel sat on the couch near his father's chair and tried not to breathe too deeply, as the smoke was beginning to make him feel nauseous.

"Maybe I'll go see her tomorrow," his father said, not looking at Daniel but instead staring at the blank screen of the TV.

"You could. But there's also a chance they'll discharge her and I can bring her home."

"Fine. Don't see how I'd be much help to her anyhow. They've got doctors to do all that. Besides, people catch all sorts of diseases in hospitals." His eyes darted to Daniel for a split second, as if visually checking whether Daniel might have brought some contagion into the house.

"She's going to need some help when she gets home, Dad."

"Sure, sure. She's got lots of church friends who I'm sure will come by every single day. They do that, you know. Every. Single. Day. It's almost impossible to get some peace and quiet around here."

"Okay. Well, they might bring in some food, but she's going to need help taking her medicines. Can you do that?"

"Of course I can do that."

"And what about the car? Mom won't be driving anytime soon, but do you guys have the number for the auto shop? A way to get it back when it's fixed?"

"Yes, we've gone there for years. We're not helpless, you know. We've been living here since you were in diapers. We know our way around. Much better than you do. How long's it been since you've been here? Ten years? More?"

"Something like that," Daniel replied.

For a while, neither of them spoke. There was just the twining smoke and the cricket pulse outside. Moonlight shone through the front window, and Daniel heard a car drive by.

He stood up. "Maybe I should go. I can call you tomorrow."

"Your family is well?" his father asked, like he hadn't heard Daniel speak. It was the way he said it, like talking to a stranger.

"Yeah. Fine. The kids are starting college this week. Mom told you, right? James is going to Yale. Julia's headed to Stanford."

His father nodded. "That's good. And your job? Still good?"

Daniel nodded.

"How much money do you make?"

"What?"

"How much do you make? I bet a lot."

Daniel felt annoyed, but he managed to respond with a half-hearted laugh. "I make enough."

"That's funny?"

Daniel bit his lip. The old man was just as he always was. Supercilious, condescending, humorless. The sort of man who didn't care what others thought, good or bad. In a flash, Daniel remembered how he used to dread when his father met his friends or his teachers.

You never knew what the old bastard might say.

But there was also something different about him. He looked so beaten. And worn out. The sunken eyes and thinning hair.

Daniel realized, too, that this was one of the first times his father had asked about his life or what the grandchildren were doing. He'd never asked about Daniel's career. At least the money was a real question. Was the old man, inside there somewhere, softening just a little?

Daniel purged the thought. Wasn't possible. This was the same man whose conversations were edgy, dark, one-sided. The man who gave orders, recited maxims, and delivered diatribes. He didn't give a damn about anyone else. Daniel and his younger brother Kenny had suffered through countless dinner-table speeches on the importance of education, hard work, and self-reliance. Daniel drifted off in one memory after another; they came on him like heat waves . . .

"Nothing means as much as honor, boys. Never forget that."

"A man's reputation is worth more than any amount of money. But money's important too. You need to make a lot of it."

"You boys have an opportunity to make something of yourselves. You have no idea what our generation did to earn your chance to be true Americans. If you don't make the most of it, I'll be very ashamed."

Once, he came home and found eight-year-old Kenny complaining about the lunch Keiko had packed for him.

"But Mom, I don't want this!" Kenny cried. "I want a regular peanut butter and jelly sandwich like everyone else brings. These fat noodles smell and if I bring them again everyone will make fun of me and say I'm eating worms. I hate this food!"

Their father had come up behind Kenny and pushed him so hard the boy had flown across the room, crashed into the kitchen table, and caused two plates and a glass of milk to fall and shatter on the floor.

Their father's face was red and swollen.

"If I ever catch you disrespecting your mother again, I'll beat you so hard you won't be able to sit for a week!"

Despite their mother's protestations, Kenny went to school without lunch for three days.

He was a cold, hard, locked-box of a man. The kind of person who didn't suffer fools or foolishness of any kind—the kind of guy who never joked and always disapproved of anything fun or frivolous. He didn't like spending money and never took a day off work from his job as a steel worker at the Douglas Aircraft Factory. He had no hobbies. Outside of work, the old man's only interest was to make his sons successful.

But for some reason, he'd always expected more of Daniel than Kenny. Maybe because Daniel was the first-born, or the better student. Bottom line, the pressure on Daniel was cruel and relentless.

It was only much later in life that Daniel learned that white people had a term for the kind of child rearing he'd endured.

Child abuse.

Perhaps not the terrible physical abuse that some children suffer—his father might shove or hit him, but he never burned him with an iron or whipped with the buckle end of a belt. No, nothing that a doctor could diagnose clinically. Instead it was an emotional abuse that could be just as wounding. Though he might be biased with selective memory, Daniel could not remember one time when his father had praised him for doing something well. It was always criticism. And brow-beatings. And what he should do better. And how much more he could achieve if he worked harder or stopped wasting time.

Just being in their living room brought back a flood of negative memories. But Daniel's mind settled on just one: the image of his ill-tempered father sitting in this very same La-Z-Boy, his body tense and rigid, his chiseled face an inscrutable mask of fury.

The Davy Crockett day.

The famous Davy Crockett movie came out in 1955, with Fess Parker, whose brave manner was every boy's dream of manhood. It seemed like a lifetime ago, and maybe it was. Daniel was ten that year, and he'd used all the money he'd saved from birthdays and recycling glass bottles to buy a coonskin cap, plastic cap gun rifle, and "buckskin" shirt. He made Kenny, five years younger, play Davy's sidekick, Russell. They were roaming the neighborhood, pretending to hunt the treacherous Indian chief Red Stick, when Johnny Caldarone and two of his friends cornered them. Johnny was thirteen years old and a head taller than Daniel. He called them chinks and said they had no business wearing American clothes. Daniel felt a hard shove, then fell and scraped his knees on the sidewalk. The bullies pushed him into the bushes between two houses, out of sight of the street. For some reason, they left Kenny alone. Now Johnny seemed ten feet tall. His father had fought in the Korean War. Daniel started to cry. They stole his cap and pulled the shirt off his back. The cheap vinyl shirt had a soft felt fringe that ran along the chest, all the way around the back. Johnny took pleasure in ripping the whole thing off. Then he picked up the rifle, which Daniel had dropped, smiled triumphantly, and ran. The three of them chanted, "Ching-chong, Ching-chong" in sing-song voices as they charged down the street.

The worst part of this random memory was the knowledge that Kenny had witnessed his humiliation. Kenny, always introverted and shy, watched silently as Daniel cried. He idolized his older brother, and it pained Daniel to lose face in his eyes.

Mrs. Longo, a nice old lady who lived in the adjacent house, found the boys and brought them home. Their mother thanked Mrs. Longo and gave Daniel a hug. He told her what had happened, and she sat with him on the couch until he stopped crying. That made him feel a little better.

Then Dad came home.

After hearing the story, his father dragged him into the living room. He sat in the favorite recliner and Daniel stood in front of him. He raged and shouted until bits of spittle formed at the corners of his mouth.

"How can you just let other kids push you around? Are you a

coward? A weakling? You didn't even fight back. I'm so ashamed." He wrenched Daniel's arm and slammed him facedown on the floor. Then he whacked him with a long wooden spoon. *Crack, crack,* the blows came hard and fast. When Daniel's mother begged him to stop, he threw the spoon so hard it chipped the plaster wall next to the TV.

That was over forty years ago, Daniel thought, but it happened right here in this room. The week after the beating his father made him start boxing classes, but Daniel didn't want to fight. Eventually the coach just let him punch a bag whenever the other kids sparred. Later, his father made him try karate, but he wasn't good at that, either. He made Daniel promise to confront Johnny and challenge him to a fight. Instead, Daniel spent the rest of fifth grade doing anything he could to avoid Johnny.

Outside of schoolwork, Daniel wasn't good at anything that seemed to matter to his father. He wasn't good at sports. He wasn't good at asking girls on dates. He wasn't tough and lacked street smarts. These were things his dad prized just as much as grades. And he could never shake the feeling that, to his father, he would always be a disappointment.

Now the older man remained silent and still, his stoic face revealing nothing except the hard-as-flint heart inside him. His uncharacteristic interest in Daniel's life had passed and now Daniel wanted to leave, but curiosity compelled him to ask one more question.

"Was that guy Joe really your friend?"

His father raised his head and looked at Daniel's face for the first time. "No."

"Did you even *know* him?"

"Yes."

"He says he knew Mom."

A flash of irritation. "He knew us both."

"He said you won a medal in the war. If that's true, how come you never told me?"

The old man still held his house keys in his hand. Now he started to rub his thumb hard against the serrated teeth of the largest one. "Medals mean nothing," he said. "Nothing good comes from war." Daniel persisted. "Joe said the government is reviewing the medals, investigating how they were awarded."

And now the softness of his father's voice surprised him. "Yes, he told me. Now I know why they've been calling."

"They called here too?"

"Yes."

"When?"

"Couple weeks ago. And a few times since."

"What did they say?"

"I don't pick up. Haven't called back either."

"Why not?"

His father didn't answer. His face, gone slack, confused Daniel. He wasn't angry. He wasn't exasperated.

He looked . . . afraid.

SEVEN

EASTERN FRANCE
Vosges Mountains
October 14, 1944

"We're sorry, Sarge. We got lost in the woods."
"The hell y'all did." Sergeant Moto was one of the few Nisei from Kentucky who, strangely enough, spoke with a deep southern drawl. "It's bad nuff Ah gotta git three squads mobilized in this soakin' wet fairyland forest, but when Ah gotta waste time accountin' for no-account jerks like you two, it makes me damn mad."

"We just wanted to scope out the area," Hiro said. "You know, know the terrain. That's good, right?"

The sarge jabbed a finger at Hiro's face. "The trouble with you is, you think it's okay to pick 'n choose what rules to follow. When we git in a firefight, it's guys like you turn tail 'n run. Are y'gonna be yella?"

"No way!"

"Better not. You prickly green recruits are a stitch in my side.

Watchin' over you is the thanks Ah get for takin' a pounding in Italy."

"You're a veteran, Sarge. We appreciate that, and we know we've got to prove ourselves."

Moto's eyes searched Hiro's face for any hint of sarcasm before adding, "Ah don't have time to write you boys up fer missin' roll, but Ah'm assignin' you to pack the crappers."

"We're moving out?" Ray asked.

"Yeah. Up in them woods." Sergeant Moto pointed northeast. "Speck of a town called *Broo-year* or sumpin'. Place is a rail and road hub, not much more. Shake a leg and get them field latrines loaded in the deuce 'n a half over there. They're gonna drive 'em back down to HQ. Take one last dump because where we're goin' it's gonna be crap where you can. Git me?"

Hiro and Ray saluted. Moto saluted back. "Ah'm gonna have my eyes on you two," he said, before turning on his heel and stomping off.

Hiro dropped his salute and began to laugh. "You see how red his face got? It gets like that when he drinks, too."

"Come on. He's a pain but we're lucky to have him."

"All right, I agree. But it's a pity we got all clean just to get stinky again hauling crappers."

They walked off in the direction of the latrines, which had been set up on a rare plot of flat ground in a clearing off the main road. Above the treetops, Ray could see snowcaps on some of the distant peaks to the east.

"And Ray," Hiro said. "I'm sorry we've gotta do this. My fault."

Ray nodded. He wasn't really mad. In fact, he was still somewhat proud of himself for bravely jumping into that pool. The endless drop played over and over in his mind. But more than that, Ray liked the feeling of doing what Hiro did. Just throwing caution to the wind.

The hanging cloth walls of the latrine area had already been taken down. On top of two parallel thirty-foot-long slit trenches sat a dozen rough pine latrine seats painted olive green. An Army deuce and a half truck stood a few yards away, ready to be loaded.

Ray and Hiro held their breath while swatting at flies as they grabbed either side of the first latrine, hefted it and side-stepped the foul-smelling trench, then loaded it into the truck.

"You scared, Hiro?"

"About what? Hauling crappers?"

"About meeting the enemy face to face."

"Me? Naw. The sarge was just tryin' to scare us. Sure, him and the Buddhaheads in the 100th got the jump on all that action in Italy. We heard about their tough scrapes and narrow escapes. But let's face it, now those guys are just one battalion of the 442nd, like us. If they can do it, we can, too."

Hiro's confidence made Ray feel a little better.

"But one sure thing came out of that fighting," Hiro added.

"What's that?"

Hiro grinned. "They proved that Nisei can kick ass."

Ray smiled. "I heard General Clark protested the 100th getting pulled to France. He wanted to keep them in Italy. We'll do all right . . . I hope." Hiro bent down to lift the next latrine. Both men held their breath. "We've *got* to," Hiro said through his teeth.

Ray nodded. He knew that every Nisei soldier was out to prove that he was just as good as any other American soldier. Prove it to himself and to his family. Prove it to all the white people in Hawaii— the *haoles*—those quick-tempered, prejudiced people who'd eyed them with suspicion, boycotted their stores, called their friends "Jap-lovers." There was so much to prove . . . and so many to prove it to, including the officers and soldiers that ran the internment camps. And, if Ray was honest with himself, there was this other thing too— shame itself. Shame weighed heavily on all Nisei. The fact that they had nothing to do with Pearl Harbor didn't matter. They were guilty by association, by the color of their skin and the slant of their eyes. It didn't matter that they didn't speak Japanese, or that they were American citizens. The bottom line was that *their* kind had perpetrated

a horrid crime that came from the land of *their* ancestors.
The shame was a burden that all Nisei silently bore, a burden
every soldier in the 442nd was fighting to be free of.

Hiro had come from Manzanar, an internment camp in central
California. He'd told Ray about it, but it was still hard to imagine the
government could throw thousands of people, including children and
old people, into prison just because they were Japanese. There weren't
any camps for German Americans or Italian Americans. The Japanese
in Hawaii hadn't undergone mass imprisonment, but that was
probably because there were too many of them—about thirty percent
of Hawaii's population was Japanese. Rounding up that many people
would have been impractical.

"Do you think your folks are getting along okay back home?" Ray
asked. They hefted the latrine into the truck and went back for another
one.

"Mom and Dad will be all right. They've got a few friends in the
same housing block. I worry about my dad's breathing though. He's
got what they call 'emphysema.' The dust around camp makes him
cough a lot."

"The mainland camps sound like a real raw deal."

Hiro shrugged. "*Shikata ga nai*," he murmured.

"What?"

"*Shikata ga nai*. It's what all the parents said about getting
evacuated. It means: 'It can't be helped.'"

"But didn't you want to fight it? To protest?"

Hiro nodded vigorously. "Of course! We're American citizens for
Christ's sake. And the camp was just terrible when we arrived—no
plumbing, no privacy, barbed wire, guards with guns. They treated us
like prisoners."

"So why didn't you?"

Hiro shrugged again. "What good would it do? You can't fight the
whole government, plus all the neighbors who hate you and the
secondhand dealers who are just drooling over the chance to pick up

your farm or truck or fishing boat for pennies on the dollar. The old folks tried to cool us down. 'Endure with dignity,' a lot of them said." After lifting the next latrine into the truck, Hiro looked away, toward the distant mountains, and repeated, "*Shikata ga nai.*"

"Did your family lose a lot?"

"Sure. Everyone did. My dad had just bought a fishing boat, only two years old, for five thousand. It was the best Japanese boat out of Terminal Island in Los Angeles. But, you can't take a boat with you to Manzanar."

"Couldn't someone keep it for you?"

Hiro scoffed. "For sure the bank repossessed it. There was no way for us to earn money in the camp; no way to make the payments. We also lost everything in our house: furniture, my Mom's piano, books, the dishes—we had to get rid of anything we couldn't carry. I think we got a couple hundred bucks for all of it. I just gave my baseball cards away to a friend of mine. He said he'd keep them for me, but I'm not holding my breath."

"I still can't believe the government did it."

Hiro didn't reply. For a while they worked in silence, until the back of the truck was almost completely full. A couple other privates from their platoon waved at them from the edge of the road. "You guys better hurry up," one called out. "We're jumping off in twenty."

"Why don't you give us a hand?" Hiro shouted. The two soldiers laughed and went on.

"What are you going to do when this is all over?" Ray asked, taking short steps as they waddled the last latrine over to the truck. Both of them were exhausted, rubber-legged, from their long hike and now from the effort of squatting, lifting, and carrying.

"I'm going to open up a landscaping business in Beverly Hills."

"What do *you* know about landscaping?"

"Me? I'm an expert. Look at all the foxholes I've dug!" Hiro grinned. "Okay, no joke. My pop was a fisherman, but I hate boats. And what other options are there?" They boosted the latrine up into the truck and Hiro began to count off on his fingers. "There's fruit growing, laundry, restaurants, and dockyard work. I don't want any of those. I figure, plenty of rich movie stars in Hollywood are gonna want a hard-working landscaper."

"Aren't you afraid they won't hire Japanese?"

"Sure, but I'll work twice as hard and eventually get the jobs. I've got to, because the other thing I'm gonna do is marry my girl."

Hiro had spent many hours telling Ray about his girlfriend, who was waiting for him back at Manzanar. Ray liked hearing Hiro talk about her, even though Hiro usually told the same stories over and over. Ray had never had a girlfriend. He'd never even kissed a girl. He wished he could learn to be as confident as Hiro was around women.

"You're absolutely positive she's the one—haven't changed your mind?" Ray teased.

"You jackass," Hiro said, smiling as he pushed Ray in the shoulder with the flat of his palm. "There's no one like her. She's got moxie. Prettiest girl in the whole camp. When I get back, we're getting married."

"But do her parents know you like to open tent flaps and piss on boots as they go by?"

"Just my bad luck I got caught! By a lieutenant no less."

"Your in-laws are probably praying right now for a son-in-law who's housebroken."

"You want me to piss on your boots *right now*?"

Chuckling, they left the truck and headed up the road to join their platoon. "Tell you the truth," Hiro said, "her parents are real strict and traditional. I tried to avoid them as much as I could. I'm sure they hoped she'd marry some college boy or doctor, but . . . by the time I get back, I'll be a war hero. Who could resist that?" He flashed another wide grin.

"War hero, huh?"

"That's right. Isn't that why you signed up, too?"

"Not exactly—"

In the distance, a barrage of explosions made both of them do an exaggerated, involuntary duck. Embarrassed, they shook their heads, shrugged. First test—they'd failed in equal measure, and now felt equally sheepish about it.

"Some artillery a couple hills over," Hiro said casually, but his voice cracked, betraying him.

"Those aren't ours. Listen, you can hear the difference. That whistling means they're German shells. They're opening up on us already."

The rumble returned. Ray felt the ground shake beneath his feet. He flinched when Hiro slapped him on the back. "Don't worry. We'll stick together. I've got your back and you've got mine, right?"

Ray swallowed, nodded, said nothing.

In the distance, the whump of the big guns continued.

"All for one, one for all," Hiro said.

"Something like that," Ray mumbled.

EIGHT

B eth Tokunaga sat on the bench in the foyer of her home and laced her running shoes. She used a pink hair tie to put her long blonde hair in a ponytail and glanced at the antique mahogany grandfather clock in the corner: 5:45 am. The house was quiet. Empty, except for Julia asleep upstairs. Normally, she found the serenity at this hour to be a welcome respite from the chaos of her daily life, but today the silence was a weight that seemed to represent the emptiness she felt . . . about her life . . . about her marriage.

Daniel hadn't called.

He'd missed their last family dinner, then he'd rushed to the airport for this emergency in California. She knew she couldn't blame him for that, but it irritated her just the same. At the very least, he could call to tell her what was happening. It would take him two minutes to let her know his mom was still alive and breathing. He should know she'd be worried.

They rarely talked anymore. Not about anything real. Nothing outside of their schedules and what the kids were doing. She stood up and opened the front door. The sky was overcast, a film of moisture coating the driveway and street beyond. She shut the door and strode between the giant oaks that straddled their flagstone front walk. Reaching the street, she turned left and started to run.

When did everything go so wrong? she wondered, searching her memory for their last big fight or the last time she'd felt so desolate. There was nothing she could pinpoint. No specific turning point. When she thought of their relationship, a wave of apathy suffused her body. She felt her legs slowing. But she wanted to sprint! To pump her arms and drive her knees ferociously to numb her frustration. Daniel never ran. *I have enough stress in my day job to get my heart pumping*, he once told her when she suggested jogging was something they could do together. It was hard to criticize someone who got up and left the house even earlier than she did each day. It was always hard to criticize Daniel. Everything he did was always more important—the problems of regular life never stood a chance in comparison.

Swarthmore's winding, wooded streets were quiet this early. She headed for the college—her favorite place to run—and took the path that went through the center of campus, past the student center, past the visitor's center and two residence halls. After a quarter mile, she came to a hill with a path that ran up to Parrish Hall. She drove ahead at a hard sprint, faster than she'd ever run it, and waited for the burn. She wanted to feel it in her legs and her lungs. The burn made her feel alive and distracted from reality. There it was. Pain. In her chest. In her side. She powered onward, slowing slightly, cresting the hill. Then a feeling of lightheadedness. Her vision began to swim. Panting, she jogged over to a tree and leaned against it.

Catching her breath, she turned and took in the view of Swarthmore's quadrangle—geometric green spaces dotted with century-old trees. A thin mist hung over the grounds, and the smell of freshly cut grass. In the distance, two students walked together, a boy and a girl, arm in arm, the girl's head seeming to rest on the boy's shoulder. Were they early risers or had they stayed up all night? Beth sighed.

What did that feel like? To be young and in love? And happy? It was hard to remember. Lots of Beth's friends thought her life was perfect. She lived in a mansion. She'd raised two wonderful, intelligent children. Her husband was a successful and world-famous cardiac surgeon who was faithful to her, as far as she knew.

Those friends didn't know she sometimes felt miserable. They didn't know how often she questioned if what she was at the present moment was all she would ever be. And she didn't know if her marriage was truly failing or if it was natural for people to simply drift apart after twenty years together.

These thoughts had brought her to the point of tears in front of her daughter yesterday morning. She hadn't even told Julia what was bothering her. Julia had merely asked why she looked so sad and Beth had suddenly started crying. Part of her wanted to explain it all to her. How she'd once aspired to go to medical school herself. How she'd started the post-baccalaureate courses but needed money for tuition and started working as a surgical technician. It was only supposed to be temporary, a stepping-stone, but then she met Daniel and her life took a different course. She never consciously gave up her dreams. Other dreams just took their place: to be a supportive wife, to raise good kids. But now, more than anything else, she wanted to tell Julia not to waste her time at Stanford. To use these years to discover something she could be passionate about, and to pursue it. To look far ahead and possibly avoid finding herself as Beth did now—unsure of what to do next.

The pair of smitten undergrads drifted away, into the morning mist. Beth straightened up. Quit feeling sorry for yourself, she thought, furrowing her brow and setting her jaw.

Do something about it. Because things can't go on like this. Something has to change.

And as she started to run, heading for a pair of gates on the far side of campus, she knew just what she had to do.

———

Daniel woke to the sound of the phone ringing. He moaned and glanced at the clock. Five am.

"Hello?" he answered, his voice thick with sleep.

"Hi."

"Oh, hi."

"Are you all right?" Beth asked. "Did you make it there okay?"

"Yes." He shook his head, trying to clear it. "Sorry I didn't call. Don't worry, everything's okay. Saw Mom at the hospital; she's doing fine. Went to the house to check on Dad . . . and by the time I made it to the hotel it was too late to call."

"We need to talk."

"Um, okay. Right now?" Daniel closed his eyes and let his head drop back to the pillow. "Listen, hon, I didn't get to bed till really late . . . remember, you're three hours ahead . . . could we do it later?"

"No."

Daniel blinked. For a few seconds, all he heard was the sound of Beth's breathing. He pushed himself up against the headboard to a sitting position.

"What do you want to talk about?"

"Us."

"Honey, I'm really sorry about the other night."

"It's not about that."

"Okay. Go ahead. I'm listening."

Daniel heard Beth clear her throat.

"We've got a big problem, and I think we've got to address it—"

"—Listen, I know I've been working a lot—"

"—Stop, Daniel. Please. I need to get all this out."

"Alright."

"It's obvious we don't talk anymore. We hardly do anything

together unless it's for the kids. I don't know why it's taken me this long to realize it but I'm telling you we need some help—professional help—if we're going to make this work. And before you say no, I should tell you that I've already been talking to someone—"

"Who?"

"Two people actually. My friend Jill is a counselor—"

"She counsels drug addicts."

"Still, she's a trained counselor . . . and also . . . Pastor Bill."

Daniel rolled his eyes. "Of course. From your church."

"That's right. He's a wonderful man. And before you knock him, you should know he really likes you and he thinks you can change."

"Me?" Daniel said. This is all *my* fault? he thought. He got out of bed and began to pace the room. "Look, I know I'm not perfect. I'm sure there's a lot I could work on, but . . . it's not like I'm having an affair or something. Look around. Is our life *that* bad? We just need to spend time together, to be together . . . just you and me. Not with your pastor. You know I'm not into that."

"It's not like he's going to try to convert you. It's just a way to help us start communicating."

"Well, why don't we just try harder at communicating ourselves, like we're doing now?"

"I'm trying to tell you I don't think that's going to work. And if you don't like taking Pastor Bill's advice, you're really not going to like Jill's."

"Which was?"

"She said, 'You already know what to do. You're just asking for permission to do it. Of course you deserve to be happy. End it.'"

Daniel opened his mouth but no words came out. He felt stunned, blindsided. Where was this all coming from? Their marital issues, which he was pretty sure all couples went through from time to time, had suddenly gone nuclear. He pictured Beth standing in the kitchen, arms crossed, lips tight in a line.

"So . . ." he said cautiously. "What exactly are you saying?"

Beth inhaled sharply. "I'm trying to tell you there is no quick fix for our problems. I know you don't like talking about it, and I know you're *really* busy . . ." She paused and Daniel heard her shut a door, before adding more softly, "Will you at least consider it? Going to a counselor with me?"

"Sure," Daniel replied, relieved she had taken the conversation down a notch. He collapsed into an armchair. "I mean, yes, I would. But I think what we really need is just the chance to spend some time together. With the kids leaving, we'll have more of that."

"Thank you," Beth said in a gentle voice that seemed to relieve the rising tension. The way she said it, almost in gratitude, touched Daniel. She was reaching out, and he resolved to meet her part way.

"Honey, I'll do whatever you want. I really do think things will get better. I love you."

"I know."

The two of them remained silent for a while. Daniel heard the hum of the air conditioning kick on in his room.

"You know . . ." Beth finally said, "I'm, um, taking Julia to the airport around noon tomorrow and there's nothing I've got going on . . ." She hesitated, then asked, "What if I flew out there and joined you?"

Daniel considered this. "Are you sure you want to? I mean, I was planning to just be here until tomorrow. Next day at the latest."

"Yes. It'll be a good change of scenery, and since you can't *work* from California," her sarcasm was playful, "we should be able to sneak in an actual date, or at least go for a walk around the block . . ."

Daniel grinned. "That sounds good."

"Besides," Beth added, "I'd love to see your mom and I might even like to meet your dad again."

"Careful what you wish for."

"What's that supposed to mean?"

"That nothing's changed. He's still the same as always. Didn't even bother to visit Mom in the hospital. Typical . . ."

"How does he look?"

"Old. Rundown. Stressed out."

"Stressed out? About what?"

"I'm not sure. Not about Mom. It was strange. He was gone all day—some guy brought him home and said they'd taken a trip to Manzanar."

"Manzanar? That old Japanese internment camp?"

"You remember," Daniel said, surprised.

"Of course I do. Why would they go there?"

"I have no idea. Worse, this guy has him all worked up about some war medal Dad got. Supposedly. Who knows . . ."

Beth gasped. "You didn't talk to him about the Army, did you?"

"No."

"Good. You know, he's not going to be around much longer. Don't you think it's time to make amends?"

"Please don't start, Beth."

"—You always say that."

"I don't want to talk about this now."

"You never want to talk about it . . ."

"Listen, hon," Daniel said, turning the conversation again to safer ground, "Why don't you go ahead, get your flight and come out here. Then you can see for yourself what's up."

Beth sighed. "Okay. I'll let you know my arrival time."

"Fine. I'll pick you up. We can stay an extra day or two. Be good for both of us."

"I'm sorry I woke you."

"And I'm sorry I didn't call yesterday. I'll see you soon and we'll reconnect then. Everything's going to be fine."

"Love you."

"Love you too."

Daniel hung up and climbed back into the bed. He tried to shut his eyes but after a couple of minutes realized it was no use trying to sleep again. Talking about his father had gotten him too agitated. He rolled out of bed, took off his clothes, and got in the shower.

Something about his father still perplexed him. It was bothering him more than his problems with Beth, because it didn't make any sense to him.

If his Dad had won a medal, why hadn't he told them about it? Wasn't he proud of whatever it was he got it for?

And why would he be afraid of questions from the government? Decades later?

It was all a troubling mystery . . . and the strange look on his father's face haunted him.

He had never seen his father look afraid before. Not when they were once driving in a rainstorm and their car hydroplaned, sliding off the Pacific Coast highway and stopping just short of a cliff. Not when he confronted Mr. Bielsky, a huge burly man whose sons had smashed their mailbox twice and often called Daniel and Kenny chinks. From across the street, Daniel had watched his dad rap on their door and engage in a shouting match with Mr. Bielsky. Bielsky was almost twice his father's size, but Daniel remembered him speaking to Bielsky like a child. Daniel had worried a fistfight would break out, but it hadn't. Mr. Bielsky had just angrily slammed the door. But one thing was certain: those boys never touched the Tokunaga's mailbox again.

His dad saw every decision in life as a choice between honor or dishonor. There was no room for anything in between. And certainly no room for fear. Because nothing was more important to him than courage. If you were courageous, you could do no wrong.

Kenny had understood that.

The sudden memory of his brother made Daniel's eyes well with tears that mixed with the hot water running down his face.

Kenny was a good boy. Honest. Loyal. Better than Daniel. He'd deserved to live a long and happy life.

And it infuriated Daniel that their father didn't recognize Kenny's death as the tragic waste that it was. He'd even made it sound *good*, in some sick, sadistic way.

An honorable death. That's what he'd said, once.

It made Daniel want to wring his neck. Damn him.

He got out of the shower and dried himself with a towel. Then he sat down, naked, on the toilet seat cover and used the towel to dry his eyes. He made a pitiful sight, but he was alone and he didn't care. Beth always asked why he hated his father. How could he even begin to explain? The reasons were so numerous and interconnected . . . and now also so distant in memory that sometimes he struggled to remember exactly what had occurred.

They were, after all, memories he'd spent years trying to suppress.

NEW YORK CITY
April 1968

"Dad? Can you hear me?" Daniel asked, holding the telephone close to his ear. He was sitting in his dorm room at Columbia University. The bruises on his arms were painful when he moved.

"Is it true?" his father's deep, brusque voice returned. It was almost a growl.

"Is what true?"

"You were arrested?" His father spat out this last word.

There was no hiding it. Daniel tried to sound confident and a little defiant when he said yes.

His father snorted. "How come you are so stupid? I told you to stop your destructive behavior. I told you to study hard so you could go to medical school. Now look what you've done—you're a criminal and you've brought great dishonor on all of us!"

"Dad, I'm not a criminal. We were protesting the war in Vietnam. It was peaceful—"

"—I saw it on the news!" his father roared. "You took over the buildings and the police had to storm in! This is worse than just wasting time standing

around and holding signs. This is serious. You're a traitor. You stand against the United States Army. You know what our people have done to show our loyalty! And this is what you do?"

"Dad, the war is wrong. It's not like World War Two. We're killing innocent women and children over there. We've invaded a country that poses no threat to us."

"What do you know of this? Are you a government official? Are you a general in the army? No! You're a stupid boy. You think you're smart, but you know nothing!"

"We're also protesting the unfair treatment of blacks. You've experienced discrimination; you know what it's like. Things can't go on like this—"

"There will always be racists. You can't change that. The only thing you can control is your own conduct. And you have shamed us. There are boys your age going over there and fighting for our country. And all you can do is stab them in the back at home. I've seen pictures of you people. You dress funny, do drugs, and have sex with anyone. To think you are one of these hooligans makes me sick."

"I don't do drugs and I'm not having sex—"

"But you are ungrateful. You know what we have sacrificed for you to be there. And you betray us. We expect you to study, so you can become a great doctor. But you are now a criminal."

"Dad, I'm sorry. I do know how much you've sacrificed for me to be here."

"Do you? Do you know that we now have no money for Kenny to go to college?"

"What?" Daniel felt like he'd been punched. "You never told me that."

"You never cared! You only think of yourself."

"Dad, I'll get another job. I'll help pay more of my tuition."

"Pah! You will never be able to pay enough. If I had known what you would do at that school, I would never have given you the money to go there. Instead of making you smarter, it just made you an educated fool. Worse, it turned you into a law-breaking delinquent."

"But Kenny has to go to college."

"No he doesn't. He's not like you. He doesn't get good grades. He doesn't like school. But that's okay, because he's hardworking and loyal. These are far more important qualities than being book smart. He'll be a good worker with me at the plant or in whatever job he wants."

"But even if we're short of money I'm sure he can go to one of the state schools."

"That's his choice. But I know he'd rather work. None of us ever went to college. And we've done fine."

"No Dad, I really mean it. Kenny has to go to college."

"Unlike you, he cares about his family. He says he doesn't want to waste our money on something he doesn't really want to do. You may be book smart, but you know nothing of the world, and less about honor. We have all sacrificed for you to be where you are. And now you have repaid us with shame. From today forward I'm not paying another cent for your schooling. It's too late for you. They will never take a criminal into medical school. You have thrown away your opportunity and spat in our faces! You should just leave and get a job!"

"Dad, please. You can't mean it."

"I mean every word!"

The words cut deeply. Daniel visualized his father's face, which, like his words, was surely set in stone.

"You're a man now. Act like a man. By the time I was your age I'd already fought in a war, gotten married, and was earning a good wage."

There was silence between them. Then Daniel heard the final, cruel cut-line—"Good bye. This phone call is already too expensive. Find some real work. And if you can't, join the Army. Fight for your country, instead of degrading it. Regain your honor. If you don't, you'll never amount to anything."

"But Dad—"

Daniel heard a dial tone. His father was no longer there.

NINE

D aniel watched her from a distance. Anne Mikado walked toward him on the sand-splashed sidewalk next to the beach, but she hadn't spotted him yet. Pairs of seagulls danced in the air overhead, twirling and spinning. A stiff breeze of salt-scented air blew in from the ocean.

Now she saw him. She waved and made a little skip in her step that made Daniel think she was rushing to draw nearer, but perhaps he just imagined it. He watched the way she moved, noticed her slim figure, and the way her black hair blew in the breeze. He marveled at how youthful she looked.

He'd suggested the same spot at Huntington Beach they'd always loved. It was quieter than other places along the long expanse of golden sand. There was a playground, and he was happy to see it was in the same spot more than thirty years later, albeit with shiny, brand new structures and soft rubber floor tiles. During the day this area was busy with kids and their mothers or nannies. But in the late evening, the playground was empty, and the surfers, high school kids, drug addicts, and homeless kept to other sections of the beach.

Anne smiled as she drew near.

"Hi," she said.

"Hi," Daniel replied, leaning against the leg of a swing set, trying to look casual.

"Do you think we might break one of these swings if we tried them again?" Anne teased. She wore a light blue sheer blouse, through which Daniel could see her white camisole.

"You wouldn't, but maybe I would. Anne, you look great. You must work out or something."

"I do, some. I teach Pilates once a week at the gym. Helps keep my mind relaxed. My body too."

"I don't have time to exercise anymore."

"You need to make time. Remember when we used to run up and down this beach together? That was before jogging got to be so popular."

Daniel nodded. "I remember. But maybe I never told you that I really never liked running. I only did it to spend time with you."

"Is that right? Then maybe I can admit to you now that I never really liked fishing. I only did it because you always took me for ice cream on the pier afterwards."

They both laughed.

Then their laughter faded, and neither of them seemed to know what to say next. Anne looked at Daniel's eyes and for a moment he felt eighteen again, looking into the face of the girl he wanted to marry.

"Should we go sit down and watch the sunset . . . like old times?" Anne suggested.

"Sure." Somewhere inside Daniel felt that tingling again. Then it was all over him. A shivery feeling.

He followed her lead. They took off their shoes and walked out onto the beach. The sand was coarse and cool underfoot. The sun burned fiercely at the horizon's edge, making the sea shimmer like an orange mirror.

"How's your mom?" Anne asked as they walked.

"She's doing well. In fact, they're going to discharge her. I'm going by to pick her up later tonight. She's almost her old self. Eating again too. I think she dodged a bullet."

"I'm so glad to hear it. And is your father doing well these days?"

"My dad? He seems all right. To be honest, I haven't gotten along with him for a long time, not since college. We've hardly spoken in all this time."

"How much time?"

Daniel shrugged, looked hesitant, as if the information were socially unacceptable. "Decades," he said flatly.

"Really? I remember he was so dedicated to seeing you succeed. And now you have. I would think he would be so proud of you he couldn't stand it."

"He can stand it alright. Proud? No. That's probably the last word he'd use . . ." Daniel stared out across the blinding water, watching the shadow surfers who hoped to catch one last good ride before the light was gone.

Daniel changed the subject abruptly. "Hey, you've not told me anything about yourself. Are you married? Do you have kids?"

"I *was* married, but my husband died. We didn't have any children."

"Oh." Daniel didn't know what to say.

"It's not that we didn't want to. We found out that we couldn't . . . that *I* couldn't."

"I'm really sorry to hear that."

"Don't be. It wasn't anyone's fault. My husband, Harold, never made me feel bad about it. We had a good marriage and he was a good man."

"What happened to him?"

"He got pancreatic cancer and died about five years ago. You would have liked him. He was smart, like you. He never went to college, but he could fix anything. He was an auto mechanic and ended up owning his own shop."

"Sounds like he was a good catch," Daniel said.

"Yes. And he was also born in Japan, so he was very good at the traditional things, like tea and Japanese history and respect—all the things my parents liked. But he was also good at everything American. He used to drive a Corvette he'd bought cheap from a customer and fixed up. We'd drive up and down the Pacific Coast Highway with the top down. Long road trips. Good times."

Anne stopped walking. They were fifteen feet from the water's crisply foaming tideline.

"And my parents loved him. That was a good thing."

"Your parents were wonderful people. They were always so nice to me."

Anne nodded, but said nothing.

Daniel looked down and around. The conversation had gone to places he wasn't prepared for. He knelt down and started digging with both hands in the sand. It was uncharacteristic of him. He wondered why he did it. To change the subject again?

"What are you doing?" Anne asked with a curious smile.

"What does it look like? Digging pits like we used to."

"To sit in? I remember now." She laughed, and the fading copper from the sun caught her in profile and made her face glow all around the edges.

He finished digging two small depressions in the sand and they sat in them, side by side, facing the darkening water. The sand wall felt cool on Daniel's back. He felt a slight chill against his polo shirt.

"So what about you? I know you're a famous surgeon. And you're wearing a ring, so you must be married. Tell me about your family."

"I met my wife Beth while I was a surgical fellow. She worked in the operating room. We have two kids, James and Julia. Both just graduated from high school."

"Do you have a picture of them?"

"I do." He took out his wallet and withdrew a small photo. It was a miniature version of the picture they'd used for last year's Christmas card. He handed it to Anne.

Anne gasped. "Daniel, your wife is *gorgeous*. Your kids, too."

Daniel's lips parted in a half-smile. "Thanks."

"No, I mean it. Your wife . . . what's her name?"

"Beth."

"She could be a model."

"Yes, she actually did do some modeling during college, just to help earn some money."

"Do you mind if I ask, what did your parents think of you marrying a white woman? I mean, did they mind?"

"Did they mind? To be honest, by that time my relationship with my dad was so bad that we weren't talking and I didn't really care what he thought. I think my mom wanted me to marry someone Japanese, but that's only because she'd always pictured it in her mind that way. Once she got to know Beth, she liked her a lot."

"She must be wonderful," Anne said.

"How can you tell, from a picture?"

"Not from a picture. But because you married her. You wouldn't marry someone who wasn't wonderful."

Daniel felt a catch in his throat. He thought of Beth and the kids and felt a hint of guilt for . . . whatever this was he was doing here with Anne. Which was? He wasn't sure exactly. Surely it was natural to be curious about this woman who'd once left his life so inexplicably. But that was ancient history, and now their lives had diverged and were different.

Weren't they?

"Do you remember the time you saved that little girl in the water?" Anne asked. "It was right . . ." She pointed up the beach, squinting against the last rays of burnished sunlight, ". . . over there, by those volleyball courts."

"I haven't thought about that in years." Daniel shook his head as the sudden memory began to take hold.

"You saw the girl in the water. She wasn't flailing or anything, but you knew something was wrong. You looked close and saw she was struggling. She was drowning, but you don't cry out when you're drowning. Her mom had gone to take her little brother to the bathroom. You ran in, swam out, and brought her back. I didn't even know what CPR was until I saw you doing it."

"You remember all that? I'd forgotten . . ."

"You didn't hesitate. You were so brave."

"Brave? No. You don't *think* in life and death situations, you just *act*."

"I suppose it's part of your everyday life now, saving people. You probably don't feel it's special when you're doing it. But it is."

Daniel didn't speak. In the distance, he watched the silhouette of a freighter slowly inching its way darkly south.

Anne continued, "You said you and your dad stopped talking to each other. But I was there when that mother came by your house and brought you a cake to thank you. Your dad was proud of you then. You could tell just by looking at his face."

Daniel did remember that. "Thanks, Anne."

The sky had gone gray, as had the water. A group of teenagers down the beach lit a bonfire from a huge conglomeration of white driftwood.

As they watched the sun disappear below the horizon, Daniel sensed Anne leaning a little towards him. Or perhaps he just imagined it? Because he remembered being together, just like this, the first time they'd come to this spot. Two teenagers, slowly drawing nearer, with nothing between their bodies but a breath of wind. And then . . . not even that.

This time, Daniel made a conscious effort to keep his body still, and his eyes straight ahead, gazing out at infinity.

⌒

"Feeling all right?" Daniel asked his mother after helping her buckle her seatbelt.

"Yes, yes," Keiko replied impatiently. "Take me home. I'm perfectly fine."

As he pulled away from the curb, Daniel waved goodbye to the orderly who had pushed his mother's wheelchair.

"I wonder what your father has been doing for food."

"Mom, he's a grown up. It's only been two days." A small, ticklish sense of annoyance flickered across Daniel's mind before he quickly got rid of it. No doubt, Keiko was as obsessive as other mothers who worry about everyone but themselves. But still, it irritated him how much attention his father could get for doing nothing when it was Keiko who needed it now.

"He's a disaster in the kitchen," she said in a dispirited voice. "I don't even trust him to boil water—you know that, right? And you remember he had a heart attack last year? He needs help remembering to take his medicines."

"You're the one who needs to remember her medicines, Mom. I'm sure he's fine." He pulled onto the 10. At nine at night, the traffic was light.

"You never told me how it went when you saw him at the house."

"It went fine, Mom. Don't worry about it. You just need to think about resting up and getting better. My mind is on you, not him."

Ignoring this, Keiko continued, "Did you talk much with him?"

"Not a lot. He'd gone out for the day with some guy, someone who said he knew you. What was his name?" Daniel tried to remember. "Joe Fukuda. That's it. Joe Fukuda."

His mother turned her head. "Joe?" She seemed to drift off into a haze of remembrance for a moment. Then she snapped out of it and said, "I haven't seen Joe in years. What did he say?"

"For one thing, he said Dad won a big war medal in World War Two. The Distinguished Service Cross. Do you know what that is? It's the second highest medal for bravery."

"Really?" She looked thoughtful. "He never told me that. Was Joe sure?"

"Yes, he was. But he also said the government had been calling his house to say they were re-looking into medals that had been awarded."

"The *government?*" Keiko said with disdain. This wasn't just a word, Daniel recalled. His mother mistrusted the political system in general but the *government* was something else again. The *government* drove her family out of their home during the war and imprisoned them in the middle of the desert, at Manzanar, for three years.

"Yes. And whatever he told Dad got him pretty upset. I don't think he was much in the mood to talk when I was there."

"I wonder what it's all about," Keiko said.

Ten minutes later they were pulling into their driveway in Monterey Park.

"I see his bedroom light on. He's still awake," she noticed.

Daniel parked the car and ran around to his mother's door, but when he got there it was already open and she was swinging out her legs.

"Go on, go on. I'm fine," she insisted.

Daniel stood close to her as she went up the short flight of stairs to the front porch, ready to steady her if need be. At the front door, he noticed a FedEx package lying on the doormat.

"Someone sent you a package," he said.

"I wonder who that could be from."

Daniel held the door open for Keiko and turned on the light.

"Oh, it's good to be home," she said with a sigh.

"Keiko!" came a gruff voice at the top of the stairs. Daniel's father was hunched over and holding the rail, wearing plaid pajamas that hung loosely on his skeletal frame. "Are you okay? How do you feel?" There was sincere concern in his eyes.

"I'm fine. They gave me a couple new pills to take, that's all. What have you been doing? What have you been eating?"

"Me? Just some dried seaweed and ramen noodles."

"Ai ya! You are no better than a teenager. I have food in the freezer. I will make some tonkatsu right now."

"Mom, you really shouldn't do that. Let's just get you settled in."

"Yes, Keiko. I'm not hungry. It's late, and you should go to bed."

"Bed? I've been in bed for two days straight. Did they call you about the car yet?"

"The insurance man called. They'll take care of it but it won't be ready for another week. They have to find replacements for the hood and fender, then they'll have to paint it."

Keiko tsk'ed and shook her head. "They'll pay for it, and then they'll double our premium next year. How could I be so stupid?"

"Mom, it was an accident. Just be thankful you survived it."

"Hmph," she emitted in reply. Her eyes fell to the envelope in Daniel's hands. "You should open that, Danny."

He examined the stiff FedEx mailer. "It's from the Department of Defense." He held it out to his father. "Addressed to you."

"Department of Defense?" The old man's face crinkled a bit in dismay.

"Might as well open it," Keiko repeated.

Daniel's father took the envelope. He slowly ran his finger into the fold, tore it lengthwise, and withdrew another large envelope— this one very fancy, his name and address written on it artfully in a style of calligraphy.

This he opened as well, and pulled out a folder, emblazoned with the gold seal of an eagle. Inside, there was one sheet of paper, with typing that filled half the page. He scanned it. And then Daniel saw his father's eyes lose focus.

"What does it say?" he asked, as he moved behind his father and began to read over his shoulder.

"Dad! It says they are considering upgrading you to the Medal of Honor!"

Keiko gasped. "You mean it's good?"

"Good? It's great!"

"But why would he get the Medal of Honor?"

Daniel looked at his father, who was still staring mistily at nothing in particular.

"Mom, I told you Dad won the Distinguished Service Cross. This says they are going to review the action that won him that medal to see if he really deserves the Medal of Honor." In his excitement, Daniel patted his father on the back, but the old man flinched and slid away.

"What's wrong?" Daniel asked.

His father didn't answer.

"Dad, tell us what this is about. What did you do in the war?"

A long silent moment. Outside they heard the squeal of car tires. At the same time, the streetlamps switched on, and a strong wind made the screen door rattle.

When his father finally spoke, his voice barely above a whisper, he said, "Listen to me, both of you. This medal is a mistake. It means nothing, except . . . *mistake*. I don't want to talk about it."

Daniel stood in front of his father and grasped the other end of the letter. "Do you realize how important this is? Not just to you, but to all of us? Do you understand?"

"No!" his father shouted, jerking the paper out of Daniel's hand. "The war was the biggest mistake of all. This brings back horrible memories." In one swift motion he ripped the letter in two, then crushed both halves into balls with his fists. "Don't answer the phone if it rings. I'm not going to talk to them about anything."

Daniel felt the warmth of his mother's shoulder against him as his father retreated up the stairs, into his bedroom, and into the void of another time, a vanished world where Daniel and Keiko were neither admitted, nor acknowledged.

TEN

VOSGES MOUNTAINS, FRANCE
Hill B, outside the village of Bruyères
October 16, 1944

It definitely moved.

Ray blinked, stared at the spot, next to the trunk of a huge oak tree, where he'd seen the branch move. The trunk was thick enough to hide a man.

He exhaled slowly and sank to his knees behind another thick tree not twenty feet away from his unseen enemy. A blinding rain was falling, reducing Ray's world to the space between the trees. He was soaked to the skin, chilled by the wind and drenched with sweat.

Ray sighted his M-1 on the branch, then the empty space where a man might jump out, but he was trembling badly. He swung his aim from one side of the tree to the other, thinking the German was just as likely to show himself on either side. In doing this side-to-side swerve, Ray's trembling hands tightened, and he gained a small advantage over his nerves.

For a long time, he waited, frozen, terrified. This day had already been filled with action. First, a German artillery barrage, causing scores of American casualties since there'd been no time to dig foxholes. Then, small arms fire all morning from German skirmishers, not a concentrated force, but just enough to slow the American advance up Hill B to a crawl. The close grown trees, creeping fog, and constant rain favored the German defenders. Before Ray's squad had been able to jump off the main road and head up the hill, a German tank had ventured forth from Bruyères and attacked their rear. One of Ray's platoon-mates had scored a direct hit with a bazooka, but the round was a dud. The tank took out half a dozen men before another bazooka team finally knocked it out.

The sarge had shown them the map. The village of Bruyères was surrounded by four hills, which HQ had designated: A, B, C, and D. Whoever controlled these heights would control the town, and the 442nd soon learned that the Germans had fortified each one. It didn't take Ray long to become convinced that his battalion had drawn the raw deal of being ordered to take the most heavily defended hill, but now, at twilight, the sounds of explosions, screams, and gunfire filling the entire valley told him there was heavy fighting everywhere.

Ray wasn't sure he was still staring at the same tree. He blinked and blinked again, peering through the driving rain. He wanted to look around and search for other nearby GIs, but he didn't dare, for fear of missing the German, who might know Ray was there, too.

It moved again!

The branch. Someone *was* there.

Once again, Ray's fingers started to tremble. He tucked his rifle stock in tightly between the side of his face and his shoulder, trying to hold his aim. More than anything, he wanted to lie out flat. He needed a more stable firing position, but he couldn't risk moving now. The sound of his own heartbeat throbbed in his ears.

Now the branch swung away from the tree. Something was coming out. Ray trained his M-1 and squinted. Clenching his teeth, he pulled the trigger.

Nothing happened.

A raven flew heavily up into the forest canopy, buffeting the air with its wings.

Ray let out a long breath. Just a *bird*?

He checked his rifle. What's wrong with this damn thing?

The safety!

God, I'm an idiot.

Ray flicked the safety off.

Feeling foolish, he started to stand up.

Then the same tree branch blurred. A fuzzy movement, indistinct but palpable. Something larger emerged. A man.

Ray swung his rifle up, finger on trigger.

He saw him clearly now—helmet shape, jacket color, 442nd arm patch.

Ray exhaled. His one-second hesitation had saved the life of one of their own. He let his M1 sag, point earthward.

The face that revealed itself from behind the tree was Nisei. The man moved off to the right with no more than a nod.

Ray felt an enormous weight lift off his shoulders. Sweat and raindrops mingled on his face, salt and sweet.

I almost shot him. I'm so turned around, I don't know which way is up or down, which way the enemy is, which way my head is screwed on. For a moment he didn't know why he was there in the muted rain in a strange forest in the middle of a battle of nerves and bullets and sheer dread.

Ray wiped his forehead and followed the other soldier.

His hands trembled, his right eye ticked, he had to take a leak bad, but out of spite and will, he forced himself not to stop and relieve himself. Let my bladder explode, better than a bullet.

~

"That's it, we're done! Let's get in!" Hiro yelled over the concussive explosions above and all around them. He lay on his stomach, peering over the edge of the foxhole Ray was in, digging furiously. The bombardment was an earsplitting pounding, punctuated by the shrill banshee whine of incoming. The shockwave from a blast overhead slammed Hiro's body hard against the earth, hammering his skull, forcing the air from his lungs. He screamed. No sound came out.

"Gotta dig deeper!" Ray shouted, spitting dirt out of his mouth. "Got to be deep enough to get our heads below ground!"

Hiro shook his head. "Forget it! This is useless. If we're gonna get hit, we're gonna get hit. A little bit of ground isn't going to save us!"

Ray looked up at his friend. "If we go deeper we'll get through this!" There was honest logic in what he said. Hiro saw it, made a face, banged his fist on Ray's helmet so that it rang. "Have it your way! Switch!"

Ray's arms were like seaweed. He couldn't feel them. He tried to climb out, but his hands wouldn't grip. Hiro grabbed him under the armpits, jerked him up and out, then dragged him away, and with a pivot and drop, was into the hole.

Ray lay flat on his belly on the cold, wet earth. He forced his mind to work. The trees overhead were exploding like Roman candles. A shell would whistle in, strike a pine tree, and turn it to a hail of white-arrowed splinters. From where he lay, he could see several dead soldiers, not from direct shell hits, but from the hurricane force of those huge splinters, each one the size of a harpoon. The noise was thunder and scream, whine and roar. It came in waves like a sea blast. Then the lethal points of knife-sharp pine.

Hiro shoveled mud as fast as he could while Ray crawled around very low to the ground gathering broken pine boughs to cover the top of the hole. They weren't much but they might be enough to save a life, or lives. He came back to check Hiro's progress.

"Okay, that's deep enough! Dig horizontal!"

"What?"

"We need to put our feet somewhere!" Ray made signs with his hands. The explosions were deafening.

A sudden, hard rain began to hammer down on them. The overhead booming increased, and with each clap of violence above, Ray's eardrums buzzed and then all sound grew faint. Then his hearing returned. Ray, face to the pine-needled forest floor, clamped his hands over his ears. Close-up, he watched individual raindrops create miniature explosions and craters in the mud. The barrage had them completely pinpointed.

He felt a tap on his leg. Hiro. He was done. Ray scrambled into the hole, right on top of his friend. He pulled the thin cover of pine boughs over the hole. After shifting around, they managed to sit upright, back to back. Hiro's face was pressed against a vertical wall of earth; Ray, too, leaned in against the dirt with his back supported by Hiro. The bottom of the foxhole almost immediately began to fill with water.

They stayed like that, wet and sweaty, filthy and tired, too woebegone to sleep. All night long they heard each other's breaths come and go, in and out, diastole, systole, as the rain came down and soaked them. The only relief was the sweet fragrance of fresh-cut pine, so that, closing their eyes and letting their minds go, they sometimes seemed to be floating skyward on the back of a raven rather than stuck in a seepage hole of dismal mud.

—

"You awake?" Hiro whispered.

Ray groaned, spat a blob of dirt out of his mouth.

"It's stopped."

Ray lifted his head, which had been pressed against Hiro's back. He tried to shift and move his sore joints. His ears were ringing.

"Yeah, it has."

Ray pushed up against the blanket of pine boughs. The branches didn't move. What's this? His hand touched something heavy, solid. A tree trunk.

"What's wrong?" Hiro asked. His face was black with mud.

Ray pushed. The tree trunk was immovable. He shifted his feet and pushed up. Hiro cursed. Ray was standing on his thigh. "Sorry." Ray worked himself into a new position, tried again. "I can't move this damned tree. It's too big."

"Let me try." They moved again, so Hiro could try.

For a moment he struggled, then, "That's really heavy. I can't move it, either."

"Can you hear any life out there?"

They both listened. Silence.

"Let's try pushing together," Ray said.

"Okay. Push it to my side. Ready? One, two, three!"

Groaning, grunting, they moved the trunk perhaps a fraction of an inch. "Again."

After a half hour of grunt work, straining every muscle in their bodies, the two soldiers moved the fallen pine tree just enough for Ray to poke his head out. A gray mist clung to the forest floor. Ray checked his watch. 0550. No sun, no dawn. "If my head can get out, so can my shoulders—that's true of animals, and probably humans," Ray said, and he proved it by twisting and turning his shoulders almost to the breaking point. At last he was out as far as his hips, and he ground them through too. Hiro did the same.

"Oh my God," Hiro mumbled. The forest floor was pocked with craters, some large enough to fit an Army jeep. Truncated trees were everywhere. The smell of sap was almost heady, but so was the smell of oil and burnt wood. The raw flesh of splintered pine and hardwood was white, and underneath, caught between trunks and limbs, were the crushed bodies of GIs. Some had hands raised, as if in supplication, others were armless, handless, faceless. Hiro found a foxhole and looked in. Abruptly, he vomited. Ray came over. Inside, there were soldiers hugging each other, skulls crushed into their necks. Ray fought back tears but they came anyway. Then he too threw up, convulsively, but only once in a great liquid stream, and then nothing more.

Ray sat down in one of the shell craters and leaned his back against the damp earth. His ears still rang. Not the ring of the night before but the steady soundless vibration of the body under siege with itself. Other noises, if there were any, were reduced to white noise. Hiro sat down next to him.

"You saved us, you know," Hiro said.

"How?"

"The tree landed right over our hole. If we hadn't dug further down, we'd both be dead."

Ray nodded. For a long time the two of them sat there, silently staring at the devastation, not knowing exactly what to do or where to begin. The ruptured earth and scorched panorama, the haunting quiet—it was as if the world and everyone in it had died, except for them. The last two survivors.

Sometime later, a voice intruded. "Hey! Dimwits!"

They looked up. A man approached, coming at them in a low crouched run, scrambling over trees like an animal. His face and uniform were almost completely covered with mud. Ray grabbed his rifle.

"Y'all two made it? Ah can't believe it. Complete stroke uh luck." The mud man came closer. It was Sergeant Moto. Ray lowered his rifle. The whites of Moto's eyes were almost blue. His brown face the crusted color of pine bark. "Any others alive?"

Ray shook his head.

"They nailed us all night. Damn Jerries. Now you guys: git off yer butts. We gotta form up 'cause they're aimin' to counterattack. And if they ain't, then our job is tuh take this hill and hold it."

Hiro groaned.

"Soldier, you wanna spend another night like the last one?"

Hiro shook his head.

"Then let's git goin'. Ain't no turnin' back. Other boys are already headin' up."

Hiro nodded, rose to his feet.

A few hundred yards above them, the *da-da-da-da* of German machine guns punctuated the silence.

The three men looked at each other. Then came the sounds of the mortally wounded and the maimed, a sound worse than incoming.

"That's where we're goin'. Our brothers are callin'," Moto said.

Hiro looked from Moto to Ray. All three of them: soaked, filthy, exhausted. "Well, what are we waiting for?" he said. "Let's go!"

ELEVEN

LOS ANGELES 1998

Beth readjusted the headrest of her seat. After the five-hour flight to LA she was anxious to get off the plane. Long flights always made her feel sticky and gross. The stale, recycled air dried out her skin and made her constantly thirsty, but whenever she drank too much she always needed to use the lavatory, which she tried to avoid as much as possible.

"I'm sorry folks," the pilot's voice came over the intercom, "Since we've arrived a little early, they're telling me our gate isn't open yet. So we'll be waiting here for about fifteen minutes."

The elderly woman sitting next to Beth in the middle seat groaned. Beth turned her head. The woman's hair was white, the pale skin over her temple paper-thin. She tapped her foot impatiently. Beth had a thought.

"Would you like to get up and stretch your legs? Maybe use the restroom?" she asked. Her hands fell to her seatbelt buckle—an offer to get up to let the woman out into the aisle.

The older woman gave Beth a pained smile. "Yes, my dear. I really need to use the bathroom, but they haven't turned the seatbelt sign off yet."

"Oh, well, why don't I ask if you can go? The pilot said we'd be sitting here a while." Beth pushed the steward call button and a slender, blonde flight attendant came down the aisle.

"I'm sorry to bother you," Beth said, "but my friend here would really like to use the lavatory. Do you think she could go?"

The flight attendant turned to look up the aisle at the cockpit door, as if trying to decide whether it was okay to break the protocol.

"The pilot did say we'd be waiting here for fifteen minutes," Beth reminded.

The attendant looked at the old woman, whose face was contorted in a wrinkle. "I suppose it would be okay, if you're quick."

"Thank you," Beth said. She rose and held out her hand to help the white-haired woman out of her seat.

"Thank you, dear," she said as she clasped Beth's hand.

Beth regained her seat and waited. The flight had been uneventful and they'd made good time. She'd tried to watch one of the movies but couldn't get into it. She'd been thinking about her conversation with Daniel.

"We'll reconnect," he'd said just before hanging up. "Everything's going to be fine."

What did that mean to him? Did it mean he'd also felt the strain on their relationship and was prepared to right the ship? Did it mean he understood the stress she'd been under to get the kids ready for college, or that he might empathize with how she felt now that her babies—they would always be her babies—were leaving home? Or was he being patronizing and just saying what he thought she wanted to hear?

Beth's anxiety about this trip had almost made her reconsider making it. She was nervous about meeting Daniel's father again, and about Keiko's health, and about what she and Daniel would talk about when they were together. Last night, she'd spent over an hour on the phone with her best friend Molly. Molly had asked her a question. *Tell me how you two fell in love*, she'd asked. *What was it about him that attracted you?*

It was a simple question. And it surprised Beth how easily the answer came to her, because the memories still seemed fresh. She recalled the happy years—when they'd dated and everything was fun, meaningful and passionate. Daniel Tokunaga was the most brilliant person she'd ever met. Beth was a surgical technician; he was a fellow in training. She was good at her job, assisting surgeons during their operations with efficiency and skill. She prided herself on knowing the steps of all the various procedures and each surgeon's preferences so she could anticipate what instrument was needed next.

Daniel was a brilliant house officer. Attendings loved operating with him; he was easy to teach and a quick learner. They knew Daniel would manage their surgical patients on the wards with meticulous care. He never overlooked anything and always went the extra mile. He was a rising star, that's what people said about him. So smart and talented, everyone knew he would one day become the chairman of a department.

In one of the first cases Beth scrubbed in with Daniel on, he stopped a new attending surgeon from making a horrible mistake by sewing in a vein bypass graft backwards onto the heart. The valves in the saphenous vein are oriented to permit blood flow in one direction. If the vein is sewn in backwards it is useless as a conduit—blood flow is impeded and the heart receives too little oxygen, leading quickly to myocardial infarction and probably death.

It wasn't the last time she saw Daniel save a life. A few days later, he brought a patient back from the dead. The chest was open and the heart suddenly arrested. The anesthesiologist freaked out. Someone shouted for the attending, who wasn't there because he was lazy and let Daniel operate on his patients—sometimes Daniel's outcomes were even better than his own. People were shouting, but Daniel calmly began to massage the heart and call for the drugs that could spark it back to life. Atropine. Epinephrine. Amiodarone. Then he shocked the heart and got the patient back. And after that, he went on with the case like nothing special had happened.

One day Beth saw Daniel sitting alone in the cafeteria and summoned the courage to ask if she could sit with him. He was dressed in formless green scrubs, and it looked like he hadn't shaved in days, but she liked the look of his eyes. They were focused and intelligent, seemingly able to take in and analyze everything at a glance. He had high, angled cheekbones and straight black hair. His teeth were shiny white. Daniel had looked up from his scrambled eggs and stared at Beth's face like he didn't know her. Then she realized that Daniel had probably never seen her without her surgical mask on. They had laughed about that and started talking. He was already post-call, which meant he'd been on duty in the hospital since the previous morning and had already worked thirty hours straight. But he didn't look tired. She'd learned he was four years older than she was. He didn't have a girlfriend. Not much time for one, he'd said with a smile.

A few weeks later, after finishing one of their cases, Daniel asked her out on a date. They went to an Italian restaurant and talked for hours, sharing stories about growing up: him in California, her in Minnesota. It seemed to her that she did most of the talking, about being into drama and singing and ballet as a young girl, and how hard she worked to earn the leads in high school and college plays, and how she'd finally decided she wanted to go to medical school and only wished she'd realized it sooner. Daniel was a good listener. He was different from the typical cardiac surgeon. He wasn't impatient, or arrogant, or at all condescending. He seemed . . . content. No matter if things were going well or poorly, he was always steady. He didn't let emotions affect him, and he rarely showed what he was feeling inside.

That was their main difference, she had realized long ago. Beth wore her heart on her sleeve. She cried during sad movies and hollered whenever James won a big point in tennis. Daniel was reserved, introverted. Maybe this was from his Japanese upbringing? she'd often wondered.

After they were married, Beth was thrilled to get pregnant almost right away. Daniel seemed happy too. And when they learned it would be twins it was like they were doubly blessed. She didn't mind stopping work. She didn't mind putting her plans for medical school on hold. And when James and Julia arrived, Beth felt her life might never be more complete than it was at that moment.

But it's tough for a mother to raise twins on her own when her husband is working 120 hours a week. There was no nearby family to help and no money for babysitters. She told herself it would get better after Daniel finished his training, but when he did, he still spent over 80 hours a week in the hospital, easy. He'd come home after completing two heart surgeries, each lasting five or six hours, warm up some leftovers from the fridge and collapse in bed with hardly a word. Beth would nurse, change diapers, run errands, all day long, never getting a break, hardly ever talking to another adult. When Daniel walked through the door, she yearned for just five or ten minutes of conversation, but he was usually too tired.

It was during those early years that she came to love the people from her church. Beth had always been a church-goer; her parents were Lutherans with roots in Scandinavia. But she'd never known true fellowship with other Christians until she found herself floundering as a mother of twins. One Sunday morning she was bone tired and wouldn't have gone to church except for the fact that she could leave the twins in the nursery and have some time to herself in the sanctuary. She wasn't above taking a nap during the sermon; she always sat in the back corner for this reason. Afterwards, she went to pick up the kids and found them in the small back room where the cribs were set up. She saw her children sleeping and realized she was going to have to wake them up and take them home and the thought of this was so overwhelming that she suddenly burst into tears. That's when her friend Molly walked in.

Though mortified, Beth couldn't stop crying and eventually blurted out how desperate she felt, like she was on the verge of a nervous breakdown. Molly listened patiently and gave Beth a hug. That very day she got a group of friends together who took turns making dinners to drop off at Beth's home for the next three months. These same four or five women volunteered to watch her twins for a couple hours every few days so she could go shop for groceries. They remained her closest friends. She would never have made it through those early years without their help.

And as the kids grew up, she and Daniel seemed to go through the motions of a marriage. Their conversations grew shorter and less frequent. Sex became routine, unexciting, and also less frequent. He stopped doing the small, thoughtful things he used to, like calling her from work for a brief hello between cases just to see how she was doing, or stopping by the hospital gift shop at the end of the day to buy her a half-price flower bouquet that hadn't yet been sold. Meanwhile, Beth concentrated on the children and found her fulfillment in devoting herself to their well-being and education— hoping to mold them to be kind, generous people who would make the world a better place. Which is exactly what she'd always wanted to do herself.

But now the kids were gone. The house was empty.

Her friends had seen this coming. Each of them had had the same advice: invest in your marriage. Reach out to Daniel. And she'd tried. At least she thought she had. She called him during the day and though he rarely picked up—most likely he was in the operating room—she always left a message. She stayed up later than usual hoping they might talk before going to bed—and they did a few times—before Daniel drifted back to staying up late surfing TV channels and watching movies.

Two years ago, she started confronting Daniel every few months to say she was worried they were having a problem. He listened attentively but said nothing. She'd even suggested seeing a counselor before, but never in a serious way. She knew Daniel wouldn't want to go. He would promise things would get better. He'd stop traveling so much to give guest lectures around the world. After the kids left home he'd take her on that trip to Europe they'd always talked about. And Daniel *would* change—he'd bring her flowers again and take her on a date or two. He'd make an effort to come home early for dinner as a family. But soon, inevitably, things would drift back to normal. And both were too busy to make a big deal about it. And life continued.

Beth felt a tap on her shoulder. She looked up.

"I'm back, so sorry for the trouble." It was the old woman who had gone to the bathroom.

"Oh, hello," Beth replied, quickly getting out of her seat.

"Thank you so much, dear. I feel much better."

"No problem." Beth returned her smile.

The overhead speaker came on: "Well folks, they've told us we can move on now to the gate. Thanks again for your patience."

Beth released a slow breath and looked out onto the sunny tarmac and the terminal building in the distance. Daniel would be there, waiting for her.

Beth emerged from the jet bridge into the terminal. She looked for Daniel in the gate area but did not see him. Where was he? Other passengers were gathering in small groups, being greeted by their loved ones. She weaved through the small crowd and walked out to the main concourse. She looked up and down the long corridor, searching faces. No Daniel.

She was speechless. She was sure she'd told him the correct time and flight number.

After about five minutes she decided to sit down and wait. By now, all the other passengers had left and she sat alone, watching travelers walking briskly to and fro.

Daniel had specifically said he would meet her at the gate, but she was beginning to question her memory and thinking maybe she should just head over to baggage claim when she saw him. He was walking toward her, not in any hurry, with a tall cup in his hand.

"Hi hon," Daniel said. "Did I just miss you come off? I went to get a coffee."

"Yes. I've been looking for you."

"I'm sorry. How was the flight?"

He took her hand and they began to walk. The day was sunny but dull because of the cloud level and the poor quality of the air. The polished, neutralizing terminal itself, like its own bright person, seemed to outshine the outside atmosphere.

"The flight?" Beth said tersely, annoyed by Daniel's nonchalance. "It was long." She let her hand go limp and Daniel let go. "Is the hotel far?"

"Not that far if the traffic isn't too bad. Did Julia get off okay?"

"It was like she couldn't leave fast enough."

"How was the packing?"

Beth smirked. "You might not like it but we ended up having to go to the post office to ship three big boxes of her stuff to Stanford."

"What? Didn't she already have two suitcases?"

"Yes, but you weren't there to stop her, were you?"

Daniel looked at her. She wasn't smiling.

"Very funny," he replied in a neutral tone of voice. He turned his head away and watched planes taxiing the runways. They walked past a dozen gates in silence.

"So what have you been up to?" Beth asked, changing the subject.

Daniel leveled his gaze from the enormity of the airport windows to the closer perspective of his pretty wife.

"What did you say?"

"I said, 'What have you been up to?'"

"Oh. Nothing much. I brought my mom home last night. Tried to get her settled back in."

"Haven't been too busy, then?"

Daniel shrugged.

"Must seem strange," Beth said. "To have all this free time on your hands."

"Well, it's not exactly like doing nothing," Daniel replied. "One thing I'm trying to gauge is whether Mom will be able to take care of herself *and* my dad. Their house is a complete mess, same as it always was. Junk everywhere."

"I've only been there once."

"Well, I don't think it's changed at all since then."

They stepped onto a moving walkway and shifted positions to avoid being bumped by two racing teenagers.

"But medically speaking, your mom is going to be okay?"

"I think so. But she won't take care of herself. She spends all her time worrying about Dad."

"That reminds me—" Beth suddenly remembered, "I meant to tell you—right before I left this morning I got a phone call from a woman at the Department of Defense, of all places. I was more than a little surprised. She started asking about your dad. When I asked why she called us, she said, 'You're next of kin.' I asked what it was about but she didn't want to say over the phone."

Daniel nodded slowly.

"They asked me if he was dead, Daniel. Isn't that strange?"

They stepped off the walkway and, a few steps further, onto an escalator going down to baggage level.

"You don't seem surprised," Beth said

"I can explain it. Stranger than the call . . . you know that World War Two medal I mentioned on the phone? Dad got a letter saying they're considering upgrading his medal. So, it's actually *good* news, but I don't think Dad sees it that way. He won't speak to anyone about it—not the DOD, and especially not to us. That's the strangest of all. Not that he was ever talkative about anything—but this reluctance to deal with an honor in an honorable way? Given his honor motto, I don't get it."

"That *does* sound weird."

"For some reason, I don't think he wants anyone to go looking into why he got a medal in the first place. But that makes no sense."

Beth furrowed her brow. "How bizarre."

"What did you tell them?"

"I said he was very much alive. Do you think that was okay?"

"Absolutely. It's the truth. I'm going to have a serious talk with him. He's got to respond to them. If he doesn't, well, one day men in long overcoats will show up at the house and scare the crap out of him. Just the letter they sent got him rattled. Imagine what Army officials would do."

They stopped at the luggage carousel just as it jerked to a start. Suitcases began to appear on the conveyor through a gap in the wall. When he saw Beth's, Daniel picked it up and led her out of the airport to the parking lot.

Beth whistled. "Nice car. How did I know it would be a Lexus?"

Daniel opened the trunk and put Beth's suitcase inside. "I'd go American but Japanese make better cars. It's just a fact."

"That's a pretty bold stereotype."

Daniel shrugged. "It's the truth."

"I'm happy with my Cherokee," Beth said.

"Because you spend so much time driving off-road, right?" Daniel dead-panned.

"Right," Beth responded without missing a beat. "Like last fall when I was driving Julia to take the SAT in a torrential downpour and the underpass to the school was flooded out and there was already one car swamped but I decided to charge through and we made it."

"Well, if it was for the SAT," Daniel said.

Beth looked at him. "Daniel, I was just kidding."

"If you say so."

He got behind the wheel and started the new silver grey Lexus. The vehicle was nearly soundless, like silk on wind. They floated out of the lot, onto a frontage road, and then onto the highway. A few minutes later, Beth asked, "What's on your mind, Daniel?"

"What do you mean?"

"You seem a little distracted."

"I do? Sorry. I guess I feel like there's a lot going on out here. You know, with my mom and all."

"Of course, I get it."

Beth gazed out the window and stared out across the sea of cars and the distant LA skyline. The traffic slowed and almost came to a stop. Daniel heaved a heavy sigh and switched on the radio. Talk radio. Rush Limbaugh. He hit the scan button and the station changed every few seconds. Classical music. Sports radio. They crawled past a broken down car on the shoulder and the traffic improved to stop and go, stop and go.

Beth switched off the radio. "Are you sure you're okay? Is something bothering you? I mean, even at home you've seemed a little . . . distant."

"Distant?"

"Like you're always tangled up in your own thoughts."

"Um hm . . ." Daniel kept his eyes on the highway and the phalanx of surrounding cars whose drivers seemed to enjoy darting in front of him without warning and for no appreciable gain. As usual, he was dealing with three or four things at once. His mother, his father, his wife, the medal. They were all on his mind contesting for a front seat. What was really important? Right now, the traffic.

Daniel jockeyed between two semis and glided well ahead of them.

"I don't think I've been distant."

"It's one of the things I think we need to talk about. Sometimes you're home but it's like you aren't really there."

Daniel briefly took his eyes off the road and turned to her. "Like I'm not there? Well, to be honest, I think the situation is that you've been overly busy with the kids and I am overly preoccupied with . . . you know."

"What?"

Daniel glanced at her again and thought, *Do I have to say it?* Beth's soft blonde hair rested on her shoulders and shrouded the side of her face so that he couldn't read her expression.

"Saving lives, hon. Isn't that what I do? I don't mean to make a case of it, but sometimes . . . the smaller details in life get reducible to a kind of white noise."

Beth crossed her arms. "I can't believe you just said that," she said. Then she leaned forward to shed her wool, frost-colored Kenneth Cole peacoat in an exaggerated way that signaled her annoyance.

Said what? Daniel thought. That I save lives? That my work is important? He gripped the wheel hard. He knew they needed to connect. This was not how he'd wanted the conversation to go. Why was it so difficult? Why was it easier to talk to Anne, a woman he barely knew anymore, than to his wife?

Anne. He felt a pang of guilt. What was it about Anne? I'm not entertaining any sort of romance with her, he thought to himself. At least I don't think I am. So why do I keep thinking about her? Is it just that elusive thing about the past? The irreducible, forever lostness of youth, of first love?

But no matter how he felt around Anne, he knew he had to solve what was going on with Beth, and soon. The distance between them . . . had they somehow grown incompatible? He'd never even remotely considered this in the past. He truly loved her. All marriages had rough patches. They would get through this.

By now the silence in the low-flying Lexus was almost unbearable. Daniel knew he had to say something.

"Hon, I'm sorry if that sounded insensitive. I'm sorry if it seems like I'm distant, but I'm really not. I've always been like this. My home is sort of in my head. You're the extrovert, not me. I've always been the quiet one."

"I can tell, Daniel, when you're not at home in your head, as you put it. Please don't patronize me like I don't know you. I think I know you better than anyone."

Daniel's lips tightened. The flow of traffic had increased again. It was hard to have an argument with his wife about mental proclivities with cars zooming into his lane.

"Okay, you're right. There's a lot on my mind right now. Not just with my mom, but my dad, too. This whole episode has given me something to think about. Like how Dad would be without Mom. Or how Mom would be without him. For some reason, I haven't thought about that a lot."

"I thought you absolutely didn't care about your dad. That's what you said, anyway."

"I don't. But my mom does, so I'm trying to do it for her."

"And how's that going for you?"

"Not well. I did try to talk to him, but he's impossible. He doesn't say anything."

"Hmm," Beth murmured. "Sounds a lot like someone I know."

Daniel bit his lip.

"Tell me this, Daniel. Whatever happened between you two—did it justify purposely preventing your children from having a relationship with their grandfather? I think that really sucks. I've only met your father a few times, but from those times he seems like a very decent person. A gentleman, even. Plus, your mom is great, and if she married him, how bad could he be?"

Daniel felt a sudden wave of disgust. Why did she always have to bring up Dad in the midst of everything else?

Beth waited, expectantly.

Finally, he blurted, "Look, maybe you haven't noticed but there's some heavy traffic going on here, people cutting in and out of lanes like this is a speedway. So let's just get you to the hotel so you can have a nice hot shower. That always makes me feel better after a flight. Don't you feel a little bit tired? Overwrought?"

Beth frowned, but she didn't say anything more.

Daniel returned to the complexity of the road, the traffic. The immensity of Los Angeles. The massivity of the buildings, the sprawl, the scarf of grey-brown smog that blurred the distance and made the highway seem surreal. Meanwhile, as he dodged and wove between the gleams of chrome, he thought, what if I were to actually tell her the truth?

About my father.

About Anne.

LOS ANGELES
May 1964

"Dad, I'm staying. I'll go to UCLA."

"No you will not," his father said. They were alone in the living room. Anne had just left, and Daniel was angry that his father hadn't been nicer to her.

"What is your problem? What do you have against her?" It embarrassed him to say it in front of his father, but he forced himself: "I love her."

To his surprise, his father's expression softened. He sat down in his La-Z-Boy. Daniel remained standing.

"Listen to me, Daniel. I understand that love is a nice thing. Wonderful, even. But in life you cannot count on love. You can only count on yourself and hard work. And when you do find someone to marry, you'll be able to rely on her too.

"But I'm going to marry Anne!"

His father shook his head. "No, son. She's a nice girl. But her family . . . I didn't want to tell you this, but her father is no good. He's not . . . reliable. He has problems with money, and I think he drinks too much. Besides, they're Japanese."

"We're Japanese!" Daniel protested.

"No, we're Americans. We've spent two generations here. I fought and bled for this country, and her father fought in the Japanese Army! I won't let *you destroy two generations of work to bring us to where we are today— you with a chance to attend Columbia University and become a great doctor. Can you imagine what you'd be throwing away to stay here?"*

Daniel was struck dumb. His father had never hidden his disapproval of Anne and her family. To him they were low-born. Commoners too base to marry into the Tokunaga family. It amazed Daniel that his father could be so prejudiced when they themselves were just scraping by. But Daniel knew his father could be irrational in matters related to honor and reputation.

"How can you say this?" Daniel said. "Anne's father has nothing to do with me, or her. Can't you see we love each other? I can still go to medical school after UCLA."

"Love is overrated. A luxury that only the rich have." His father paused and looked away. And for a moment Daniel thought he might actually be tearing up. But with a quick sniff his father turned back to him with a serious face. "Sacrifices must be made in life, for the good of others. For the good of the family. You must learn this. Our family honor is bigger than you, or me. It's the work of many generations. I won't let you ruin it, or make us step backwards. Your mother and I have worked tirelessly to put you in a position to go to Columbia. You will be the first in our family to go to college!"

"I know you've worked hard, Dad. And I'm grateful. But can't you see how important this is to me?"

His father's face grew cold. His voice had a knife's edge. "You will not marry a Japanese. You will go to Columbia and become a great doctor. That is your privilege, and if you choose to view it this way, your sacrifice. You can't rely on love. Love can disappear and feelings can change. But no one can take away your education. You're smart. You're smarter than your brother. Smarter than me and your mom. You should go to college. Love can come later."

His father's rare compliment passed Daniel almost unnoticed. Under normal circumstances the praise would have made him happy, but now it rang hollow. His father rose from his chair and moved toward the stairs. Without looking at his son, he raised his hand and gave a careless wave.

"I'm tired, have to work tomorrow. End of discussion."

Inside, Daniel boiled with rage. He wanted to grab his obstinate father by the neck and squeeze. He wanted to tackle him and kick him in the ribs. But he stood there, frozen, unable to move or react. He loved Anne more than anything in the world. They had to be together. And yet, he realized the old man held a power over him that was impossible to defy.

I hate you, he thought maliciously as his angry eyes burned holes in his father's back. And for the first time in his life, he truly wished his father was dead.

TWELVE

VOSGES MOUNTAINS, FRANCE
October 17, 1944

"I see three nests. Interlocking fire," Lieutenant Okimoto, a native of Bainbridge Island, Washington, reported to the eight Nisei soldiers gathered around him—all that was left from the squads that had endured the overnight shelling of Hill B. The lieutenant was thickset and heavy. In another time and place, with more food and less exercise, Ray could picture him as a sumo wrestler.

"Should we wait for reinforcements?" one private asked.

Okimoto shook his head. "It'll take at least an hour for battalion to get a decent force here. They're gonna use dozens just to clear the dead and wounded back down the hill. Meanwhile, Jerry's getting stronger. There's a good line of supply on the backside of this hill. If we wait another hour, we'll be going up against eight machine guns, instead of just three."

Ray gritted his teeth. How could nine guys possibly take out three machine guns? How many of us will die trying to get up this damn hill? All of us? His clothes were soaked and a chill breeze made him shiver.

Okimoto was already giving out orders.

"We've got to flank them, if we can. Keep quiet and let's slide to the right. Spread out. Use grenades. Stay low and quick. This is what we trained for. Let's get it done."

Ray looked at Hiro, who nodded grimly.

The rain had stopped, and for the first time in a day, Ray felt like he could open his eyes fully. He looked forward, through thin grey mist, and knew that ahead lay men who intended to murder him. He wanted to shrink behind a tree and curl up in a ball, but he knew this was impossible. He also felt the urge to vomit, and dry heaved. Nothing came up. Embarrassed, he wiped spittle from the corner of his mouth and glanced at the other men, but no one was paying any attention to him.

The others were beginning to fan out. Ray advanced slowly, crouching, going from one tree to the next. The forest floor was a spongy carpet of pine needles. He peered up the hill. The forest was dark, but he squinted and thought he could make out the gun emplacements Okimoto had seen, three of them arranged roughly in a semicircle. When he found a dense thicket of young hemlock to hide behind, he stopped. Not wanting to go any farther, he reached down inside his khakis and ran his fingers across the knots of his *senninbari* wrapped tightly around his waist. He'd reluctantly promised his mother to always wear the strip of white cloth with the thousand stitches, for, in doing so, the wearer was protected on any field of battle. Each stitch was done by a different woman, and his mother had spent days going to different ladies' patriotic meetings and church groups, where hundreds of mothers gathered to get their sons' *senninbari* filled. Near the end, his mother spent hours standing outside the grocery store asking random passersby if they would please place a stitch. He knew it was a silly notion, but right now, it made him feel a little better knowing that white cloth was tied firmly around him.

There was no one else in sight. How far had he lagged behind? He stepped out of the hemlock shadow and forced himself to advance a little more, to another tree, and then found himself hiding behind a large granite boulder. He went on like this for a few minutes, running and hiding, but there was no enemy gunfire, and no sight of the other Nisei. Where had they gone?

Then, a flash of brazen white light, a burst of gunfire that seemed to come out of the ground itself, forty yards ahead. Ray saw two Nisei crumple, the attack coming from another gun nest, well-hidden, on their right.

Ray dropped to the ground. The other three machine guns opened fire. Bullets zipped past, slicing tree branches, ripping the ground. Ray froze.

Oh my God, oh my God, oh my God.

He peeked out, and found himself at the convergence of a murderous crossfire. The perfect ambush. He tried to melt into the ground, and wondered if the enemy had purposely set up three easily seen gun nests to drive attackers into the path of another, perfectly hidden one.

Ray's eyes moved toward his fallen comrades. One KIA. The other, still moving! It was Lieutenant Okimoto. From what Ray could see, he'd been hit in the leg and was trying to crawl, roll and slide back down the hill.

Suddenly, the hidden machine gun opened up again and hit Okimoto in the back. He sprawled and lay still.

We've got to get out of here, Ray thought. He turned and, at a crouch, started to run. Almost immediately, strong arms reached up and tackled him to the ground.

What the . . .? Dazed, Ray lifted his rifle, but the man knocked the muzzle away. It was Hiro.

"Get over here!" Hiro hissed.

"Hiro! We've got to fall back!"

"We can't leave him." Hiro said, pointing at Okimoto. Ray

looked. The lieutenant was still alive. Shot twice, he'd begun to crawl ineffectually.

Helping him would be suicide. But, still thirty yards away, there was no way he would make it on his own.

Ka-BOOM!

A huge explosion twenty yards behind them. Ray pitched forward, felt a flash of heat across his back. He looked backward in time to see a body fly six feet in the air and come down with a hard thud. Another Nisei scurried toward the body—"

"Freeze!" Hiro shouted. "Mines!"

The horror of their situation now dawned on Ray. Unable to advance, unable to retreat, six guys left against four machine guns, one of which they couldn't see but which could see them the minute they lifted their heads or stepped out from behind a tree. He wiggled down into the deep bed of pine needles and pressed his face against cold, hard dirt. The smell of resin and redolent earth filled his nostrils. He'd give everything he owned for the chance to surrender right now.

"I've got to get him," Hiro said.

"What?"

Hiro pointed at Okimoto, then signaled to two other Nisei whom Ray hadn't even realized were close by.

Hiro put his rifle on the ground. "Cover me," he said. And before Ray could say another word, Hiro was scrambling up the hill.

Ray fired in his wake, again and again, into the trees, hardly aiming. He emptied his clip, and heard other rifles echoing all around him. Bullets from all four machine guns peppered the ground around Hiro, who, remarkably fast, ran and dove, rolled and crawled toward the lieutenant, never stopping, always moving. One soldier threw a grenade at the enemy which exploded ineffectually but added to the din.

Somehow, impossibly, Hiro reached Okimoto unscathed. Ray saw Hiro flat on the ground, pulling Okimoto by the arm into the relative protection of a shallow depression in the ground behind a group of thick tree trunks.

Hiro shoved Okimoto's grenades into his own satchel, adding to his stash. Ray saw him throw one, and, three seconds later, a puff of dirt and an agonizing cry above the sound of gunfire. He'd hit the hidden nest, now a smoking ruin with a dead body slumped over the small berm that had hidden it so well. Like a Jack-in-the-Box, another German soldier stood up, seemingly out of nowhere, turned and started to run. Hiro grabbed Okimoto's rifle and fired two shots into the German's back, dropping him.

The other three machine guns vengefully intensified their fire, with total command over the patch of ground where Ray and the other remaining GIs hugged the ground, shrunk behind trees and dared not move.

Then, one Nisei soldier did. On Ray's left. It was Sergeant Moto, running at the nearest gun nest, trying to get close enough for a grenade. But he was not a fast runner. Tense seconds, all eyes on him, Moto seemed to plod up the steep slope in slow motion. German bullets tracked his steps, chipping the ground, chewing the earth at his heels. He drew back his arm, holding the grenade.

Please, Ray prayed, as he gave covering fire.

Then, Moto's body seemed to collapse and fold in half—Ray watched him take the pummeling impact of a half-dozen rounds. His body slid downhill until it came to rest ten feet in front of Ray. He could see the sergeant's eyes roll around. He coughed blood. The front of his jacket, wet and black. There was nothing Ray could do, but the isolated moving eyes of the other man were on him, as if he might do something miraculous.

Ray's heartbeat raced. What now? he thought. We're reduced to a bunch of privates. Where's Hiro?

Ray craned his neck.

He saw Lieutenant Okimoto, but Hiro was gone.

Ray quickly scanned the field, left and right, looking for his friend.

There he was!

Hiro was further uphill, running through the woods. Ray lifted his head to see better. A burst of bullets chomped at the trunk of his tree and he scrunched back down. He could still see the remaining machine guns, arrayed to their left and slightly uphill, their black barrels protruding from the brush the gunners had placed in front of rough log barricades.

There came a sudden explosion—the nest to Ray's immediate left. Two bodies in grey uniforms seemed to do a ragdoll dance up and out of the brush. Tossed forward, they flew and flopped and landed without making much of a sound.

It had happened so quickly Ray hadn't time to figure it out, but now he knew that Hiro had pitched in a grenade from behind. And there he was now in the midst of the twisted, melted machine gun, looking for survivors.

Ray joined the others in firing at the other two nests, whose machine guns now threw lead in jerky spasms, uncertain of what to hit.

To Ray's surprise, Hiro now ran straight at the next gun emplacement. He sprinted, then stumbled on the uneven slope, grabbing at his belt for another grenade. The machine gun swiveled and was on to him. It stuttered maniacally. Little founts of flame spat from the barrel.

Hiro was there. Running. And then he wasn't there. He was on the ground, in a disfigured heap.

"No!" Ray yelled.

Hiro didn't move.

They killed him. Oh my God, they killed him.

Ray felt a hot wave of rage crash down on him.

Without thinking, he gripped his rifle and stood up straight. On his left and right, the other Nisei rose up too. A man on his left charged forward.

"Banzai!" he hollered.

And then a chorus of "Banzai!"

101

And Ray went, too, filled with unreasoning hatred. His only desire was to run his bayonet through the heart of the German who had killed his best friend. The Nazi gunners redirected fire at the oncoming attackers. The first man out groaned as he took a hit to the stomach and went down.

Ray felt splinters of bark sting his cheek as bullets struck all around him. He ran toward Hiro's body, and then, Hiro moved!

His arm flew up.

He's alive!

Hiro followed his arm's roll and turned his body closer to the nearest nest. From only six or seven feet away, he tossed a grenade, and did a swift back roll downhill.

The gun emplacement seemed to implode and explode at the same time. Metal fragments, clumps of dirt went everywhere. A moment later Ray scrambled to the place where Hiro had stopped his acrobatics.

Hiro's face was dotted with mud and oil spatters. He was smiling.

"I got 'em?"

Ray shook his head in amazement. "You sure did."

"Am I all right?" Hiro patted his body everywhere from head to toe.

"I tripped and fell down. Played dead—and figured I *was* dead when that burst came. But I wasn't. He missed me by a mile."

"You lucky son of a bitch!"

New grenade blasts. Rifle fire. They both looked up and watched their comrades assaulting the fourth and final machine gun.

Then, the guns went silent.

Ray sucked some air. It tasted of cordite and smelled of burnt flesh, oiled steel, and hot dirt.

Black and blue-grey smoke wafted downhill and away into the woods where it tangled in the pine trees. Ray looked up. For the first time in the Vosges, he could see a tiny patch of blue sky through a small gap in the trees.

THIRTEEN

LOS ANGELES 1998

"Daniel, is that you?"

"Anne?" he said in a low voice, holding the phone close to his ear and cupping his other hand over the receiver. Sitting on the bed, he glanced at the bathroom door. It was partly open and he could see Beth's lovely naked profile through the translucent glass shower door. The narrow waist and flaring hips. The model's breasts too perfect for a mother of two.

"Yes, it's me. I hope I didn't wake you."

"No, no. I just woke up."

"Oh good. How's your mom?" Anne asked.

"She's fine. I brought her home."

"That's good news. Are you going to leave soon?"

"Me? I'm not sure. Maybe in a day or two."

"I see. I was wondering . . . do you think we could meet sometime today? There's something I want to talk to you about."

Daniel felt his heart beat faster. He sat up straighter, and cautioned himself to tread carefully. "Uh, sure, I think I could manage that. Are you sure you don't want to just tell me now?"

"No. I want to tell you in person."

"Okay. Maybe I'll come over to the hospital after you finish work? Would that be good?"

"That would be perfect. Could you meet me around six in the cafeteria?"

"Sounds fine. I'll see you then."

Daniel hung up and rested his head against the headboard. He couldn't help feeling a little nervous excitement at Anne's mysterious call. What could she have to tell him?

"Who were you talking to? Was that your mom?"

Daniel jerked his head toward Beth, who was now drying her hair with a towel in the bathroom.

"Uh . . . no, not Mom. Just an old family friend."

"Oh really? Who?"

"Just someone I saw when I visited Mom in the hospital, wanting to know how she's doing."

Beth started to get dressed. "Well, it's great that your mom has so many friends she can count on to help her through this time."

"Definitely," Daniel said.

He had decided to spend the day at his parents' house helping them clean out their junk. Beth had wanted to come, but Daniel had convinced her that her presence in the midst of the chaos would be counterproductive. Better for him to take a taxi over to the house this morning and let Beth drive by later. He didn't add that he was sure relations with his father would be tense at best, and it was preferable to keep Beth's exposure to his toxic family to a minimum.

Now Beth seemed perfectly happy with the plan. She was excited about visiting a friend from college who lived in Westwood and could drive her around Hollywood and Beverly Hills. Thinking quickly, Daniel figured when the time came to see Anne, he could find some excuse to go to the store and stop by the hospital on the way.

He felt guilty about not telling Beth the whole truth, but at the same time, he needed to know what Anne wanted to tell him. What it could be, he couldn't guess, but he felt sure of one thing: this day would be one to remember.

⁓

"You and Dad really shouldn't be living by yourselves anymore," Daniel said to his mother. "For one thing, the house is too old and just about everything needs fixing. You don't want to deal with plumbing leaks and electrical problems, do you? The yard is another major headache. Why don't you move into a senior living facility? There are some really great places now. Even nearby. You could still see all of your friends and have a social life."

Daniel now believed his time in California could best be spent trying to get his parents into a better living situation. Not a nursing home. Not one of those dire, family-run dumps that smelled like a toilet. But a place where retirees lived in condos and never glanced twice at the yard wondering if the yardman was going to show up on time. In these newer facilities, residents played golf every day, made new friends on the tennis court, played bridge to their heart's content, and no longer worried about meals because there was a fine dining room that served elegant food three times a day. This was the kind of place Daniel had in mind. He would love to get them into one of these upscale condos, and he could pay for it, too.

He had mentioned this to his mother a couple of times in the past, but she'd merely listened and then smiled so politely that Daniel knew she had no intention of moving. "Your father wouldn't hear of it," she reminded him.

But now on this trip Daniel had seen the house, which was more of a mess than ever. His dad had a history of heart trouble—a heart attack and two coronary stents last year—and now his mother's hospitalization had gotten Daniel worried. If his mother came down with a serious medical problem, there was no way his dad would be able to take care of her. That was his real fear. He doubted his mother would consent to leave California to live with him in Philadelphia because his father would never agree to it. So, what he had to do was get her into a better situation here and now . . . or at the very least, work toward that goal.

And this unpredictable morning, much to Daniel's surprise, his mother said: "Maybe you're right, Danny."

Daniel wasn't sure he'd heard right.

Keiko sighed. Her eyes swept over the dining room, where they were standing together. Daniel followed her gaze. He remembered how much it had embarrassed him as a kid to bring friends over because of this room; it looked shabby then and was even worse now. The surface of the dining table was no longer visible, completely buried under mounds of five-year-old newspapers, piles of expired coupons, clothes in need of mending, and year-old Halloween candies in creepy wrappers. His mother was the worst hoarder he'd ever met, next to his father. They fed off each other, keeping useless stuff because the act of throwing anything away was anathema to them.

"We're getting older," she admitted, "and I know we can't stay here forever. It's probably just a matter of time."

How much time? Daniel wondered.

He said, "Mom, how about we get started now? It's going to take a lot of work to clean up the house and throw things away. It's not going to happen overnight. But I can help you while I'm here. We could start in this room by going through all the paper and stuff together. Anything we want to throw away, I'll take to the porch. I can fill up the recycling cans."

He waited hopefully for a positive response.

"Danny, why don't you just do it?"

"What?" He wasn't prepared for such a quick consent.

"I know we've got to throw things out, but it's too hard for me. Why don't I go make lunch and you can do it."

This was better than he could have hoped for. He felt like someone had taken his real mom and left an impostor behind, but he was going to seize the opportunity.

"Absolutely, don't worry about anything. If there's something I think you might want to keep I'll ask you."

Five minutes later, Daniel wondered if his mom's apathy was really a sign of her age. No doubt his father's grouchiness and maybe her own mortality were weighing heavily on her.

With these thoughts, he found himself partly wishing they'd had the same old argument all over again.

Two hours later, Daniel's four, three-foot high stacks of old newspapers, magazines, and junk mail were stacked and tied with cord out front. The tabletop was clear, the first time he'd seen it this way since the last real Thanksgiving meal they'd had together during his last year in high school. His back hurt, but this was a once in a lifetime opportunity to throw things away, so now he turned toward the dish cabinet. He opened the top drawer and found it filled with knick-knacks and tchotchkes. Among other things, there was a green plastic soldier from a Cracker Jack box, a letter "A" Scrabble word tile, and a red Jolly Rancher that might be a decade old. Daniel sneaked a peek at the kitchen, half-expecting his mother to pounce and stop him. But her back was to him. She was at the sink washing dishes. He began to scoop things into a large plastic garbage bag. He kept a few things, like a framed photo of his mother's parents, and an old Leica camera that was probably broken but looked like an antique.

He'd almost finished clearing out the first drawer when he uncovered a faded yellow envelope in the back corner. It was the old-fashioned kind that closed by wrapping a red string around a circular tab. Curious, he looked inside and pulled out a faded yellow sheet of paper.

It took him several seconds to realize he was holding his parents' wedding certificate. He ran his fingers over his parents' names. The certificate stated: Los Angeles, California. February 5th, 1945.

He froze on the date.

1945?

Mom and Dad got married in 1944, he remembered. He'd been born in March of 1945. How strange.

"Mom?"

"Yes?"

He walked into the kitchen. His mother was filling the rice cooker with water.

"Look, I found your marriage certificate." He held it close so she could see. "But it says 1945. You got married in '44, right?"

His mother adjusted her glasses. She took the paper from his hand.

"Danny, I can't believe you found this. Good boy."

"What about the date, Mom? Your anniversary is July 4th, 1944, right? You and Dad got married on Independence Day, at Manzanar, didn't you?"

"Yes, that's right."

"Then why does this say 'February '45?'"

Keiko seemed puzzled. She looked closer at the paper. "This paper is wrong," she concluded.

"How could that be?"

"They made a mistake. That's all."

"But it *says* Los Angeles."

Keiko furrowed her brow and looked down at the paper again. After a few moments, she said: "Manzanar wasn't a legitimate place to them."

"You mean the government?"

"They just said everything was LA." Keiko put the paper on the kitchen table. "Now go back over there, I'm busy cooking. Your dad is going to be hungry."

There was something in the way his mother spoke—rushed, higher-pitched than normal—that made Daniel a little uneasy. As she lifted the rice and water-filled bowl from the sink to the rice cooker, she spilled some water over the edge.

"Mom, slow down."

"I'm fine. Why don't you just—go back to cleaning up in the dining room."

"Wait a second." Daniel picked up the marriage certificate.

"What's wrong?" a rough voice intruded.

Daniel looked up to see his father standing in the doorway. He wore brown dungarees and a button down khaki shirt with a rumpled collar. He'd been mowing in the backyard and there were blades of grass stuck to his sleeves.

"I stopped to refill the gas tank, heard you talking. What'd you find?"

Keiko snatched the certificate from Daniel's hand and held it up, her hands trembling. "Danny found this. Our wedding certificate."

Daniel's father took the paper, and grunted. "What of it?"

"The date's wrong," Daniel said. "You were married in 1944, right?"

The old man squinted at him and then examined the document. Daniel watched the tight line of his mouth turn down and form a frown.

"I told him it was a mistake," Keiko interjected. "Just a silly mistake. It says Los Angeles instead of Manzanar. You know, just a mistake."

Daniel's father looked up, nodded. "You know the government. Always making goofy mistakes like this. Some dumb secretary typed the wrong thing."

"You sure? Because the chances they'd get the date *and* the place wrong are pretty—"

"—what business is it of yours?" his father said, raising his voice and sticking out his chin. "It's just a piece of paper. Why do you care so much anyway?"

"I *don't* care. I mean, all I was asking is *why* . . . I thought there must be a logical explanation."

"There is no explanation. Forget it."

"Ooo-kay," Daniel mumbled. A sense of futility overcame him. No one could penetrate his father's samurai armor.

Now he pointed his index finger at Daniel. "This has always been your problem. You stick your nose in other people's business. I don't care that you're a big shot rich doctor. That doesn't make you a man. And it can't change what you did, and didn't do. Things would have been better if you'd just minded your own business and left other people alone."

"Things would have been—?" Daniel felt a wave of prickly heat from head to toe. He was suddenly so furious he could barely breathe.

"What *things?*" He took a step forward and came in close to his father's face. They were almost nose to nose. "Do you mean our family? Do you mean the grandkids you never get to see? Do you mean the freakin' Vietnam War?" Daniel sucked his teeth, drew a breath. He saw his anger mirrored in his father's eyes. "You better not mean what I *think* you mean, because Kenny died because of *you*, not *me!*"

Daniel saw a flash of light and felt a sharp, sudden pain on the left side of his face. His head snapped to the right. He saw fizzy little stars before he closed his eyes.

His father had struck him, open-hand, very hard.

Though dazed, Daniel balled his hands into fists and got ready to return the blow. His father, eyes ablaze, jutted out his chin as if daring him to take his best shot. He drew back his right fist. As he started to throw the punch, Keiko suddenly threw her body between the two of them.

"No!" she shouted.

Daniel pulled his punch, but not before the forward momentum brought him crashing into Keiko, who toppled to the floor.

Daniel gasped and took a step back. His mother curled up into a ball and started to sob.

"—Daniel!"

It was Beth, standing at the front door. She came into the kitchen.

110

"What in God's name are you doing?" she cried.

Daniel blinked. He was still dizzy from his father's assault. He looked down at his tight fists. He unclenched them.

In a low, bestial growl, the old man said, "You have no right to speak your brother's name to me. He died with honor. You lack honor. He is dead and you are alive. But better to be dead than to live as a coward."

Before Daniel could respond, his father stormed out of the kitchen and went through the back door, slamming it as he left.

"Daniel, what is happening here?" Beth demanded in a voice he'd never heard her use before.

Daniel surveyed the small room. A tea kettle sang on the stove. Outside, his father's mower made a choking sound, then roared as it chewed grass. Daniel sagged against the kitchen wall. He felt lightheaded. Then, loose-limbed and a little loopy, he slumped into the nearest hard wooden chair at the kitchen table.

Beth knelt beside Keiko and wrapped her arms around the older woman's shoulders. "Mom, are you okay?"

Daniel took short breaths and tried to calm himself. I've got to get out of here, he thought. He looked at Beth, the concern and confusion in her eyes. No one spoke. Keiko's soft, birdlike sobs were the only sound against the mower's persistent, high-pitched moan.

Then came a funny little cry over the noise of the motor, followed by the crashing sound of glass breaking as the mower came to an abrupt stop.

Without thinking, Daniel rose and went to the back door. He looked through the screen to where his father had fallen—he'd crashed into the patio table, shattering the glass tabletop. His face was twisted in agony, and small rivulets of blood streamed from his scalp where a glass shard had slashed him. He lay on the cement patio, hands clutched together at his chest.

Daniel moved swiftly, went to his side, touched his shoulder. Keiko and Beth followed, faces registering shock.

Daniel looked up at them. "Call 911, he's having another heart attack!"

FOURTEEN

VOSGES MOUNTAINS, FRANCE
October 19, 1944

W e're lost, Ray thought. He was beginning to hate the wooded hills of France. With every step, his feet squished inside his boots. He'd forgotten what dry socks felt like. When it wasn't raining, which was rare, ground-level fog reduced visibility to a matter of yards, soaked his jacket and pants.

He paused, looked around him. The thick fog weighted the leaves of the deciduous trees and hung in the pines. The only person Ray saw was Hiro, fifteen feet ahead of him, a mere shadow in the mist. Ray quickened his step to catch up. The thought of being alone on this hillside unnerved him.

"Don't lose me," Ray said, as he drew up to his friend.

Hiro looked back. "Keep up, then."

"Where's the rest of the squad? Haven't seen anyone but you for a half-hour."

Hiro shook his head. "That replacement sarge should have forced us to stay together, 'stead of trying to cover more ground. Far as I can tell, we're going where we're supposed to: straight up this hill. Problem is, now that we're separated, fair chance we'll accidentally shoot one of our own guys in this soup."

Ray peered to the south, into the rags and wisps of mist and imagined he could see the whole village of Bruyères at this elevation; but, like everything else, the valley and village below remained shrouded in fog. After the conquest of Hills A, B, C, and D, the 442nd had liberated Bruyères. That was yesterday. Today most of the town was reduced to rubble. Shell-shocked townsfolk leaked out of their cellars, one at a time, surprised to see their liberators were Japanese Americans.

The celebration was short-lived; soon German artillery, positioned on hills beyond the ones already secured, began to bombard the town anew. The villagers scurried back to their hiding places.

Next day, squads went into the hills to find German artillery, or, equally important, good vantage points from which enemy spotters might be directing their fire. Ray and Hiro were on one of a number of unnamed hills, searching for enemy emplacements.

Hiro leaned against a tree and took off his helmet. "Let's stop for a minute." He drew a pack of Lucky Strikes out of his pocket, tapped out a cigarette, and lit it. "Lieutenant said the top of this hill would be a prime spot for spotting artillery. All I know is, we've got to reach the top and hope for a break in the weather. If the others have beaten us there, fine."

Ray sat down on a fallen tree trunk. Its bark was moss-damp and slippery. "I'm in no rush to find out. Hopefully, this is just an empty hill." Ray took a swig from his canteen. The water tasted stale rather than fresh, metallic rather than natural. He sipped some, washed the inside of his mouth, and spat it out on the ground. "So how do you feel?" he asked Hiro.

"About what?"

"About what you did."

Hiro looked into the mist.

Ray continued, "You're a hero, man. Everyone saw it. We were pinned down, getting chewed up. You took out three machine guns and saved the lieutenant's life."

Hiro smiled wryly. "I'm no hero. I know it probably seemed crazy."

"Suicidal."

Hiro shrugged. "Don't ask me why I did it. Just seemed the thing to do."

"Captain heard about it. Said he's going to write you up for a medal."

"What do I care about a damn medal? Right now I just want new socks."

"Me too."

The two men laughed.

"And maybe some of Mom's beef stew over rice," Hiro added. He drew on his cigarette, exhaled a draft of blue smoke into the grayer fog that had crept in and enclosed them.

Ray groaned. "Don't talk about food. You're torturing me." His grumbly stomach made him think of the D ration in his pack, his last chocolate bar, and then his mouth began to water. He spat and decided to save the candy bar for later. "This is what we signed on for—no good food, no decent water, no telling if we make it to nightfall."

Hiro took a deep drag and leaked smoke out of his nostrils. "That's it, more or less. I expected as much."

"Really?" Ray took off his helmet and scratched his wet and itchy scalp. He wondered how anyone could picture this indecisive mess they were in, this hell on earth where you went forward on an empty belly not knowing anything. "And still, you wanted to join up?" he asked Hiro.

"I did. Anything to get out of Manzanar. Besides, I was no good at school, and the only real job there was farming. I hate farming as much as I hate fishing."

"What did your folks say? About fighting?"

Hiro crushed his cigarette ember under his heel. "They didn't like it. Hell, a lot of people didn't like it. Can't say I blame them. 'Why should we fight for a country that treats us like prisoners?' a lot of them said. Some Issei called us traitors. Just for enlisting."

"So why'd you do it?"

"To me, the choice was, go back to Japan or stay in America. I could never live in Japan. I don't even speak the language. But I knew if I was going to stay I'd need to prove to other Americans that we were just as good as them. That simple. And that's why I'm fighting. Maybe if I do this, and prove I can kick ass with the best of 'em, then maybe, just maybe, my kids will have a better life. *Kodomo no tameni.*"

"What?"

"*Kodomo no tameni.* Another old folks saying. It means, 'for the sake of the children.'"

"For someone who doesn't speak Japanese, you've got your sayings down anyway."

Hiro shrugged. "You saw those signs along the roads in Mississippi, didn't you? Signs in LA said the same thing: 'Only good Jap is a dead Jap,' 'Japs not welcome,' 'Don't serve Japs.' Maybe you don't see them in Hawaii, but in the rest of America, it's different, and it gets to you. After a while, part of you feels like you *deserve* to be insulted, or worse. All because you're basically, from birth, inferior." Hiro glanced at Ray. "Well, I *know* it's not true. But it flashes through your head just the same. Thing is, I don't want my kid to have that flash-feeling I do sometimes . . . someday, when I have a kid, maybe it'll all be different."

After this, the two men sat without talking. Ray was sure Hiro had seen worse than he had, white people full of hate. There was nothing he could say to mitigate what his friend had already said. The quiet was healing.

The only sound was the occasional breeze that pierced the fog. When the wind died, the fog spewed its thick porridge of gray, coating the trees and dampening the men's spirits as well as cutting off their visibility.

Ray broke the silence. "So, you're already thinking about kids?"

Hiro smiled. "Oh yeah. Big Thanksgiving dinners, lots of grand-kids, people to take care of me when I get old—all those good things come from having lots of kids." He tapped out another cigarette, lit it, took a deep drag. "Besides, I'm looking forward to teaching my son to play baseball. I think I'm gonna be a better dad than mine was. I want to have a lot of fun with my kids. That's my dream."

"Heck, who wouldn't want a dad like you? All fun and games."

"No, they'll learn to work hard too. Damn hard. I won't be their friend, I'll be their *father*. And my son's going to be a doctor."

"Really?"

"Yes. A real doctor. An *American* doctor—not one of those old Issei healers who mixes herbs and doesn't know squat. My son will go to college, a good one, and make it into medical school."

"Do you realize how hard that'll be? Even if he wasn't Japanese?"

"We'll do whatever it takes. Times have to get better for our kind. What else are we fighting for? A father's got to make things better for his sons, if he can . . ."

"It must've been hard, going up against *your* father . . . when you enlisted, I mean."

"He came around. We had a talk. He knows a thing or two about war; he went to military school in Japan and his uncles fought in Japan's war with Russia. He was scared for me." Hiro dropped his voice and began to imitate his father, "'When you go to war,' he told me, 'you have to believe you will die. Do you expect to live? Do you expect to come back here to marry that girl? You must forget her, and us. Because if your love of life is too strong, then you won't be a good soldier, and you'll probably make a dumb mistake and be killed in some meaningless way. The Japanese are such good fighters because they expect to die. Do you? I know you don't. So you'll be a bad soldier, and you shouldn't go."

117

Ray nodded. "That actually makes sense." He paused. "You don't have some weird death-wish, do you?"

"Course not. I don't bank on dying." Hiro took a long pull on his cigarette and released the smoke, which came out a little bluer than the surrounding mist. "I told my father it's different if you believe in what you're fighting for. I can still fight well if I believe that I can make my country better for my kids."

"Change his mind?"

"Probably not. He's worried about me. First he says I'll be too careful, then he thinks I won't be careful enough."

"Gee, I wonder where he gets that idea?"

They both laughed. Hiro flicked ash at his boot top, then kicked it off.

"Well, you sure sound a lot like *my* dad," Ray said. "He thinks like you. He'd say we owe America a lot, and we've got to earn our rights as citizens, for the next generation, if not ours."

"So, why'd *you* join up?"

Ray's smile fell. He looked into the mist and wondered what was on the other side, and whether there was one. Maybe the whole country was misted-over. A German ploy.

The truth was, he didn't want to be there at all. When the 442nd first formed, thousands of boys from Honolulu had jumped at the chance to join the Army. But not Ray; he didn't want to go to war. His father had seen a recruiting poster, brought it home, and handed it to him. He'd said, "This, you do. It is your chance to become a man, to gain honor." But even though he desperately wanted to make his father proud, Ray continued to avoid the recruiting station. Several more of his friends and cousins joined. Each battalion filled their quota and shipped out. Ray told his parents he intended to apply for a training program to become a welder at the Pearl Harbor drydocks. Getting a full-time job, bringing home extra money, and helping the war effort—these were sure ways to please his father.

But the war wasn't going well. The Japanese had captured

Singapore, the Philippines, Hong Kong, Wake Island, and Guam. They were threatening Alaska and many thought they might come back to invade Hawaii. Anti-Japanese sentiment was very high, and Nisei sons felt increasing pressure to enlist and show their patriotism.

And then—the awful day when the FBI came to their home. Ray's father worked as a crewman on an eighty-foot tourist boat that sailed out of the Ala Moana marina. Their cruise, which sailed around Diamond Head to Koko Crater at sunset, had been very popular with Japanese tourists before the war. The FBI was questioning anyone who had had contact with native Japanese, or anyone with a boat that might have been used to pass intelligence or fuel to Japanese subs. Ray's father was just a lowly deckhand, but two G-men came to question him, and when they searched the house they found Ray's shortwave radio.

The dark-suited G-men were livid. "How come this hasn't been reported? Japs aren't allowed to have radios!"

Ray's father tried to show them he had cut the wires that enabled transmission beyond the islands. He tried to explain that the radio had been a very expensive gift for Ray's last birthday, and that he thought the ban was only on radios that could transmit long distance.

Without another word, one G-man snatched up the radio, stomped out to the backyard, and smashed it on the driveway. The wood casing splintered into fragments. Ray watched, horrified, wanting to cry. He'd loved his radio, which he'd used to listen to stations in San Francisco, Los Angeles, and even the Philippines. He'd begged his father not to turn it in, and, against his better judgment, his father had acquiesced.

Then the FBI arrested Ray's father and held him for two days. He returned home sullen—he wouldn't speak of his ordeal, and it looked like he'd aged a year under the inquisition. The family's Japanese friends heard about the arrest and began to distance themselves. Better to be friendless if the only friends you have are possible traitors. And finally, though the notion of war terrified him, Ray knew that he had to enlist. It was the only thing he could do to regain his family's honor. "Well?" Hiro asked.

Ray rubbed his eyes, returned to the present. He cleared his throat and said, "Why'd I join? You know, to help the war effort. To defeat the Krauts. To get off the islands . . ." Ray cleared his throat again, spat. "Mainly I did it to earn my dad's respect. The last thing he told me before I left was, 'Do not dishonor the family.'"

Hiro slapped Ray on the back. "Perk up, you're making him proud just by being here."

It embarrassed Ray to retrieve this painful memory of his father's travail and his eyes suddenly, and uncontrollably, welled up with tears. He glanced away, drying his eyes with his sleeve. "Let's mount this hill," he said. "Sooner we do, sooner we can be back in town for hot chow."

The two men plugged along for another half hour, always moving upwards and peering through the fog for squad mates. The straps of Ray's pack were beginning to dig sharply into his shoulders. He regretted carrying his spade, gas mask, and first aid kit. Hiro made a habit of forgoing these items, and his pack was much lighter. And there had been no signs of enemy activity all day: no nearby artillery blasts, no mechanized sounds of tanks or trucks, no small arms fire. Nothing but fog. Ray cheered himself with the thought that today was going to be a good day, maybe the best day in a while. It made no sense to think that way, but then, it made no sense to think the other way.

Ahead of him, Hiro crouched behind a fallen tree, his arm raised into a fist. Twenty feet behind, Ray froze. They stayed like that for what seemed like several minutes. Finally, Hiro lowered his arm, waved him up, and Ray came forward.

There was a small clearing—the top of the hill at last. In the center was a small rectangular cottage made of gray fieldstone. Smoke rose lazily from its chimney and merged with the blanket of dark clouds. Little patches of short grass peppered the otherwise dark, bald ground. At the far right edge of the clearing a milk cow was penned in a split-rail enclosure.

The Germans were here. Ray saw a gray Opel truck with an open bed and machine gun mounted over the cab. The truck had come up a small dirt road which led down the other side of the hill, to the north. A thin, gray-coated soldier leaned against the side of the truck, smoking a cigarette, facing the road.

Hiro leaned in close to Ray, whispered, "Two more in the house. I saw them go in with the family that lives here—parents and two kids."

Voices rose inside the little farmhouse. Guttural shouts in German. Rapid protests in French. A child's whimpering.

Ray scanned the tree line. The woods were empty.

We're the only Americans here, he thought.

"This is the perfect place to bombard Bruyères from," Hiro murmured. He stuck up a thumb and jabbed it back in the direction from which they'd come, to the south. "On a clear day you could see the whole village."

"What are you thinking?" Ray asked.

Before Hiro could say anything, there was more noise in the farmhouse. Shoutings. Stomping. A woman's high-pitched screaming. Then the back door flew wide open and a young blonde girl dashed out. She ran desperately, falling, getting up, running wildly again.

Then she turned and headed straight toward Ray and Hiro.

A bald, stocky German soldier appeared in the open doorway. He raised his rifle and aimed at the girl.

Hiro's M-1 was up in an instant, but he hesitated to pull the trigger. The girl was running in and out of his line of sight. There was nothing to be done.

As Hiro and Ray looked on, a man in farm clothes came up behind the soldier in the doorway. He threw all of his weight against the bigger man, and the soldier's shot went wide.

The blonde girl made it into the scrub a few feet from Ray, then she dove, flat out, and lay facedown in the dirt.

She lay still for a moment. Ray was so close to her, he reached out and touched her arm. Startled, she recoiled like an animal. She stared at Ray in complete lack of comprehension. The girl's light green eyes peered out between a shock of wheat-colored hair. She looked at Ray, then Hiro, then back to Ray who saw her expression turn from abject fear to total surprise.

Obviously, the French farm girl had never seen Nisei before.

We're invaders from outer space, Ray thought.

But the girl didn't move and neither did they.

All the movement was taking place in the doorway of the farmhouse. The man, apparently the girl's father, was struggling with the soldier. While the two wrestled, another gray-coated soldier appeared behind them. An officer. His uniform was creased and neat and he moved with silent ease as he withdrew a Luger from his holster.

Ray, Hiro, the girl—all eyes were on this silent, second man. He spread his legs apart, one in front of the other, extended his arm, pointed the pistol at the base of the farmer's skull.

The gun fired and a film of red decorated the open door. The dead man kicked as if still alive, but his skull was shattered.

The girl shrieked.

Both Germans looked to the woods.

Hiro lowered himself as much as he could. Ray grabbed the girl, clasped his hand hard over her mouth, and flattened himself like a pancake.

The officer stood motionless, his Luger still faintly emitting smoke.

The supine soldier got up, dusted himself off.

Inside the farmhouse a woman was screaming.

The officer took several steps into the yard, listening, searching. He scanned the tightly woven trees, the low underbrush.

And then he looked right at them.

FIFTEEN

LOS ANGELES 1998

"Dad? Can you hear me?"

Daniel saw his father's eyes open a crack. "We're in the hospital. Just got you out of the ER and up to the floor." His father shifted his head, looked left, then right. He glanced down at his bare chest, where EKG leads sprouted like vines out of his body. Through the windows, bright, dust-moted beams of sunlight cut through the institutional, green-walled room. A bouquet of deep red roses Keiko had brought gave the room a pleasant, homey touch, but they were overcome by the stale hospital smell, the harsh antiseptic and metallic austerity of the place.

Daniel was shocked by his father's frail appearance. His chest emaciated, hollowed. His skin whitish, paper-thin. Daniel gave an involuntary shiver. This man was barely a suggestion of the strong father of his childhood, the big man who'd shown him love only through firm discipline, always pushing him to do better, daring him to rise to occasions he couldn't even visualize.

123

He watched his father's eyes roam the room, from the hanging IV bag to the tubes delivering oxygen to his nose—all the symbols of his mortality in plain sight. A pathetic sense of irony overcame Daniel. This was the same man he'd secretly wanted to be and did not want to be. He thought about how powerful, how unyielding his father had once been, and he remembered the times when one word of praise was all it had taken to thrill him and make him the happiest boy in the world.

"Daniel . . ." his father whispered.

Daniel drew his bedside chair closer and leaned forward.

"Feeling better?"

Instead of answering, his father pulled at the restrictive nasal tubing.

Daniel put his hand out to stop him.

"Dad, you might have had another heart attack. You've got morphine in your system and that will make you a little groggy. Best to just settle back now."

His father's hands sort of wilted, dropped to his sides. He peered at Daniel curiously.

"Where is your mother?"

"She just left to pick up some food."

There was an implacable moment of silence, and for some reason, Daniel eased the chair back away from the bed.

What should I say? he pondered. That I'm sorry?

He'd never felt comfortable talking to his father. Even in his youth, the conversations were one-sided. His father gave advice and he listened. That was the order of the day . . . to be quiet and obey.

Daniel felt his stomach clench as he thought of all he could say to break the uneasy silence. *I'm sorry for arguing and getting you upset. I'm grateful for everything you sacrificed, for the years you worked, so I could succeed. I forgive you for being too hard on me.* He knew it sounded like a speech, but maybe that's because it was.

As he silently reviewed his feelings, he studied his father's diminished face and wasted frame lying in the hospital bed among machines that both restrained and demeaned his mortality while at the same time preserving his life. So there was the deepest irony . . . that and the things he wouldn't say because there were other, less pleasant things that would have to come first.

But now the hard truths came one after another.

I wish you hadn't tried so hard to toughen me up. I wish you'd let me stay and be with Anne. I wish you would've listened to me about Kenny. I wish you could've respected the choices I made. I wish . . . but a wish was just a wish. And he knew these things he wished to say, were unsayable. His father would never hear them. Not now. Not ever.

"Daniel?" his father muttered softly.

"Yes?"

With effort, the old man sat up straighter. "I want you to take care of your mother."

"Of course, Dad. But you're going to be fine. We'll be out of here by tomorrow . . . you'll—"

"—This time it's different, Daniel."

The bedside cardiac monitor emitted intermittent beeps. The old man closed his eyes, but Daniel didn't want him to fall asleep. His thoughts settled on the questions that only his father could answer.

"Dad?"

The old man's eyelids fluttered open.

"Would you please tell me about the war? I mean . . . you never talked about it. We didn't know you were a hero, we need to—"

"—I'm no hero. Don't use that word."

"But you did something great, didn't you? And they want to honor you for it. Besides, Mom and me—"

"—You and your mother need to give it up, this foolishness."

His father's slack face tightened slightly, but his eyes remained glazed and sad. He stared unsteadily across the room at the wall where an ugly abstract painting depicted a splash of sea, a storm-tormented boat. Daniel followed his father's gaze. Maybe this clichéd image

125

suggests something to him, he thought. Maybe the mood of it anyway. Finally, his father spoke. "The war was a bad time. The worst time of my life. In war you do terrible things. You make mistakes . . . you kill your enemies and cripple your friends. You do things you can never take back."

His father winced, as if his memories were more physically painful than his hospital incarceration.

"I should never have gotten that medal."

He looked at Daniel with hawk-like, intransigent eyes—the old dominance, the mean man of Daniel's fearful childhood, the one who'd made him do things he didn't want to do.

Then his father looked up at the white, empty ceiling, and then away, out the window where he squinted at a sharp angle of sunlight and seemed to see something in it that he, Daniel, could not see. Daniel wanted him to explain more, but he moved on, and Daniel didn't interrupt because it was so rare for him to talk at length about anything.

"I'm glad you did not go to war, Danny. I know I have given you a hard time about it. But by going to medical school, you missed the war, and that was a good thing. And now you *do* do honorable work. You help people. You save lives. I . . . ." He paused, his eyes moist.

Daniel blinked. He could hardly believe what his father was saying. A small tear crossed over the older man's cheek, but he made no effort to wipe it away.

"If something had happened to you your mother would have died from grief. It's true you gave me heartache. I still disagree with the way you went about that disrespectful protest of yours . . . in college. But at the end of the day, you did what you planned to do, what you had to do to fulfill your destiny. You still became a doctor."

And now there was the glimmer of a sly grin at the corner of his father's mouth. "Of course it would have been better if you had become an ophthalmologist or a dermatologist."

"What?"

"More money. Everyone knows those ones make the most money."

Daniel did his best to laugh but it sounded a little choked. "Dad, I make plenty of money."

"Oh, sure . . . but not like those guys. The eye doctors and the skin doctors, everyone knows they make the most. And you work so much harder than they do. But then again, at one point I did worry you might become a pediatrician because you liked kids. That would have been worse. They make very little and work very hard. So I think we are lucky."

His father was smiling. He'd actually made a joke. A first.

Daniel didn't know whether to laugh or cry. Or accept whatever it was that was coming out of his father's mouth. Truth?

It felt strange to be having such a normal conversation with a man who'd never had one with him. Under these circumstances, it was tempting to forget his earlier mental review, his father's harshness, his brow-beatings. For the moment, Daniel would forgive but not forget.

Nothing was ever good enough for the old man. If Daniel earned a 98 on an exam, his father would ask where the other two points had gone. He'd often berated Keiko for being too easy on Daniel when it came to cello practice. His strictness had made Daniel a great cellist, but then, when Daniel had told him he was thinking about applying to Juilliard, he became angry and insisted medical school was the only option.

That or the Army, which is what had happened to Kenny.

The way it was, Kenny had graduated from high school in 1969. There was no money to send him to college, his father had said, but Daniel always felt he'd only said that to hurt Daniel. Kenny could have gotten into a state school or at least a community college, but Daniel knew the reasons his father gave ran deeper.

Kenny wasn't much of a student. Truth be known, he wasn't made for it. Reading, writing, math—Kenny had struggled with them all. Whereas college had seemed to be a natural part of Daniel's future,

Kenny had never wanted to go. Most kids didn't. Most just got a job. But the draft changed everything. Or it should have, Daniel thought, if you were someone with any common sense. Anyone who didn't go to college was 1-A, fodder for cannons, as they said it then. To get a 1-Y you had to have an arm missing or a broken back or the eyesight of a turtle. A draftee could graduate from high school and, after a cursory boot camp, find himself in the jungles of Vietnam three months later. Daniel told Kenny to apply to college. He could see the writing on the wall. But his younger brother refused. The last face-to-face conversation they'd ever had occurred the month before Kenny graduated. They were playing basketball at a park near the entrance to their neighborhood. Kenny was on the varsity team and had no trouble beating Daniel one on one. His little brother was also three inches taller than he was—almost six feet.

It was dusk. The setting sun cast a bronze glow over the park. In the distance, a middle-aged woman let her dog off its leash to run. Otherwise, Daniel and Kenny were the only ones there.

"Do you want to die overseas in another country's civil war?" Daniel asked his brother after finishing their last game. "Please think this through," he pleaded.

"You don't *know* I'll get drafted," Kenny replied.

"The odds are more than good."

The two of them began walking home. Kenny bounced the basketball as he went.

"I'm not made for college," he said. "I'm no good at it."

"You could try harder. Make passing grades."

"What? Cs and Ds? Where's that going to get me? And that's about the best I could do. I hate school. It would be a waste of four years."

"But even if you just go to community college you'll miss going to Vietnam. They're calling it miniature hell, Kenny. It's that bad."

His brother's feet came to a halt. He slapped the ball between his hands and held it. Turning to Daniel, he said, "For me, going to college would be the coward's way. Dad's right."

"*Dad* told you not to go?"

"Yeah. He says I shouldn't be afraid to serve my country."

"Don't listen to him. He's crazy. All he cares about is that goddamn family honor. You know, that old country idiocy."

Kenny shrugged. "I think I'd be good in the Army. I'm tough. I can follow orders. Maybe it would be good for me."

Daniel shook his head, trying desperately to think of something he could say to change his brother's mind. "Small hell isn't good for anyone."

"Why not, if it makes you a man? Plus, it'll make Dad proud. I'm not like you, Danny. You've got everything going for you. Someday you'll be a rich doctor. And what will I be?" Kenny looked away. "This is the one thing I can do to make him proud of me too."

"No, Kenny, you—"

"—It's too late anyway. I can't apply and get into school before the next draft call. Whatever happens is going to happen." He made a quick fake move to pass the ball at Daniel's face and Daniel flinched, jumping back. Kenny laughed, grabbed his brother around the neck with his arm.

"Don't worry about me, big brother. I can take care of myself."

One month later, Kenny's draft number was ten. He would definitely be called up. Daniel called him from Boston to beg him to go to Canada, or claim to be a conscientious objector, but Kenny laughed at these ideas. He was ready to go. Ready to serve.

One month after he arrived in Vietnam, during the middle of Daniel's second year in medical school, Kenny was killed when the Huey helicopter he was riding in was blown out of the sky by a Viet Cong rocket-propelled grenade.

"Where is your mother? I'm hungry."

Daniel's mind returned to the hospital room. His father had been speaking of the past and he wanted to keep their conversation going, to redirect him back to the war, to find out what heroic thing he'd done. But then there was a knock at the door.

A young doctor entered. The cardiologist.

"Dr. Tokunaga? I'm Dr. Kim. It's an honor to meet you."

Daniel shook hands with him. To Daniel this cardiologist looked awfully young, probably in his mid-thirties. The knot of his tie was halfway undone and the Littman stethoscope draped around his neck was tangled up in the collar of his wrinkled white coat.

"Hello, Mr. Tokunaga," Dr. Kim said, addressing Daniel's father. "The good news is that your cardiac enzymes came back normal. I'm thinking you might not have had a heart attack at all—"

"—But my chest really hurt."

The cardiologist nodded. "We can do a cath to check your heart vessels. I know you had two stents last year. But we might want to do an upper endoscopy first." The doctor saw his patient's confusion. "I'm sorry. I mean, we can take a look at your stomach with a small camera we place down your throat."

"You think this is reflux?" Daniel asked.

"Maybe. Like I said, his enzymes were normal, and his EKG . . ." The doctor picked up the strip of paper coming out of the machine at the bedside, ". . . looks pretty stable compared to the one he had six months ago. If it's not reflux then it might be a stomach ulcer. Have you been under a lot of stress lately?"

Daniel's father shrugged but his eyes stayed riveted on the cardiologist.

Ever since the government started hounding him, he's been wound tight as piano wire, Daniel thought. His mind went to the possible endoscopy. He knew his father wouldn't like having to swallow a thick rubber tube that snaked down the esophagus into the stomach. But then—who would?

"The answer is yes," Daniel said. "Dad's been under some stress recently. So I suppose it's not a bad idea. But I'm not sure he's up to it right now." He said this in a soft, low voice, not really hiding it from his father but not broadcasting it either.

"We'll sedate him. He'll be comfortable," the cardiologist said reassuringly.

Daniel glanced at his father, whose face was set in stone as usual.

"What do you think, Dad?"

His father raised his shoulders, let them fall slowly. He sighed loudly.

Daniel took this as acceptance. If his father was anything, he was stoic.

"Okay, let's get it done," Daniel said.

"Great, I'll call the GI specialist and have it scheduled for this afternoon."

The doctor jotted his orders in the chart. As he turned to leave, a new face appeared at the door.

"Hi, Daniel—"

"—Anne . . . what a surprise!"

She wore knee-length black leather boots and a stylish burgundy blouse. In her hands was a vase filled with yellow carnations. She smiled at Daniel, then turned to his father and smiled at him too.

"Uh . . . Dad. Do you remember my friend, Anne Mikado? It's been a while, maybe you—"

The old man nodded, his face showing neither surprise nor pleasure.

Don't you remember her, Dad . . . the girl you kept me from marrying?

"Mr. Tokunaga, it's nice to see you again after these many years," Anne said in her smooth, diplomatic way. She placed the flowers on the table next to the bed. "I just found out you were admitted. So sorry you're in here, but it's good to see that you're doing alright."

The old man offered a faint smile and bowed his head briefly and formally.

"Thank you for your kindness," Daniel said to Anne.

Anne placed a small brown paper bag on the bedside table. "I brought these *inari* for you, Mr. Tokunaga."

The old man's face lifted. Her gift was a hit.

He peeked into the bag and, grinning, reached for a morsel of sticky rice wrapped in sweet tofu skin. He smiled warmly at Anne. "Thank you very much," he said to her.

"Dad, wait. You can't eat that now, you're going to have that endoscopy test."

His face tightened as if a screw had been turned. "Oh, crap."

Anne giggled at the sudden way he said this. "Don't worry," she said. "It will be waiting here when you get back. I won't let anyone else eat it." She looked at Daniel, then winked at his father.

What a gentle charmer, Daniel thought. Even now, surrounded by all the tension of the past, she'd cut right through simply by being so thoughtful and relaxed.

Then, for a nanosecond, Anne's eyes wandered to the visible scar, almost a faded purple, on Mr. Tokunaga's shoulder. She looked away, but too late—he'd seen the mild surprise, the curiosity, all in a flash, then instantly covered by her sweet face. The old man misses nothing, Daniel thought.

"That scar? I got shot in the war," the old man said so softly and matter-of-factly that Daniel was not sure Anne heard him.

"I was very lucky to keep my arm," he whispered almost to himself—yet his eyes were on Anne. "Lucky that the field hospital in France had penicillin. I was in that place for two months, healing. After that I got to come home."

"You're a hero, Mr. Tokunaga."

Daniel's father looked vaguely out the window. "The boys who didn't come home, *they* were the heroes. Not me."

Beth got off the elevator and looked for signs pointing the way to her father-in-law's hospital room. She was still trying to process the day's events, especially the surreal scene at the house. She honestly had no idea what to think. All she could do was go along, like a spectator watching a film with so many twists and turns that she had no idea what to expect next.

She located the room, and when she came to the door she saw it was partway open. She stopped. Through the gap she saw a slender woman. Asian. Quite pretty.

Beth recognized Daniel's voice. The woman laughed at something Daniel said, and the way she did made Beth pause. Then Daniel said something Beth couldn't quite make out, but his voice was animated, with an energy behind it that she hadn't heard in a long time. Now the woman reached over and touched Daniel's hand. They knew each other.

Who is this person and what is she to my husband?

Beth knocked on the door and pushed it open.

"Hello everyone," she said.

She smiled at Daniel, then her father-in-law, then the stranger. The woman's eyebrows lifted for a millisecond, betraying surprise, and perhaps, apprehension? But in the next moment she was wearing a welcoming smile.

Beth moved to her father-in-law first. "Dad, you look a lot better." At the bedside, she leaned over and gave him a quick kiss on the cheek.

The old man did his usual formal nod but there was something less mechanistic about it. "Beth, thank you for coming all this way to visit," he said.

"Of course! How could I not?"

"I mean, it's very good to see you."

Beth smiled and looked at Daniel with an expression that said: *You see, don't you? You have him all wrong. He's a wonderful man.*

"You gave us quite a scare yesterday," Beth said.

"We're having a couple of tests done today," Daniel interjected, trying to sound cool and professional, though deep inside he felt somehow almost boyishly out of place. "Beth, this is Anne Mikado, an old family friend."

"Don't call me 'old,'" Anne protested with a smile.

"Sorry!" Daniel blurted, too loudly and seriously, betraying his nervousness.

Beth laughed politely and offered her hand lightly to Anne. "Hello. It's a pleasure to meet you." Beth didn't see a wedding ring. The two women briefly clasped hands.

"—And to meet you, as well," Anne returned warmly. "But please excuse me. I'm actually supposed to be working right now in the hospital. I just came to say hello." She turned to leave, but then turned back and said, "So good to see you again, Mr. Tokunaga."

"Thanks for visiting," Daniel's father replied. He gave her a half-smile, but his eyes glittered a little.

Two pretty women can always gladden a man's heart, Daniel thought.

Anne left and Beth took a seat in the chair next to Daniel.

"So, Dad . . ." she said. "Tell me what you've been up to for the last few decades."

All three of them laughed at the same time.

⁓

Alone in the hospital room, Daniel and Beth waited for his father to return from the endoscopy procedure. They talked in low tones as the sun filled the room with an orange glow that was beginning to go red as the sun descended.

"So, who was that woman, Daniel?"

"I told you, a family friend. She works here in the hospital. We knew each other in high school."

"Is she the one who called you this morning?"

Daniel paused. "Actually, yes, she was."

Beth shook her head sadly. "Alright. I think you better tell me what's going on."

"What do you mean? Nothing's going on."

"Seriously? Women don't walk around the hospital dressed like that. And they don't find you all that funny unless . . . argh!" Beth clenched her fists and threw back her head in frustration.

"Honey, I literally just ran into her the day I arrived because she happens to work in the hospital. She was a good friend of our family and we knew each other a long time ago. I don't know what you're suggesting, but you don't need to worry."

Beth looked away and took a deep breath. "Fine. Let's change the subject."

"Fine."

They sat there, in silence, for a full minute. The empty bed, the setting sun, his wife's irritation, made Daniel anxious. He looked down and traced the pattern in the floor tiles with his eyes.

"Hasn't it been obvious to you that I'm not happy?" Beth stated matter-of-factly.

Daniel looked at her face in the reddish wash of light. It was the lovely face of the woman he had fallen in love with, but now the pastel shadows made by her cheekbones gave her a haunted look.

"No," Daniel said at last. "I mean, I never thought you were *unhappy*. It's impossible for any of us to be happy *all* the time. If you wanted us to communicate more you could have just said so and we would have made time." In his mind every problem was a paradigm with an answer at the opposite end.

Beth released a deep and pained sigh. "I've done that many times in the past. You might make a small effort, but it never lasts. And I don't make a big deal about it because we're both so busy. But something has to change, Daniel. Sometimes you're just so detached . . . so . . . so distant. You come home to eat and then spend what little time there is left watching whatever sport or movie's on all night. I go to bed; you're still in front of the TV and it's like . . . well, it's like I don't even exist. What am I to you if you don't want to talk to me? Sometimes I feel like . . . furniture or something."

"I wouldn't go so far—"

"—I would. Did you know that I've been going to a new church group every Friday afternoon for almost six months?"

Daniel watched as an airplane sliced through the sunset cloud layer, appearing one moment, disappearing the next while his eyes followed its path. The sound of the jet engines diminished as the fan in the AC kicked on, cooling the room. It was a distraction. He needed something to keep him from thinking about yet another problematic situation—there was already his father, his mother, his work, and now there was Beth.

"I knew you went somewhere on Fridays," he said. "But you never told me where exactly."

"You never asked. And you're obviously too busy to care."

"Baby, I'm a *surgeon*. Not just some guy with a job—"

"—Don't play that card, Daniel. I've heard it too many times. You know, it would be good if we had at least one conversation a day. Maybe that's all I'm asking. Just one heart-to-heart each day. To sort of keep up with what we do, what we feel, where we're going and who we're with."

"Truthfully, Beth, we've both been very busy—you with the kids, me at the hospital. We're both under pressure. Each of us in different ways, right?"

Beth snapped. "Damn it, Daniel! You aren't listening to me! You think we're like one of your patients you can just fix? We aren't! I'm trying, Daniel. I really am. But you're not. And unless something changes quick, we're done."

Daniel sat speechless. The threat of divorce scared him, but his first reaction was an overwhelming sense of injustice. He'd worked so hard for so many years, from residency till now, eighty hours a week, going in, middle of the night. He'd never cheated on Beth. He'd always tried to be a good and honest father. Why was it always his fault? He knew he could do better, but he didn't deserve this. He wasn't a mind reader, after all.

While these thoughts rolled about in Daniel's mind, his silence spoke volumes to Beth and had the unintended consequence of making her even angrier.

"What's wrong with us, Daniel? Do I not excite you?" She cupped her breasts indignantly with her hands. "Am I not attractive to you anymore?"

"Don't be silly," Daniel managed to say.

"Am I boring to you?"

The question lingered. Daniel knew he needed to say something right, something straight and true. It had to be something helpful or he'd find himself in deeper trouble.

"No, of course not."

"Because you don't look at me or talk to me the way you did with that 'old family friend' a couple of hours ago."

Daniel didn't know what to say. The chirp of cardiac monitors and squeaking shoes from outside in the hall were the only sounds with the exception of the whirring fan.

"Just tell me what you want, Beth."

She threw up her hands. "I've tried, Daniel, I've really tried. It's like we're just roommates living in the same house."

There was a knock at the door and a custodian opened it wide. He was an elderly Asian man with a mop in a rolling bucket and a trashcan on wheels. He saw Beth's face and took a step back. It was dusk and the room had grown dark, but now that the door was open Daniel could see his wife's face by the fluorescent blaze of light from the hallway. There were tears in her eyes.

The gray uniformed man glanced awkwardly at his watch. Then he pointed at the trashcan in the corner, and Daniel nodded. With a look of relief, the maintenance man quickly emptied the can and left on squishy, gum-soled shoes.

Another look at Beth's face and Daniel knew he had grossly underestimated the depth of her feelings. This was not a heart problem he could fix with a suture or a shock. This was a completely different kind of heart problem—one he didn't know how to mend. At this realization, he felt a tinge of fear. Nervously, he began to dry Beth's eyes with a tissue.

"Beth, I'm sorry. I know I've been preoccupied with work. I know I can do better." He looked into her eyes, and their sorrow took his breath away. "Please give me another chance," he said, as he reached out to embrace her.

Beth pulled away. She shook her head as fresh tears rolled down her cheeks. "We've fallen out of love, Daniel. I think it's too late." Then she walked out of the room.

Daniel stood up, alarmed. "What?" He ran into the hallway. "Beth! What are you doing?"

Nurses and doctors looked up and stared. Daniel caught up to Beth, took her by the arm, and gently pulled her into an alcove with shelves piled high with linen.

"Don't say that! Why would you say that?" he said, trying not to sound as scared as he suddenly felt. "I love you. Please give me another chance. I'll do better, I promise. Please."

Why didn't you tell me? Daniel also wanted to shout. But even now, to himself, the excuse rang hollow. It was his fault for not seeing the signs. In an instant, he remembered a multitude of small events, a half-dozen missteps, so many foolish things he wished he could do over.

Our last anniversary, when I forgot to even write her a card.

Her last birthday, when I believed her when she told me not to get her anything, because I figured we each get whatever we need whenever we need it.

And yes, the countless nights of staying downstairs watching TV instead of spending time with her.

"Beth, I'm so sorry. You're right. I've taken you for granted—for a long time. I haven't made the effort I should've. I'm guilty as charged. But I swear to you, I haven't strayed from your side. It's just maybe . . . maybe I wasn't there to know I wasn't there. If you know what I mean."

Tears rolled down Beth's cheeks. Daniel hugged her close. She was trembling.

"Beth, please say something."

A monotone voice over the hospital PA system: *General surgery to GI suite, stat. General surgery to GI suite, stat.*

Daniel froze. He let go of Beth.

"What is it?" Beth asked.

"Dad," he said, already turning swiftly into the hall.

"Where's the GI suite?" he said sharply to a startled nurse.

"Two floors down," she replied, stepping back to get out of his way.

Daniel ran down the corridor. Beth followed him. He skipped stairs in the stairwell and, two floors down, saw the double doors labeled Gastroenterology. He pushed hard through them.

There were already half a dozen people gathered outside one of the rooms: attendings, residents, technicians, nurses. Daniel came forcefully into the room, heard a protest—*get the family out of here!*—Daniel ignored it, dodging two men in scrubs.

And there was his father. The head of his bed was up, and he was coughing, choking, and spitting up blood.

"Where's the surgeon? Call the OR!" the doctor standing at the head of the bed shouted.

A man in blue scrubs entered and accidentally bumped Daniel from behind. Daniel spun round and glimpsed his I.D. One of the surgeons.

"What happened?"

"Found an ulcer, tried to biopsy, profuse bleeding."

"Can you stop it?"

"Can't see anything, stomach's full of blood. This patient's on aspirin and Plavix—prior MI and stents, too."

"Perforated ulcer, or just bleeding?"

"Don't know. Can't see a thing."

"Exploratory laparotomy," the surgeon said. "Type and cross eight units, stat. Let's get him up to the OR."

Daniel stared, helpless. Beth appeared beside him. He tried to stand in front of her to block her view. At the same time two nurses wheeled his father past both of them, out the door. Daniel saw his father's face. He was obviously in agony. Fighting for breath. *Dad, can you see me? I'm here.*

But then he was gone, down the hall. Daniel followed, but stopped as the surgeon and his team pushed the bed into an elevator.

"What's the patient's name?" the surgeon asked.

A nurse read the chart. "Ryoji Tokunaga."

The doors slid shut.

Daniel looked at his own frightened reflection in the stainless steel doors.

Then he whispered the words he'd wanted to say before they closed.

"He goes by Ray."

SIXTEEN

VOSGES MOUNTAINS, FRANCE 1944

The clouds parted and a beam of sunlight gleamed off the Nazi's wire-rimmed glasses. Two fiery lenses and the man's hard-boned, immovable face bore into Ray. Was he looking at him or was the German seeing beyond him into the bracken that lay behind Ray and the girl? Ray held his breath along with the child. He waited for some sign of discovery. But the wire-rim man told him nothing.

The thin, helmeted soldier who'd been smoking beside the truck was now inside the farmhouse. He seemed not to care when mother and son went to the father's dead body. The little boy shuddered, wailed. The woman knelt in the doorway and sobbed.

Now the wire-rimmed officer shouted an order, then took three steps toward the woods, and hesitated. He turned back to the house and stood still for several seconds. Then he faced the forest again, as if, somehow, he could will the woods to part and reveal their secret.

Again, the Nazi reversed his position and re-entered the house.

Ray released a long pent-up breath. Slowly, he moved his hand away from the girl's mouth. Her pale eyes were frozen with fear, but she didn't scream. She whispered several things rapidly in French, none of which Ray or Hiro could understand. Then she impulsively jumped up and started to make a run for the farmhouse. Hiro caught her ankle and brought her down fast. Before she could rise again, he held her close to his chest. For a while she fought against his superior strength, then she wriggled and squirmed, and after a minute, her body went limp. Hiro shouldered off a rivulet of sweat from his face.

"What now?" Ray whispered.

Hiro stroked the girl's forehead. She looked unconscious.

"Should we go back and find the others?" Ray asked. "We've found this place. I'm sure we can find it again."

Hiro looked at him. "We're supposed to take and hold anywhere that's good for artillery."

"But there's only two of us."

Hiro did not answer. He was silent for so long that Ray wondered if he'd forgotten Ray was there. The Germans in the house conversed loudly. The helmeted soldier used the sole of his boot to push the dead body clear of the doorway. Then he dragged it further into the yard. The mother hadn't moved; she was still crying. The soldier casually took a fistful of the mother's yellow hair and hauled her inside. The door shut, muffling the woman's cries.

Hiro said, "We should take them now." He looked into Ray's eyes. "We can do this."

"Just us? There's more of them."

"Only three, and we'll have the element of surprise. Wait, and when we get back here there'll be a whole company of Jerries with a lot more firepower."

Ray's heart began to beat in a strange elliptical pattern. "I'm not sure . . ."

There was a new, high-pitched shriek. The boy. The door swung open and the two soldiers emerged. The bald, heavyset one gripped the child by the arm, but the boy kicked and clawed, so the man scooped him up with one arm and caught him in a headlock. Inside, a flash of blue, the woman's dress. Then the officer, chasing her, laughing.

The door closed again.

Outside, the soldiers laughed as they carried the boy around to the front of the house.

Inside, the sound of upturned furniture, a crash of dishes.

The little girl was alert and wide-eyed now, studying the house with wild uncertainty.

"We're going in." Hiro said. "Now."

"Are you sure—"

Hiro's face flashed with animal determination. "You know what's happening in there. I'm not going to live the rest of my life haunted by this. We can do it. Listen, I get the fat one with the boy. You get the helmet head by the truck. Quickly and silently, so we can still surprise the one in the house. Got it?"

Ray's throat went dry. He looked at Hiro, then the girl.

"Well? You got my back?"

The girl's stare unnerved Ray. Her eyes pleaded for something to be done to save the rest of her family. Ray agreed, but he had none of Hiro's passionate conviction, none of his winner's mentality. This was the land of the lost and nothing good could come of it. Still, he nodded.

"Okay," Hiro said. "Let's go."

Hiro darted into the clearing. Ray crouched low and followed, leaving the girl behind the thick trunk of a maple tree. The ground was thick with slippery fallen leaves.

The Germans with the boy were out of view, opposite side of the house. Sounds from inside grew louder: a thump and a shout, a table scraping on a bare wood floor.

At the southwest corner of the house, they pressed up against the structure's rough stone wall. Hiro unsheathed his bayonet and held it up. The steel was shiny and new. Ray fumbled to get his out of its scabbard. Should he leave his rifle behind? How could he carry it and stab someone at the same time? He could leave the gun here—but—then he'd be defenseless if the enemy spotted him first.

Hiro glanced around the corner. He ducked back and pointed at Ray, then towards the truck. Ray understood: my guy's still at the truck. Hiro patted Ray on the shoulder and nodded. Then he disappeared around the corner.

Ray drew a short breath and then—his feet wouldn't move.

Go! He wanted to follow. He strained to lift his foot, willed his legs to action. But his feet remained planted on dirt. In his skull, panic alarm. It felt like his heart might burst from his chest and fly out like a crazed bird.

He heard Hiro moving around the side of the house. Then a grunt, a groan, the boy's high-pitched voice keening.

Ray didn't move.

The soldier by the truck cried out.

Ray looked around the corner, saw the soldier running toward the house, unholstering his pistol.

There's still time, move! Come on! Get your rifle up!

But Ray didn't move. He ducked back behind the corner.

Hiro's voice: "Don't shoot! Don't shoot!"

Ray looked down at his hands: white-knuckled, rifle in one hand, bayonet in the other.

He didn't know what to do.

A sudden burst of German invective.

Hiro again, "Don't shoot!"

Ray dropped the rifle and the bayonet.

He ran away from the house, back to the protection of the forest.

SEVENTEEN

LOS ANGELES 1998

Daniel had been in medical school for only four weeks when he attended his first anatomy class. The students entered a large, well-lit room with thirty cadavers lying naked and supine on stainless steel tables. The room reeked of formaldehyde, forcing Daniel to take short, abbreviated breaths through his mouth. Each cadaver lay under the eyes of four students who were prepared—or maybe not quite— to dissect it.

Daniel's group named their cadaver "Harry" because he had a massive amount of pubic hair. It seemed insensitive, but paradoxically, naming their cadaver was one way of de-humanizing it. Naturally, it was important to respect that these were real people, people who had generously donated their bodies for the education of the Harvard medical students; but, it was also necessary to find ways to distance oneself, or one would never be able to make the first cut. Daniel found that this was especially true when he dissected the hands. To him, the hands were the most human part of the cadaver.

The part that gave him goosebumps.

His father's hand was like that. Gray and sallow. When they brought Daniel and Keiko to view Ray's body, Daniel felt the need to touch it, and he did. This was the hand that changed my diapers, picked me up when I fell off my bicycle, and shook my hand when I went off to college, he thought. Now it felt cold, rigid, and so absent of life it might not have ever been a living hand that had once helped others to live.

Now Daniel stood in the rain beside Ray's grave, listening to his mother's pastor deliver a sermon on the twenty-third Psalm. Daniel kept one arm around Keiko, who stood beside him, as he held a black umbrella over both their heads. Roiling storm clouds in the distance threatened heavier rain, but Daniel found it fitting, as if the weather matched the occasion, and his mood.

There were only ten other attendees. Ray Tokunaga did not have any friends. There were a half dozen ladies from Keiko's church who had come to support her. Beth stood across the flag-draped casket, still looking stunned, though three days had passed since Ray's death. They'd both agreed the twins should stay in school and not travel to the funeral. Daniel was particularly glad the kids weren't present. He didn't want them to see this. His horrible, dysfunctional family. It was too late to shield Beth from knowing the garish truth, but he could at least protect the kids. They shouldn't be burdened with any of this, he thought. This was the family he was ashamed of, and he couldn't escape the truth that he was the one most responsible for failing it.

His father, dead after a life of hard work and sacrifice, estranged from his son and grandchildren because Daniel couldn't be the bigger man.

His mother, looking stoic but undoubtedly hurting, after forty years of heartache that Daniel could have easily alleviated with something as simple as an occasional visit or even just a phone call.

His wife, ignored and taken for granted. His beautiful, wonderful wife whom he had driven away with sheer apathy. Nothing could have been easier for him to ameliorate. How could he be so blind? For all his accomplishments, all the lives he'd saved, the honors he'd received, in the end—what were they all worth? Nothing, in comparison to the people gathered in this small space of just ten feet, one already dead.

The weight of his failure drove him to despair.

The pastor had finished. A lone bugler sounded taps as the casket was slowly lowered. Daniel was grateful to the kindly funeral director who, after learning Ray was a veteran, had arranged for the flag, the bugler, and even two Army pallbearers.

Her face a mask of grim forbearance, Keiko dropped the first shovel of dirt into the hole that would hold Daniel's father for the rest of time.

A week later, Daniel was at home with his mother, going through his father's things. He could tell Keiko was saddened, but overall he thought she was holding up better than she might have. It was strange how when the surgeon came to tell them that Ray had bled out during surgery and died, Keiko didn't cry. She didn't say anything; she just nodded and looked away.

After the funeral, Beth returned home to Philadelphia while Daniel took two additional weeks to manage his father's affairs and help his mother. Daniel hadn't taken two weeks off in his entire life, but he knew he couldn't leave Keiko alone. She was a very sociable woman, used to having people around her, and she felt somewhat abandoned in the empty house.

And maybe I need her companionship too, Daniel thought. Plus, I know that on her own, she'd never do anything with Dad's stuff. His clothes. His shoes. His toiletries and piles of old paperwork. All of it will still be here a decade from now if I don't help her clean it out . . .

It was a Saturday afternoon, and Daniel was back to cleaning out the drawers in the dining room. He cleared out drawer after drawer, going through the motions of a man half-awake. Since his father's death, his mind seemed to drift often, like a ship in search of an elusive, fog-bound harbor.

There was a knock at the front door. Daniel came out of his reverie. He looked up, turned around. The door was wide open for easy access to the porch, where the old man's impersonal-personals were piled up for Goodwill.

Through the screen door, he saw someone, but there was a dream haze before his eyes, as if he'd been deeply asleep.

"Anne, what a surprise . . . how are you?" he said as he opened the door.

"I'm fine. The question is, how are *you?*" Before Daniel could even answer, Anne said, "So very sorry about your father."

"Thanks. I'm sticking around to help my mom handle all of this." He waved his hand toward the dining room, which was full of scattered piles of paper, used and dead ballpoint pens, a half-dozen pairs of eyeglasses and lots of crisp, yellowed postcards from the 1950s. Most of the dinette drawers were half-open, stuff falling out of them onto the floor. The dining room chairs were shoved haphazardly against the wall, one hooked into the other upside down.

"I was wondering if you'd call me," Daniel said.

"I almost did," Anne replied. "Several times. But I felt sure you'd still be here sorting things out for your mom. Is Beth still here?" She glanced around, half-expectant. She looked from Daniel into the living room where Ray's old recliner and the ancient television resided.

"Beth went home."

"Oh."

"Well, please come in and sit down." Daniel led her into the living room. They sat next to each other on the beige couch against the far wall.

"Can I get you something to drink?"

"Oh no, I'm fine."

"Alright."

They sat there not knowing exactly what to say. The window was open and they heard the rhythmic slapping of a ball hitting a leather glove—two boys playing catch in the yard back of the house. In the distance, a car honked, a flock of blackbirds bickered in a nearby mulberry tree. Then silence but for the rhythmic striking of leather.

"Is your mother here?" Anne asked.

"No. Her friends from church took her to lunch."

"Oh." Anne's eyes circled the room and returned to Daniel. It was clear to Daniel that whatever she wanted to talk about was not easy to bring up. And yet, she'd come here just to tell him. He waited, listened. A full minute passed; the baseball boys got into an argument about who would do what, and how.

Finally, Daniel broke the ice: "Anne, what is it you wanted to tell me?"

He saw that her dark eyes were moist.

Anne touched her cheeks lightly with a tissue she found in her purse.

"Sorry," she whispered. "This is a little hard for me. I've wanted to say this for such a long time."

"Say what?" Daniel felt a tickling sensation, a small alarm that went off behind his eyes.

"The reason why I left."

"Oh." Daniel swallowed. "I'd like very much to know about that," he said. "All these years I've wondered."

Anne smiled, but the tears continued to flow.

"Oh Daniel . . ." she said so faintly that he could barely hear her.

"Why did you leave?" he asked. "I remember when it happened. I was going to go against my father and stay at UCLA so we could be together. I was so sure we were going to get married. But then suddenly you were gone and I never heard from you again. Honestly, I never knew what to make of it."

"I *had* to go. My parents decided to go back to Japan. They made me leave with them."

"But why didn't you write me? Or call? Anne, I was devastated. Depressed. I didn't know what to do without you. I always suspected—"

"—What?"

"That you met someone else."

Anne laughed bitterly. "That didn't happen."

"Then, it must have been . . ." Daniel took a deep breath, exhaled slowly.

"What, Daniel?"

"My father must have *said* something to you, or *done* something. Anything to keep us apart. Am I right?"

Anne bowed her head and brought her hands together to cover her face. Her shoulders trembled, then shook. She was crying hard now.

"He did, didn't he?" Daniel said, his voice rising. A wave of anger swept through him. "Damn him. Tell me, did he talk to you? Did he say something crazy to your parents?"

"Yes," Anne replied softly. "But it's not what you think."

"It's not? Then tell me."

"You're right. Your father did not want you to marry me. I understood why. Your family was more established than mine. You were Americans. Your father disliked mine because we were from Japan and my father had fought America as a soldier in the Japanese Army."

"No one could have helped that. It was nobody's fault. Besides, that's history."

Anne nodded. "I know, but that was how he felt. And we knew it, my parents and I. They also discouraged me from seeing you, because they had their own sense of honor. They did not want me to marry into a family that felt they were better than ours."

"I would never have made you feel that way."

"I know, I know. But that was what *they*—my parents—felt. You know how it is. We can't go against our parents, who sacrificed so much for us. And your father did come to see my father. They knew each other from the Japanese Association in town. But it wasn't about us."

"It wasn't?" Daniel was surprised.

"My father was in trouble."

"What kind of trouble?"

"He was never good with money. He wasn't good at a lot of things. I think the Japanese defeat in the war affected him badly. He lost all his friends. His parents were killed in the firebombing of Tokyo. He came here because there was nothing left in Japan. No work. No friends. And I think he felt guilty that he had survived when all those he loved died. So he came here and always had trouble finding a job. His English wasn't good. He'd work at the docks unloading ships, or sometimes washing dishes in a restaurant. But then he'd gamble and drink and half the money would be gone before he brought it home to my mother. You remember that little house we owned in Torrance? Remember how small it was?"

Daniel remembered. Anne's home had been a two-room, one story structure with the kitchen and eating area in the back. The front room served as living room and bedroom for Anne and her parents.

"The bank came to foreclose on us. The mortgage payments weren't very much, but even they were too expensive for my father. His desire to return home to Japan was not surprising under the circumstances. By that time the Japanese economy was just starting to recover. He'd heard there were jobs. But he was too honorable to just leave and not pay his creditors, so he was stuck . . . and that's when your father came to us."

"What could my dad possibly do? He was strapped himself."

"Well, he'd heard that my father needed money. I remember when he came to the door. Both of them were very formal. They bowed to each other. My father asked me to leave, and I went into the back room with my mother, but we could hear everything they said. Your father asked how much money we needed and as I remember it

151

was about five hundred dollars. Your father asked what my dad would do in Japan. He said there was a new car manufacturing plant with good, stable jobs. And then your father said he would give us the money to pay off the rent so we could leave. I remember at that moment my mother's mouth fell open in amazement. She drew a breath and looked at me wide-eyed. She, too, desperately wanted to go back to Japan, and this offer was like a miracle."

Daniel shook his head. "What did your father say?"

"He politely refused, as was the custom. Your father insisted. This went on three times. Then my father said he would pay back the loan with interest within a year and your father said that was fine. We heard my father's voice telling us to come into the room. We did and I saw them shaking hands. My father was beaming. He'd been so depressed and now it was like he had new life. My mother and I bowed ceremoniously to your father, to thank him. And then your father just left."

"He didn't say anything about *us*?"

"No."

Daniel tried to process everything but it was a bit too off the wall—too unusual to sort out so quickly. How could a poor man save a poorer one? But he could easily intuit why his father had made the offer. "He must have done it mainly so that you would leave and we'd split up. Simple as that."

"Actually, I don't think so. My father told me your dad had also loaned money to at least two other Japanese families he knew—loaned it to them when they'd gotten themselves into a hole. And when he looked at me that afternoon he smiled in a kind way. I really think he was just trying to help us."

"But if he didn't tell you to stay away, why didn't you come back? Or write to me to explain?"

Anne sat up straighter and slid down the couch, away from him. Daniel stiffened. What could be coming next?

"Daniel, I did it for my family's honor. And out of love for you."

"What? That doesn't make sense."

"Listen. Try to understand. We knew your father did not approve of our marriage. The money he gave us got us back on our feet. My father's job in Japan was good, and he regained his self-respect. He felt indebted to your father, deeply indebted, as only the formal Japanese can feel. He wasn't offended that your father thought his son was too good for me. He understood it. It's part of our culture. After the way your father helped us, my dad would never do anything that would shame your family, nor would he do anything he thought your father disapproved of. And neither could I. I couldn't do that to my parents. In such a situation I knew they would lose face."

"That's crazy! That's why you gave up on us? Just like that? Anne, we loved each other." Daniel's eyes were wet now with confused emotions—sorrow for lost and unrecoverable time.

"Daniel, you must understand what a terrible sacrifice this was for my family's honor. I cried and cried for months and months, every night. But that wasn't all. That wasn't the *only* reason I never wrote you."

Daniel breathed deeply, wiped his cheek. The rapidly hastening emotions were almost too much for him.

"I did it because of how much I loved you."

"You're not making sense," Daniel said, bewildered.

"If I had stayed, then you wouldn't have gone to Columbia. You would've stayed here at UCLA and that would have limited you. I knew you would do something great with your life. And look at you, you have! You're saving people's lives every day. I didn't want to be the reason that held you back. Your dad and I felt the same on that score. We both wanted the best for you."

Daniel felt a ball of heat rise uncontrollably in his chest, and now it radiated to his head and into all of his extremities, even his fingertips.

"That's the reason? Ridiculous! I could have gone to UCLA and still gone to any medical school I wanted to."

Anne shook her head. "You don't know that. We would've gotten married and probably had kids—there was no reason to believe I couldn't back then—and then you'd have the responsibility of providing for a family. Daniel, you went to Harvard Medical School! Do you really think you would have gotten in there from UCLA? Attending Harvard set up your whole career . . . there's no doubt of that, is there? And do you really think you would have chosen to endure all those years of training with no money coming in while you had a family to support? No. You might never have become a doctor at all."

"Who knows?" Daniel's voice was heavy with sadness. "We could have made it work."

"I'm so sorry, Daniel. I thought if I wrote you or told you where I was you'd move heaven and earth to be with me. So I decided it was better to cut off ties. Then it would be easier for you to move on . . . but I'm so sorry, Daniel. I'm sorry I hurt you. I'm sorry if I couldn't see another way."

Daniel felt warm tears run down his cheeks. He was speechless.

"I started to write you dozens of letters that I always tore up and never sent. I loved you, too. You have to know that."

Daniel wiped his eyes with the back of his sleeve. He realized Anne had suffered just as he had, and probably even more—she'd made an impossible decision and lived with that burden all these years. At last, he knew the truth.

"I doubted it for so long because you just disappeared. But now . . . thank you for coming to tell me. For helping me understand. And Anne, I . . ." he met her gaze, ". . . I'm very sorry your husband passed away."

Through her tears, the corners of Anne's mouth turned up in a wistful smile, as if sifting through a lifetime of memories. "Me too. But I'm glad you're happily married. Your wife is more beautiful in person than even in her photograph. Your kids must be so smart, just like you."

"Thanks for saying that. Yes, I'm very lucky, though I hate to admit I've had some failings in the family department. I'm working on that."

Anne startled him by laughing. "Daniel Tokunaga, I don't think I've ever seen you look so serious about anything."

Daniel grinned. "Well, we all have to grow up sometime."

Anne stood up.

"I'm so happy for you, Daniel. Happy that you found love, and have a great family. I learned a lot from you, and I'll always be grateful to you for that."

Daniel rose. He blinked the tears out of his eyes and nodded. They embraced, but only briefly. Then she turned and went out the door.

Daniel watched her move delicately into her Honda and drive off. She didn't look back.

⁓

After Anne left, Daniel went up to his old bedroom, plastic garbage bag in hand. Pieces of the past, one after another, went into the mouth of the bag. It was one large mouth to feed, and then another. After stripping his old room, he took apart his father's, then back to the dining room where he'd started out that morning on the china cabinet. There was a small closet to one side of the hutch, and there Daniel discovered a musty stack of National Geographic magazines on top of which was a dented Florsheim shoe box with a bootlace wrapped around it multiple times.

Daniel lifted off the cover, expecting to find a bunch of yellowed baseball cards. Instead, the contents were neatly arranged: folded-up bank statements, newspaper clippings, and an envelope of old photos. This had to be Dad's box, Daniel thought, because he always did the finances, paid the bills, and saved the receipts.

He was about to throw the bank statements into the black maw of the garbage bag when he noticed they were from Citizens Bank. That's strange. Dad exclusively used Bank of America. The checkbooks Daniel had found in his father's desk, the ones he used to pay for everything, were from Bank of America. Come to think of it, I'm pretty sure there aren't any Citizens Banks anywhere near here.

Curious, Daniel looked closely at one of the statements. It showed almost no bank activity, just a few dollars of interest on a balance of about three hundred dollars. He looked at another, and then another. Each statement covered an entire year, from January to December. The only withdrawals he saw went to "BNP Paribas," in January and July, $100 each time. Each withdrawal was preceded by a deposit for this same amount.

BNP Paribas had headquarters in Paris. Daniel knew that from his surgical travels worldwide . . . *but who did Dad know in France?*

He scanned some more statements and every one showed the same $100 going out, twice a year. Some statements were old. Very old. At some point his father had moved the money to Citizens from Bank of Los Angeles—the papers from this older bank were faded and brittle. The earliest one Daniel found was from 1946.

He heard a noise in the kitchen. Keiko was recently returned from her shopping trip.

"Mom, can you come take a look at this?"

Keiko came into the dining room wearing a white apron. She held her hands up in the air—they were wet and covered with flour.

"I just started wrapping *gyoza*, Daniel, can this wait?"

"I found these old bank statements. Dad was sending money to a bank in France. Did you know about this?"

"No." Keiko looked puzzled as Daniel showed her several of the statements.

"That's quite a bit of money for back then. I never knew a thing about this."

"You've no idea who he knew in France?"

156

"Let me wash my hands and take a look at it more closely."

While he waited for his mother to return, Daniel sought an explanation on his own. He looked in the box, searching for some missing piece of information. There was a military patch with a logo that showed a hand holding a torch. This was the logo of the 442nd Regimental Combat Team, his father's World War II unit of Nisei soldiers. The words under the torch-bearing hand were: "Go for Broke," the regiment motto.

Digging deeper in the box, Daniel found a newspaper clipping from *The New York Times*, July 16, 1946.

The headline—"Truman awards Nisei 442nd Regimental Combat Team unprecedented 7th Presidential Unit Citation at White House." Beside the text was a photo of men from the 442nd, a row of Japanese American faces, stiff, solemn, standing at attention. The President, dressed in a dark raincoat, walked down the line reviewing the troops.

Now Daniel worked through the stack of old photos and set them on the dining room table. They were small black and white prints, only a few inches square. Many were of scenery: hills and trees, a church in a village, the sea. Daniel realized these were from his father's war days. He'd always liked photography, so Daniel wasn't surprised he'd had a camera with him. And now a bunch of the pictures had people in them, Nisei soldiers. He recognized his father in some of them; to Daniel he looked very young, even younger than his son James looked now. There was one photo of his dad posing with two other guys in front of a tank, and another one of him alone in which he held his rifle up in front of him. There were close-ups of other soldiers, too, some of them in goofy poses, others standing at attention. The last photo in the stack was of a young French woman. She wore a cardigan and her hair was up in a bun. Pretty, Daniel thought.

"Mom, come and look at these old photos."

Keiko re-entered the room drying her hands with a towel. She sat down at the table.

"Here, check these out," Daniel said, handing her the snapshots.

"Danny, where did you find these?"

"In this shoebox."

"I have never seen them before."

She went through them slowly, one by one, seeming to linger on the faces in each picture. Wanting to give her some time to look them over, Daniel turned back to the drawers to check that he'd cleared them all out. He opened the top drawer and there, resting alone at the bottom, was the folded marriage certificate he'd found the week before. The paper was crisp, the ink faded. Compulsively, he opened it up and stared at the date: 1945.

A typo? I don't think so.

Then a thought occurred to him. He turned back to the table and picked out the photo of Ray holding his rifle. His face was out of focus but his left hand tightly gripping the gun was front and center, and clearly visible.

"Mom, you told me you and Dad got married before he went to the war, right?"

"Yes, of course," she answered.

"He was traveling from Hawaii to boot camp in Mississippi and stopped at Manzanar for a couple weeks to visit some friends. That's how you said you first met and fell in love. A whirlwind romance, isn't that what you called it?"

"Yes, that's right."

"Then, if he was married, how come he's not wearing his wedding ring in this picture?" Daniel showed her the snapshot.

Keiko studied it. Her face paled.

Have I hurt her feelings? Daniel wondered. That would be cruel after all that's just happened.

But something in the tone of her voice told Daniel she was hiding something.

She was never a good liar, he thought. Not when I was little, not now. I could always see the truth behind the trick.

"Your dad told me he didn't wear it on purpose," Keiko finally said. "He said it might get in the way and he also didn't want to lose it."

"Mom . . . are you telling me the truth?"

"Of course I am!" she fired back.

"Because I could call up Joe Fukuda right now and ask him if Dad was married during the war. That would settle it, wouldn't it?"

Daniel said this without fully considering its import. Right now might not be the time to be questioning his mom, pressing her for distant, unwanted memories so soon after her husband's death. He glanced at her. She seemed to be thinking of things long put away like the pictures in the shoebox, and not liking whatever it was she was remembering.

Suddenly, without warning, she erupted.

"Joe Fukuda? Don't you talk to that man! He's not a friend to us. He should never have come around here. He's the one who got your dad so upset and stressed out in the first place. If he had left us alone, maybe Ray would still be here!" Keiko fell forward, into Daniel's arms. He hugged her tightly. She was crying freely, crying for the first time since Ray had passed.

They stayed that way for a few minutes: Keiko's tiny body quaking in Daniel's arms.

I don't want to hurt her anymore, Daniel thought. But . . . I've got to know the truth.

"Mom, please explain this to me. Dad is gone and nothing's going to bring him back. Whatever it is, whatever you may be hiding, you can tell me. It's all right."

She pushed away from Daniel and drew a deep breath. Looking up toward the heavens, she whispered, "Oh, Ray, Ray. Why are you not here to say this? Why did you have to go and leave me with all these unanswered questions?"

"What are you talking about?"

She wiped her eyes with a tissue. "Danny, you should sit down."

Daniel brought another wooden chair over to where she was sitting and sat down facing her.

"Danny, I love you."

"I know that, Mom—"

"—Shh. Listen to me now. Dad loved you, too. I know it was hard for him to show it. I know you two disagreed. Still, he loved you very much. He just wasn't comfortable showing his feelings. He couldn't say he was sorry, even though he wanted more than anything for there to be peace between the two of you."

"I know that, Mom."

Keiko looked at Daniel searchingly. At last, she shook her head and looked down at her knees.

"Danny, your dad was not your real father."

EIGHTEEN

VOSGES MOUNTAINS, FRANCE 1944

Ray lay flat on the ground, soaked in sweat. He could smell the fear coming off him. He was a mess. But the little French girl stared at him, hopefully, he thought, and he looked helplessly from her to the farmhouse, back and forth.

This was a conundrum. A Gordian knot. A nightmare in broad daylight.

And it was impossible to see what was happening in front of the house or inside it. Then the wind picked up. A flurry of leaves spun around them, doing little pirouettes, and then some large solid raindrops began to fall.

Hiro was helping the thin gray-coated soldier carry the dead body of one of the other German soldiers. Another man kept his Luger trained on Hiro. Even from a distance, Ray saw his friend had taken a pistol-whipping, his face battered, his nose bleeding. Ray understood that the dead man had been killed by Hiro, and now he was captured and it was all but over. What could Ray do? Was it too late to do anything?

After stowing the dead man in the truck, Hiro was ordered to sit with the body. That much Ray could see.

Hiro's face—he saw that, too. The old angry resistance was still there, would always be there. Ray wondered why he didn't have any himself. Why was he so fearfully passive? He did not feel that way, but his body acted that way.

A sudden poke in the ribs. Ray turned, startled.

It was the girl. Who else would it be? Her pale green eyes bore into him. She pointed to the house using her hand, fingers folded and one pointed, as if it were a pistol.

Ray glanced at his own empty hands, and then to his M1, which lay in the dirt behind the house some thirty yards away.

A sense of shame, of uselessness, overcame him.

Suddenly the girl pounded Ray with her fists. Ray blocked her blows. He didn't know what else to do except keep low.

There was a new sound, an eight-cylinder engine, a truck, climbing the mountain road and groaning up into the front yard. It was another Opel, but this one carried six soldiers in back. It also towed a 105mm howitzer that looked huge next to the tiny house. They had studied German artillery. This cannon could hurl a shell more than seven miles.

Ray ground his teeth.

He was about to make an irretrievable decision.

There, it was done, in his mind. All other thoughts were gone, banished.

He turned from the girl and ran down the hill and vanished into the woods.

NINETEEN

LOS ANGELES 1998

"What do you mean Dad wasn't my real father?" The idea was impossible; yet there it was. Neither false nor true. Merely absurd. Before Daniel's mind could even take it in, he broke into a cold sweat. His heartbeat began to accelerate.

"He never came to Manzanar before going to the war. I was pregnant," Keiko said, "that is, even before I ever met him. I met him after he was done fighting. He came to the camp. He promised to love you—"

"Wait a minute." Daniel shook his head. "Slow down. You've got to explain this—whatever it is—from the very beginning. Right now it just sounds like a very bad joke."

Keiko slid her chair closer to Daniel, and then reached out to hold his hand. For a moment he let her do this, but then he withdrew his hand.

"Just tell me the facts," he said, "from beginning to end. Tell me clearly what happened."

"Just the facts." she repeated, nodding. Then, speaking slowly, as if she were addressing a small child, she began to tell her story.

"During the war, I was at Manzanar with my parents. I had a friend there . . . a very serious . . . boyfriend."

Keiko glanced at Daniel's face. He returned her look with an open, emotionless stare with no reproof, no surprise.

"We were very much in love," she continued, "but then he went off to the war. We said we'd get married after he came back, but five months later, I learned he'd been killed. I was sad and frightened, not just because I loved him, but because I was already pregnant with you. I didn't know what to do. It wasn't like it is now. Having a baby out of wedlock in those times was greatly disapproved of—worse, it was deep dishonor on the family—my mother and father.

"Then one day, Ray Tokunaga came to Manzanar. He asked to meet me. He was my fiancé's best friend, and he'd brought me his personal things: his dog tags, his uniform, a picture he'd always kept of me. I broke down in front of Ray and started to cry and then I couldn't stop crying because as I said I was seven months pregnant, hiding it the best I could . . .

"I was lucky in that my body was small, my belly was not so big. I wore oversize clothes, and may have fooled some people who didn't look at me closely, but my family . . . they must have known something was wrong. I was desperate and depressed. I even thought of killing myself."

Daniel listened silently, caught up in his mother's words. He'd never heard her speak with such emotion, and her words touched his heart, even if he didn't like what she was saying. If she had killed herself, he wouldn't be there listening to her. His own sense of impermanence just then was measureless. He felt her words cut to the quick, and it made him realize that life was but one breath away from death, the blink of a firefly on a summer night. As a surgeon he knew this to be true, but as a surgeon he at least had some control, albeit small, over the fragile beating of a human heart. His mother's words he had no control of, nor what she might have done before his birth. The thought of it struck him like the reverberation of a gong.

Keiko went on with the story. "Ray listened to me. He let me cry on his shoulder. He held me. I didn't know anything about him, but I told him everything: about the baby, about not knowing what to do. I was so shamefully embarrassed, but I was at the very end of my rope.

"Ray told me my fiancé had been like a brother to him, and he called him a hero. He said, 'I have known many men in my life but none like him. He was the most courageous, most fearless man you could imagine. He would do anything to save another life.' We parted that night but I couldn't sleep. I tossed and turned and had nightmares. The following day, before Ray had to leave, he came to see me. He asked me if I would like to marry him."

"Just like that?"

Keiko nodded. "Just like that. But he was so sweet about it. He said we would *learn* to love each other, but that right now, it was important not to bring dishonor to my family."

"But he didn't even *know* you!"

"Yes, that is true. But he was willing to do it, not just for me, but for my family and his best friend whom he called his brother. He said, 'It is fair and right that we should do this.'"

"What did you say?"

"I said yes, of course."

"But *you* didn't even know *him!* He could have been a crazy person, a liar, a drunk, who knows what . . ."

"What choice did I have, Danny? I knew that he cared enough to listen to me, and to offer to marry me—and I felt so very lucky at that moment because he was giving me a second chance."

"Did he . . . was he . . . I mean, do you think he was—"

"—in love with me?" Keiko shrugged. "I don't know. I don't suppose so. A lot of boys were interested in me at the time. I was 'cute' they said. But I was a mess that day, no make-up, circles under my eyes from lack of sleep. I couldn't have been cute that night, but I was just so grateful to him, for *saving* me." Tears appeared in her eyes.

A hundred pictures flashed through Daniel's mind. Mom and Dad walking in the park without holding hands. Mom leaving to visit her sister in Seattle once a year, never giving Dad a hug or a kiss when they'd dropped her off at the airport. Long car rides in which each of them talked to him, but not to each other. No smiles or laughter, never any touching or common niceties of the married kind.

"But Mom . . . tell me the truth . . . did you love him? Did you love each other?"

"Ahh—you young people are always obsessed with love. Love only lasts a few years. It feels good, but it's not what makes a marriage last."

"You didn't answer my question. *Did you love him?*"

"Yes . . . I mean . . . I felt grateful to him. So very grateful to him . . ." Keiko's voice trailed off and she looked away. But a moment later, she looked at Daniel and spoke with sudden conviction: "We didn't have a perfect marriage, no marriage is. I suppose we were incompatible in many ways, but I tried very hard to be a good wife, and he was always faithful to me. Even more importantly, he promised to love you, and he did . . . in his own way."

In his own way? Daniel thought. The person his mother was describing was a stranger. His dad had never been tender-hearted or a good listener, not to Daniel. *Why didn't he show more feelings toward me? Why didn't he ever ask me what I thought? Why didn't he ever tell me that he wasn't my father?*

"Do you really think he loved me?" Daniel asked. His voice was flat, his tone without feeling, and the sound of it almost surprised him.

Keiko watched him with wide, searching eyes. "Oh *yes*, Danny. As much as he could have loved anyone. I know he didn't show it. It was too hard for him to show it. Something happened to him in the war, and it changed him for the worse. His parents once came to visit from Hawaii, and his mother was shocked by how much he'd changed. She told me that, before the war, he'd been fun, carefree, almost naïve. He'd even tell jokes! Can you believe that? Your father, I mean, Ray, telling jokes and stories, being light-hearted? I never saw that part of him. His mother said he was a different person—after the war. Whatever happened on the battlefield ruined him. Haunted him. He never laughed. He never joked. He had bad dreams, night after night. It was like living itself took a toll on him. I mean to say, being spared may have done that. Then life just wore him down like another kind of war, a silent, invisible one. He worked so hard, poor man, and he felt the weight of his responsibility, the burden of being a husband and a father, so deeply that it dragged him down." Keiko paused to inhale deeply, a tremor of memory and hard times shuddering through her small frame.

"There were times when I actually thought he was afraid of loving anything or anyone too dearly—like he would never give us his whole heart because doing so would mean taking the chance of getting hurt. Loving wholeheartedly means taking that risk. When something happens to the ones you love, the pain can be unbearable."

"Or maybe he didn't feel like he deserved to be loved," Daniel wondered aloud, almost hoping it was true because it was exactly how he had felt as a child, exactly how his father had *made* him feel.

"He always cared about you so much, Danny. Remember the phrase he'd use sometimes? *Kodomo no tameni.* 'For the sake of the children.' It's what our parents used to say about enduring racism and their time in the camps. We suffer and struggle because we hope the next generation will have it better than we did."

Daniel heard his mother's words; he listened to everything she said, but his mind kept returning to what seemed to him a single, incontrovertible truth.

The man who was supposed to be his father had lied to him. Any day of his life he could have told the truth, but he hadn't. Their relationship was simply a lie built upon other, hidden lies.

Keiko was still talking, ". . . and, I think what he was trying to do, what he really wanted, was to raise you to be more like your real father, to be courageous and tough. A winner."

My real father . . . Daniel thought.

Keiko reached over to the pile of photos. She carefully picked one up by the edges and handed it to Daniel. It was a photo of Ray and another man. They were standing in front of a Sherman tank and had their arms around each other's shoulders. Both were smiling.

Keiko pointed to the other man. "This is a picture of your real father. His name was Hiro."

TWENTY

MANZANAR RELOCATION CAMP,
CENTRAL CALIFORNIA
January 1945

He got off the bus in Lone Pine, a small town seven miles south of Manzanar. A thin skein of fresh snow dusted the hard-packed, wind-driven ground of Main Street, which was deserted. The thermometer attached to the front of Clark's General Store read twenty-one degrees, and Ray turned his collar up against the biting wind. He hefted his gunny sack up on his right shoulder, the side that hadn't been injured, and followed the dirt road leading north out of town. In the distance the crinkled, snow-sluiced Sierra Nevada seemed surreal against the cobalt sky. All of it was beautiful and forbidding to Ray. Not to mention lonely.

He'd arrived at the Army hospital in Los Angeles the week before, where the doctors were unimpressed by his wound, which had healed considerably. They discharged him after only a couple of days.

After being in France, Ray thought southern California was other-

169

worldly. Fine weather, manicured lawns, movie theaters, diners—it was hard to believe that life had gone on, more or less normally, while he'd been fighting.

The racism was another thing. It was just the way it was in the stories Hiro told—malicious and without heart. Ray went everywhere dressed in his uniform, bright-colored campaign ribbons sewn on his chest, including a special one denoting he had received the Distinguished Service Cross—but white people still stared at him with hatred in their eyes. More than one mumbled, "dirty Jap," under his breath, saying it softly but just loudly enough for him to hear.

In a barbershop, Ray had an unpleasant stand-off with the owner who proudly stated before his other patrons that he didn't "cut Jap hair." Polite people, if you could call them that, had a way of not looking at him, pretending he wasn't there. However, their children often stared with eyes brimming with hate and fear, and sometimes a confused and diffident mixture of both.

Despite the cold, walking the deserted road to Manzanar felt good after the long inert hours on the bus. The snow-capped, sawtooth Sierras to his left cast endless shadows across the desolate plain, dotted with sage brush and Joshua trees. The sun was an hour above the western horizon when Ray began to make out a row of low buildings in the distance. Drawing closer, he wondered if he'd happened upon a large Army base. That gave him a chilly feeling. Had they built a base next to the camp? He saw row upon row of long barracks, dozens of them; the size of the site amazed him—it had to be at least a mile square.

He reached the southeastern corner of the base. Through the barbed wire fence he saw the barracks up close. Plywood. Tar paper. Just like the Army barracks at Camp Shelby. A few kids rounded a corner and ran into view. They were kicking a ball. They were Japanese and paid him no mind.

This was Manzanar.

The eight tall guard towers were wooden sentinels, immense

scarecrows of a wintry fallow field. The soldiers on watch barely looked at Ray; their eyes were turned inward. He arrived at the entrance gate. A gust of early night wind formed a small vortex, a dust devil of dirt and snow. Ray shut his eyes and lowered his chin against his clavicle. When he looked up, there was a soldier peering at him from the shelter of his sentry box.

Ray took a few steps forward, and waited.

The guard, a freckle-faced private, was puzzled. A visitor? A Nisei soldier at that. For several seconds the stunned man stared at Ray, who finally cleared his throat and nodded at the corporal's stripes on his own shoulder.

Now the private jumped to his feet.

"I'm here to visit some friends," Ray said. His frost white breath appeared like smoke in the cold air.

"Yes, sorry. Uh, it's rare to have visitors here. Did you walk all the way from Lone Pine?"

Ray nodded with a faint, almost imperceptible smile.

"Who are you here to see?" the private asked.

"Matsuo and Furiye Fukuda."

"Okay. Let me check those names." He ducked into his hut and came out a moment later with a clipboard. "Fukuda, Fukuda . . . only about a hundred Fukuda's," he said chuckling. Then he looked up and his smile evaporated. Ray was not amused by the man or his manner. "Um, okay, here they are. Let's see." The soldier traced his finger across the page. "Oh, I'm sorry. You just missed them. They left the camp last week."

"Left?"

"Yes, the internees have been free to leave for some time now, at least a month."

This was the first Ray had heard of it.

"Is this true of all the camps?"

The private lifted and lowered his head. "Yup. Far as I know. President Roosevelt signed the order just after he got re-elected. People are free to go. Every week buses take a bunch back to Los Angeles, but some are still here."

Ray felt the pit of his stomach tighten. He'd come all this way for nothing. For several seconds he stood in the frigid, gritty desert air staring through the gate. He thought of the things he'd brought for Hiro's parents: their son's dog tags and lighter, the uniform he'd spent hours trying to scrub the blood out of, and the medal they awarded him posthumously for taking out the machine guns. There were also a few snapshots, from the voyage to Europe, from France, and one of Keiko.

Keiko!

The sentry had put the clipboard away and was now studying him, perhaps trying to decide whether to let the corporal into the camp to bunk for the night, seeing as there were no buses past six in Lone Pine and the sun was already almost gone, but the man's face showed indecision. The long shadows of nightfall were seeping into the camp, making it harder to see.

"Private?"

"Yes, sir?"

"Can you check one more name for me? I know one more person . . . someone who's hopefully still here."

"Sure." He picked up the clipboard.

Keiko. What was her surname? Ray didn't know. He remembered there'd been a letter from her in Hiro's cigar box, the one in which he'd kept the photos and lighter. Ray unslung his gunny sack and untied the top. He reached deep down in with his good arm— Hiro's things were in the center, along with Ray's camera, where they'd be most protected. He felt the hard edges and corner of the box and wriggled it out.

By the dim light of the lamp posts beside Manzanar's entrance, he read the return address: Keiko Yamada.

"Keiko Yamada, please."

The private flipped through the pages to the end. "Yamada,

172

Yamada," he mumbled.

"She would be a dependent," Ray added. "A student."

"Okay, that helps."

"Here, got it. Daughter of Daisuke and Suri Yamada. Yeah, she's still here. They haven't left."

Ray exhaled slowly.

"They're at 10-12-B."

The private saw Ray's confusion.

"Sorry. That's Block 10, Barrack 12, room B. Just go that way—" the private pointed, "—until you reach the main central avenue. It's a firebreak, really wide, you can't miss it. Go down it about a quarter mile and you'll see Block 10 on your left. Each building has a number, find Barrack 12. Then, room B."

Ray cinched up his sack again and hefted it on his shoulder.

"10-12-B," he repeated. "Thanks."

He passed through the gates, turned right, and came to Manzanar's desolate, darkening central street. The avenue was packed dirt, flanked by row upon row of identical barracks, each building about 20 feet wide by 100 feet long. Few people were out, hurrying from one building to another, too cold to linger outside for long. He resumed walking and passed a lonely wooden flagpole with the Stars and Stripes fluttering atop.

It was hard to imagine living in a prison camp like this for three years. Ray saw the barbed wire outer walls and imagined them closing in. Time, he thought, would crawl like a slowly dying snake. One, and then two of Manzanar's residents stopped to stare at him. They knew his uniform and the 442 patch on his shoulder. People in the camps had followed the 442nd throughout the war. They were proud of "their regiment."

The camp's streetlights fluttered on in a weak, desultory way. A mother called her child to the mess hall for dinner. Ray neared Block 10. He saw a man walking slowly with a cane. Ray went over to him and asked, "Excuse me, can you point me to Barrack Twelve?"

The man had a kind, weathered face with a sheepherder's watchful eyes. There was a large mole on his cheek, a solitary hair growing out of it.

"Yes. It is that way," the old man said, pointing. "The fifth building on the left."

Ray nodded and said thank you.

As he passed a latrine, he side-stepped inside. It was nothing but a long narrow hall with no privacy, built on a concrete slab. He wanted to wash the dust off his hands before meeting Keiko.

He counted twelve toilets, six pairs arranged back to back, with no partitions. Two men sat on toilets, spaced as far apart as possible but still in plain sight of each other. Ray diverted his eyes, discomfited, but the men were lost in their own thoughts as custom dictated. Against one wall was a metal trough and water spigots. Ray went to a spigot, ran the water—it was ice cold. He washed his hands, then glanced in a tiny cracked wall mirror. With his still-wet hands he patted down his windswept, dust-woven hair. Then he clawed his fingers through it very quickly and a little sandspur came off on his hand and stuck in his palm.

Back outside, he saw a middle-aged mother hustle her daughter out of a door at the end of Barrack 12. Others emerged from nearby buildings and headed toward the mess hall for dinner. They all wore thick winter coats and wool hats. The cold made them move quickly, but several of them paused, then bowed slightly to him as they passed. Their silent respect for his uniform.

Ray trotted over to talk to the mother who had come from Keiko's barrack. She was using her hand to shield her daughter's face from the wind.

"Excuse me, ma'am. Do you know Keiko Yamada?"

"Keiko?" She nodded. "Of course."

"Do you know which room belongs to her family?"

The woman looked back and pointed. "They are next to us. That door, on the side."

"Thank you."

Ray now saw that each long building contained four separate rooms. He went to Keiko's door and climbed the short flight of stairs. Hiro had told him once that the Manzanar barracks were built off the ground because of tarantulas that sometimes traveled in large numbers. *Herd*, Hiro had said. He smiled, thinking of it, hoping there were no tarantula herds this evening.

He knocked on the door and waited.

Then came a young woman's voice from within, "Come in."

Ray opened the outer wood-framed screen door, and then the inner door made of rough pine planks. Inside, he found himself facing two ancient green Army blankets hanging from clotheslines that formed a sort of anteroom and blocked his view into the living space. He looked down. There were empty knotholes in the floor and the clotted smell of detritus and guano that mingled with the smell of dirt. Some of the holes were plugged with old newspaper. Lifting his head, he drew a deep breath and noticed the building itself had a dry wood and resin smell. The bite of the wind was gone, but a chill remained. He ran his fingers along the rough single plywood walls, feeling channels of wind that whined and moaned through knot holes and cracks between the boards.

"Hello?" he said.

He heard a little gasp, and then a chair scrape across the floor, making a single grotesque sound.

"Miss Keiko Yamada?" he called.

There were soft steps, moving closer. Beneath the aged Army blanket partition that smelled of dust and wool he saw a woman's slippered feet. Then her hand appeared where the two blankets met and drew one back.

She looked just like her photograph. Raven hair, cut short in a bob. Her almond eyes looking bright and beautiful. He could see her surprise . . . who was this strange, beribboned soldier?

Ray removed his cap. "Excuse me, Miss Yamada. My name is Ray Tokunaga."

"Yes?"

Ray took a cold deep breath, swallowed. "Miss Yamada . . . Keiko, I came to meet you because I was a friend of Hiro's."

Keiko gasped, the back of her hand went to her mouth, then dropped.

"I'm sorry to shock you like this."

She fumbled for the wall to steady herself.

"Please, let me . . . maybe you should sit down."

Keiko leaned against a small table. She shook her head. "I'm sorry." She bowed. "I don't mean to be rude. Please come in." She drew back the blanket more, and Ray ducked his head under the clothesline. A bare bulb hanging from the ceiling cast a dingy light around the room. The apartment was small, only twenty by twenty-five feet. Hiro had said usually two families of four or five each shared one apartment.

Eight or nine people in a room like this? It seemed impossible.

Ray noticed the rough plywood partitions that separated the apartments from each other, but he realized there were no ceilings, just empty space above the walls, which was why he could hear a half-dozen voices echoing up and down the long, wind-whipped building.

There were four steel cots, a small coal-burning stove, a chest of drawers, and three chairs. The stove had a number ten can with some sage on it. The scent of sage sort of lay upon the smell of lye soap that had been used to scrub the warped floorboards.

"Please sit," Keiko said. Ray did; his roughhewn pine chair wobbled. She sat down opposite him and rested her hands in her lap. She wore a grey flannel dress that seemed two sizes too big for her.

"I'm sorry I can't offer you any tea. We aren't allowed to have electric water heaters in here."

"Please, don't bother. I'm fine."

"You came all this way . . . to see me?"

"No, actually. I came to find Hiro's parents. I have some of his things."

"They've left."

"I know. The guard at the gate told me."

"They were terribly broken up. They wanted to get out of here as soon as they could." Her voice trailed off as her gaze drifted to the rafters above. "It's been very difficult," she said softly. "For everyone."

"I'm so sorry for your loss. Hiro was my best friend."

Keiko nodded. "Now I recall: he wrote to me about you. He said he felt lucky to have a friend like you. He said you were *serious* . . ."

Keiko glanced at him, afraid he might take offense. But Ray grinned, and so did Keiko, and they both laughed softly together.

"Compared to him, I suppose I was . . . a serious man."

"What did you bring back?"

Ray reached into his gunny sack and brought out Hiro's uniform, the contents of the cigar box, his medal. He stood up to lay these things out on the straw-filled mattress of the nearest cot.

Keiko came closer. And again her hand covered her mouth as she studied the items, one by one. Then she stroked the clothes very gently, as if afraid of damaging them. Ray watched her in fascination as she knelt down and brought her face close to Hiro's jacket, drew in a deep breath. "It smells a little like him," she said. Then she touched the medal. "Why did he get this?"

"He took out three German machine gun nests single-handedly, and probably saved my life and the life of half a dozen other guys. He was a hero."

"A hero . . ." Keiko repeated softly as she rubbed her belly with her left hand. "Is that when he died?"

"No. That isn't how it happened. It was two days later. I was with him."

"What happened then?"

Ray didn't reply. The sound of one of the other barrack doors slamming shut jarred the silence. Footsteps and a man's voice saying something in Japanese. The wind whistled through a broken-paned window. A couple of male cats grappled and yowled under the knothole floor.

"Please," Keiko said, "I really do want to know."

Ray looked down at the sad floorboards, swept bare and sanded smooth by a thousand broomings and scrubbings. "He was killed trying to save a French family from the Germans."

A small tear formed at the corner of Keiko's eye, hovered, then slowly descended. She sat down on the bed. Outside, a pair of giggling girls walked past the window, their laughter seeming out of place in this moment of solemnity.

Ray reached out to touch Keiko's hand. "He never thought about himself. He only wanted to help others."

"Oh . . ." Keiko's body went soft and she collapsed on the bed, falling across Hiro's things. She buried her face in her hands. "He's really gone," she murmured. Ray shifted uncomfortably. "All this time I hoped . . . I thought . . . there might have been some mistake, but you were there. He's really gone, isn't he?"

Ray watched her cry softly for several minutes.

Voices around them lowered; there were a few hoarse admonitions to children, and in the adjacent room the sound of feet scuffing to a far corner so Keiko could have a modicum of grief and privacy.

"I'm so sorry," Ray mumbled. "I miss him, too. I wish sometimes that it was me who died rather than him."

Keiko looked at Ray, her face damp with tears. "Oh, don't wish that, please. You were a good friend to him. Thank you for coming to see me and for showing me these things." Her gaze slowly returned to Hiro's uniform and then fresh tears came to her eyes.

Somehow her words made Ray feel worse. He wanted to help her, to do something for her, but it seemed there was nothing he, nor anyone else could do. Her sorrow was too deep.

Keiko wiped her eyes with her sleeve. "I should feel better; it's been a long time. But I don't know what to do." She inhaled sharply, then whispered, almost inaudibly, "I'm pregnant."

"I'm sorry, what did you say?"

"I'm pregnant," she said under her breath. Then she motioned for Ray to sit closer to her on the bed.

"I don't know what to do. Hiro and I had only one night, right before he left. I realized I was pregnant about a month and a half later. I didn't know what to do, but I knew Hiro would, so I got through each day telling myself he'd be back soon." Her words tumbled out rapidly. "And then the telegram came. He was dead. He wasn't coming back." She tugged at her oversized dress. "I'm hiding it, but it's getting harder. The showers are open here, everyone can see you. That's why I shower quickly in the middle of the night, when there's no one else there. I haven't told anyone, but when my parents find out, oh!" She looked up, shaking her head hopelessly. "When everyone finds out, I'll be so ashamed. There will be great dishonor on my family. My parents will be so angry. I wanted to leave, but I have nowhere to go. My parents lost everything in Seattle. They were tulip farmers, but we lost the farm. Now they want to stay here as long as the camp stays open. But what should I do? What *can* I do?"

Ray put his arm around her shoulder, rocked her back and forth lightly, ever so lightly, and as he breathed in the sweet scent of her hair, he thought of Hiro.

TWENTY-ONE

LOS ANGELES 1998

Daniel blinked the tears out of his eyes. He was having trouble seeing the car in front of him. After leaving his mother's house, he headed for the hotel where he'd been for over two weeks. In the dark, red tail lights swam fishlike in front of him, leaving a momentary arc of color. He wiped his eyes on his sleeve.

He wasn't my father.

How could he not tell me?

How could she not tell me?

He was equally mad at his mother for hiding the truth. A secret this momentous seemed unfathomable to Daniel, who lived in a world where knowledge—good, bad, and indifferent—could mean the difference between life and death. The unknown was the one main negative that all doctors fought against, though at times, ineffectively. One thing he knew: he could never have kept a secret the way his supposed father had.

That's just one more example of why we were so different, why we never got along.

Daniel's mind darted through a maze of contradictions. The father and son who were nothing alike. The father who liked to build things with his hands. The son who did not. The father who never read a book in his life. The son who read all the time. The father who was tough and strong. The son who was tough in the operating room but not on the street. The father who was a war hero. The son who was a coward when school bullies picked on him. The father whose temper was quick to flare. The son who hardly ever raised his voice and had no temper at all.

Thinking about it, Daniel realized that his brother Kenny resembled his father in ways he never had.

They were so similar. The way they looked. The way they talked and acted. Their preferences and view of life as a strategy won over by being physically tough and alert and always ready for the next unexpected curve or blow.

Daniel wondered—if I'd been his real son, would he have treated me differently?

The saddest thing of all in Daniel's mind was that even when the old man's time was running out, he'd still had no intention of telling Daniel the truth.

He couldn't stem the tears. They kept flowing, like his random thoughts. He bit his lip, trying to keep the car straight, trying not to look at the maniacal freeway traffic, squeezing into spaces that hardly existed.

And the thoughts and the tears kept coming . . .

Was my real father more like me? Or rather, was I, am I, like him?

Daniel felt a sudden passion to know everything there was to know about this mystery man: *Hiro.* Daniel spoke the name out loud and it sounded strange.

A name that has never passed my lips before, he realized. Who was he? In his picture he is smiling, carefree, young. Was he a hero? I wonder what he did and what made him who he was. He probably never knew his fiancé was pregnant with his child, never knew he was going to be a father.

Daniel pulled into the hotel lot and parked the car. He sat there, eyes red and wet, uncertain of what to do, what to think, and what to make of this mess his life had become. He wanted to curl up like a baby. He wanted Beth to hold him in her arms. But Beth wasn't there. He was alone.

He picked up his cell phone, took a deep breath, dialed Beth's number.

"Hello?"

"Hey, it's me."

"What's wrong?"

One last tear ran down Daniel's cheek, and he dried his eyes with his fingers, wiped his face with his hand.

"My mom told me something," he said, his voice faltering. "Something crazy. She told me . . . she said . . . my dad was not my father." Saying this, Daniel's usually composed voice cracked. "He . . . he . . . was best friends with my real father, who was my mom's boyfriend. You know, at Manzanar. But, the way she explained it, my real dad got killed in the war."

"Oh, my God, Daniel . . ."

"He wasn't my dad, Beth! He lied to me, the old bastard! Every day of his life, he lied to me!"

"I'm so sorry . . . this is totally crazy. Are you sure?"

"Yes."

"How could he do that? I don't understand . . ."

"I don't know what to think . . . a while ago I was so blurry-eyed I thought I might crash the car. I've never felt so confused in my life."

"Daniel, take some deep breaths and let's talk this through."

He felt as if his life were ebbing away, like a ghastly tide, taking every shred of sense he had and leaving him so empty he thought he might just curl up and die on the seat of the car—or worse. The thought of suicide rushed through his brain, compounding the desperation that made him feel completely alone. Even Beth's voice wasn't enough to hold him. He floated out with the tide of loss and desolation.

"Honey, you shouldn't be alone. Not now. Can you please come home? Can you get a flight tomorrow?"

Daniel started to sob again. But it was dry this time, like coughing. His chest rose and fell and yet the tears wouldn't come and he wanted to wrap his arms around Beth and hug her so hard, but his body felt flimsy, like tissue paper in the wind blown out to sea.

Finally, he managed to speak. "I'll get a flight, Beth . . . I want to come home."

—

The next afternoon Daniel went to his mother's house to say goodbye. He'd wanted to leave immediately, but the only flight he could get on less than twenty-four hours' notice was a red-eye leaving late at night. He knew his mother might be at her regular church meeting, but he went to the house anyway. He wanted to get the goodbye over and done with, and then he'd just wait at the airport. He also wished to get as far away from LA as possible. He wanted to vanish.

As he pulled up to the house, he saw a big Buick Regal parked on the street in front.

I've seen that car before, he thought. Where?

Then he placed it—Joe Fukuda's ugly chunk of metal.

Why is *he* here?

Joe was waiting on the front porch. It irked Daniel to see him; his mother wouldn't be happy with this untimely visit. Neither would his father, if he were still alive. The irony of this gave Daniel the bit of extra strength he needed. He decided to get rid of Joe quickly.

He parked the car and got out. Joe sat in Ray's old rocker, which was yet another peevish annoyance—just seeing him there where he didn't belong but seeming to be content with himself when nobody else was.

"What are you doing here?" Daniel said.

Joe removed his blue, duck-billed "WWII" hat from his head. He wore a plain grey sweatshirt and dark green trousers.

He looks like a bum who's come for a handout, Daniel thought. I'd love to just dump him off that chair.

Joe stood up. He'd brought a small bouquet of daisies that lay dispiritedly on the floor by the chair.

"I come to pay my respects to your mother."

"She's not here. I'll tell her you stopped by."

"Can I wait?"

"I'd prefer you didn't. We're going through a lot right now, you know."

Joe nodded respectfully. He bent down, picked up the limp flowers, and placed them neatly on the seat of the chair. Then he walked past Daniel and headed for his car.

Halfway there, Joe stopped. He slowly turned and asked, "You know if your dad ever talked to the government about his medal?"

"He didn't speak to anyone."

"I'm flying to Washington D.C. tomorrow for an interview."

"*You* got a medal too?" Daniel asked, surprised.

"Oh, not me. My brother. He was the one who died in the war. I never did anything special and the whole mess was almost over by the time I got there." Joe kicked at a pebble on the sidewalk and shoved his hands into his pants pockets. "Anyway, I'm real sorry about your dad. I just wanted your mom to know that."

Joe walked to his car and had his hand on the door handle when Daniel realized Joe might know the answers to some of his questions.

"Mr. Fukuda, wait a minute. Let me ask you something."

Joe looked up.

"How did you know my mom?"

"At Manzanar. We were both in the camp from '42 to '45. She and I were in the same high school class."

"And you met my dad in France?"

"Not exactly."

"What do you mean by that?"

"I didn't fight with him."

"Then where did you meet? And one more thing, why didn't you guys get along?"

Joe moved his head to one side and spat out of the side of his mouth. Then he brushed his lips with his hand. He cocked his head, left and right, making sure no one was anywhere near except the two of them. "He never said anything to you about it?"

"No."

Joe walked around the car and came closer to Daniel, until they were only an arm's length apart.

"I didn't meet your dad until after the war. He . . ." Joe's brow furrowed and he spat again. "Truth is, I never trusted your dad."

The insult gave Daniel an eerie feeling. He too looked around, as if expecting the old man himself to come walking around the corner of the house.

"Why didn't you trust him?"

"Well, it's complicated," Joe said. "You see, Ray made a friend during the war. His best friend. But when he came home he stole his best friend's girl."

Daniel laughed sharply. He enjoyed the look of surprise on Joe's face.

"That's what you held against him? You've got it all wrong. By the time my dad met my mom, that so-called best friend was already dead. He didn't *steal* her."

Joe opened his mouth to speak, but Daniel cut him off. "What's it to you, anyway? It's none of your business . . ."

Were you in love with my mom or something? he wanted to add. Is that what this pathetic visit is really about?

Joe looked puzzled but he recovered quickly and said, "Boy, you don't know much do you? It mattered to me because your dad's best friend was my older brother, Hiro, and Hiro was going to marry your mom. They were engaged, by word, anyway."

Daniel was stunned.

Joe Fukuda . . . my uncle?

"But . . ." Daniel managed to sputter. "But . . . your brother died in the war. He was gone. You're not making any sense. Why shouldn't my dad have felt free to marry my mom?"

Joe came a little closer. "Listen, kid," he said quietly. "I don't expect you to understand. All I'll say is that your dad could have saved my brother, but he didn't. That's why my brother died and that's why I wanted to wring his neck when I found out Keiko had married him."

Daniel's mind tried to process this new and impossible information. It made no sense. "You're making this up," he said. "How could you ever know something like that?"

Joe's face tightened. "Ask your mother," he said. "She told me."

Then Joe Fukuda turned on his heel and walked to his Buick. He got in and drove away.

Daniel stood there watching the car, frozen, for a long time. At some point, he did an uncharacteristic thing. He lay down on his back in the yard that his father had mowed for the last time. He lay very still, arms outstretched, and closed his eyes. The world went away.

When he finally opened his eyes again, the crickets were cricketing in the fringes of the yard. Night had come and a mockingbird was singing a drunken aria in the old man's avocado tree. Daniel sat up stiffly, his back damp with dew, and wondered how long he'd been out.

TWENTY-TWO

MANZANAR RELOCATION CAMP,
CENTRAL CALIFORNIA
January 1945

After 4 am Ray gave up trying to sleep. He hadn't slept well for three months, and hearing every cough, wheeze, sneeze, and snore in the Manzanar barracks didn't help. The insistent odor of sewage crept into the room like an unwanted animal. He banished it with his mind control, but after a while it was back, begging to be noticed.

But worse than the early morning septic smell was the face of Hiro. It, too, was an imprint that returned, again and again. Hiro was burned into his brain—Hiro's face, his expression the moment before he died, his look a recurrent, intractable image of untimely death that demanded Ray's attention even when he was asleep. Hiro's eyes followed him everywhere; so did the last words he'd spoken to Ray.

"*Shikata ga nai.*"
It can't be helped.

There were worse things than insomnia, like his nightmares. He lay on a cot in an otherwise empty room whose occupants had already left the camp, two rooms down from the Yamada's. Lying on his back, he stared up at the darkness, waiting for the coming of dawn. Would it ever come?

He thought now of Keiko's parents, whom he had met last night after dinner. They seemed pleased to meet him, but sad to be reminded of Hiro. Ray could tell they were very traditional: Keiko's mother did not say a word. Her father, a short, gray-haired man with calloused farmer's hands, spoke to Ray as an equal and was impressed to meet a member of the 442nd. Keiko, her little sister, and her mother left the barracks to allow Ray and her dad to talk, though Ray felt bad that the women were forced to walk outside in the cold. He could still see their dark shapes, moving around, going nowhere, and then huddled against the wind like strange birds that had landed in the wrong place.

Finally, the red glow of dawn needled through the barracks' knotholes and dusty windows, and Ray sighed. He'd been mulling it over all night. It was a hard decision. He felt sure about the *right* thing to do. Wasn't that enough? If it was right, then that was the only way. He chastised himself: only selfishness held him back from doing what honor and duty demanded. And yet, there was also . . . hope. Hope for a life of happiness? Was he giving that up?

What right did he have to hope? Or to reach out for happiness? There was none of that for him.

He'd made his decision, and now that he knew what he needed to do, he felt like getting it over with.

He put on his boots and walked out the front door. Cold air hit him like an iron fist and reminded him of the freezing nights in the Vosges, in the foxholes. Hustling across the road to the bathroom, he was surprised to find a half-dozen men already awake and using the showers. There was a palpable steam in the air and the carbolic smell of Lifebuoy soap. Ray breathed it all in as he brushed his teeth and washed his face. For once he felt he was not in the desert. He felt alert and alive.

When he returned to his room he rearranged the contents of his gunnysack. He would leave some of Hiro's things with Keiko: the letters, the snapshot of her, some incidental mementoes like the miniature version of the New Testament issued by the Armed Services, and a curious shell casing wrapped in French damask. The other personals of Hiro he'd carry with him until he could locate Hiro's parents, or his younger brother, Joe.

There was a noise outside, an opening door, the light scuffing of feet. Ray opened his door and stuck his head out. It was Keiko, already dressed for the day, wearing a long, gathered skirt and an oversize serviceman's blue woolen sweater.

"Psst," Ray hissed.

Keiko stopped and turned around in the street.

He motioned to her.

She hesitated, undecided, glanced back toward the room with her sleeping parents and sister. No one was stirring. She walked slowly to Ray and stepped gracefully up the worn wooden steps. He held the door open for her as she entered the room.

Ray gestured at a chair, while he sat on the bed.

She sat down, and they looked at one another for several awkward seconds. Ray wished he'd taken the time to comb his hair. Keiko sat with her arms crossed, looking lovely, if vulnerable. Twice she rubbed her hands together, breathed into them; it was very cold.

"Keiko, I—"

"Shh," Keiko urged, putting her finger to her lips. She got up and sat beside him on the bed.

Now Ray leaned close and spoke into her ear. It was almost easier this way, not looking at her face. He stared at the wall.

"Keiko. I'm glad we have a chance to talk alone. I want to ask you a question. You can say no, if you want to, but I thought about it all last night, and if it's of any help, I want to do it."

Keiko remained perfectly still.

Ray took a deep breath.

"Would you marry me?"

Keiko gasped and leaned away so she could look him in the face. Ray held her shoulders with both hands and drew her close to him again. Softly, he continued what he'd planned to say, "I know it's strange, we hardly know each other, but I was thinking about your baby. . . and your parents and . . ." he turned to look at Keiko's face, but she averted her gaze, and suddenly, Ray felt terribly embarrassed. He wanted to run away. But it was too late. He mumbled, "I know you probably wouldn't want to . . . but I just wanted you to know . . . if you want to . . . I'll do it."

There, he'd said it. But Keiko hadn't moved or spoken. What an idiot I am, Ray thought. He hung his head. I've never felt so stupid in my life.

Keiko raised her right hand and touched Ray's chin. Then, with both hands, she softly lifted his down-turned head.

"Would you? Really?" she asked, her voice full of wonder.

Ray said, "Yes. I could take care of you. We'll go to Los Angeles and I'll find a good job. Together, we could start a new life."

"What . . . what about . . . my parents?"

"What about them?"

"We just met you; they hardly know you. This is so sudden." Keiko paused and her hands touched her belly. "But . . . I can't wait much longer. If I do . . . oh . . ." she cried once, then stopped herself.

Heavy footfalls just outside the door. They both held their breath until the unseen person passed. Ray turned back to Keiko. He could see her thinking, worrying, struggling to make a decision.

Finally, she said softly, "I would have to leave now. We could just go."

"You mean elope?"

Keiko nodded.

Ray thought it through. "Yes, I think we could. I could take you back to my place in L.A."

"And what would we tell people, later on? All my friends . . ."

"The truth. We met, decided to go to L.A. and get married. In nine months or a year we can tell them we had a baby."

Keiko closed her eyes and pondered the momentous decision. Then she opened her eyes and looked deeply into Ray's. "Ray—have you really thought this through? Being a father? Having a baby?"

"It's Hiro's baby," he said, speaking his friend's name in a way that showed that this was reason enough for him to love her child. Ray pressed his lips together and let his gaze drift down to her belly. "I would raise him to be like Hiro. Someone Hiro would be proud of."

"But you don't even know me. Would you really do this . . . for me?"

Ray nodded. "Yes. And for Hiro, and your parents as well." He held her hand. "Maybe we can learn to love each other, Keiko. I mean, really fall in love. But right now, we have to act. Do you want to come with me?"

Keiko's eyes were wet, glistening. She came close and hugged him. "Yes, I will. I will marry you."

Ray used his thumb to gently wipe a tear from her cheek. She smiled to ease the embarrassing silence. Then she hugged him again. This time, more tentatively than before.

"Thank you," she whispered. She released him from her embrace. And she bowed three times.

TWENTY-THREE

LOS ANGELES 1998

"Danny, what are you doing out here in the dark?"

Daniel lifted his head and shielded his eyes from a blinding set of headlights. "Who's that?" he asked.

"My friend from church drove me home," Keiko replied. "I crashed my car, remember?" She waved to her friend, saying all was well, and the car slowly pulled away.

Daniel stood up slowly and stretched his legs.

"Mom, we need to talk."

She busied herself with her house keys. "Talk? All right, but let's go inside."

Daniel thought his mother looked tired herself. She was very active in church and prided herself on teaching a class on traditional Japanese dance. Usually fit and energetic, now she looked worn down.

It's been a tough week for both of us, he realized, but there are so many things I still don't know.

Inside the house, Daniel sat at the small kitchen table while Keiko started to boil some water for tea. Daniel watched his mother as she brought the teacups out of the cupboard. Her movements were spare, rhythmic, as if nothing were wrong, everything was just the way it was, and would always be. But she was a great cover-up artist. Not only did she look tired, but her usually tight face seemed to sag, the corners of her mouth runnelled on either side. This night she looked every bit her age.

"So . . . what I wanted to tell you, Mom . . . Joe Fukuda stopped by today. He brought you these." He placed the sad, fallen-petaled daisies on the table.

"He did?" Keiko glanced at the flowers and made a face. "I'm glad I wasn't home. What did he want?"

Daniel had thought of a dozen ways to broach the subject but none of them—even in his mind—sounded right. He decided to jump right in. "Mom, for starters, Joe's my uncle, isn't he?"

Keiko dropped the dragon-decorated tea tin, which fell to the floor, showering the yellow linoleum with a dark peppery rain.

Daniel got down on his knees and began to hand-sweep the dragon's blood tea. Keiko steadied herself, both hands on the counter. Daniel made a pile of tea and then stood and helped his mother to a chair. Then he got a broom and a dustpan and did an impeccable job of sweeping up.

"Is that what he told you?"

"He said he was Hiro's younger brother. True?"

Keiko's lips tightened. "Yes. What else did he tell you?"

"He said Dad could've saved Hiro, in the war, but he didn't." Before Keiko had a chance to deny this, Daniel added: "He told me you said so."

Keiko didn't speak for a while. Daniel put the broom and dustpan back where they belonged in the narrow closet by the stairs. The kettle sang a high-pitched, piercing tune, and Daniel switched off the heat and let the kettle song drop an octave or two. He then selected a nice green tea in the cupboard. He put two tea bags from the box into blue china cups, poured the hot water, and watched the little curls of tea-steam rise swiftly and disappear. After this, he leaned with his back to the counter, waiting while the tea steeped. He was in no hurry now; neither was she. After what seemed a long time, Daniel placed Keiko's cup on the kitchen table, and she made a sudden move to touch it, but withdrew her hand.

"Too hot?" he asked.

She looked at him and shook her head gently. Then she stared into her cup like she was searching for something she'd lost there.

Finally, she spoke. "I did tell him that," she said. "After I married your dad and we started sleeping in the same bed, I realized how badly the war had affected him. He couldn't sleep. I'd wake up to go to the bathroom at three in the morning and find him in front of the radio, listening to static. He'd eventually collapse from exhaustion and have terrible dreams. He talked in his dreams, like he was having conversations with Hiro. This was very frightening to me. When I tried to wake him up, he'd think I was fighting him, and he'd push me or try to hit me. After a while I learned to leave him alone. If he was in our bed I'd go the family room and sleep on the couch during those dreams of his."

"Did Dad ever tell you what happened to Hiro?"

"He wouldn't do that. No, I suppose he *couldn't* do that. But many nights he'd mumble the same things over and over. He'd say: 'Sorry, so sorry,' or, 'I can't save you now,' or even 'Hiro, please forgive me.' On one of those really bad nights I tried to wake him up and he punched me in the face." Keiko's left hand touched her cheek, as if she could still feel the blow. "When he woke up and realized what he'd done he was so sorry, he cried, really cried. I'd never seen him cry before. I held him in my arms and told him how he'd been saying all these things in his sleep. I told him what he'd been saying, and that's when he told me the bitter truth."

"What was it, Mom?"

"He said he was unable to forgive himself . . . he could have saved

Hiro, he said, but he told me he was a coward and ran away. It was his fault Hiro got captured and killed. That's all he said. The next day I asked him to tell me more but he refused to speak of it again. By this time we'd been married almost a year. I was still curious, but I knew never to bring it up. Now I'm not even sure if it's true. It was just something he said."

"But what if it *was* true?"

Keiko shrugged. "I decided that it didn't matter either way because if it was true, I needed to forgive him. Do you see? There was no other way. Nothing was going to bring Hiro back, so I just let it go."

"But I don't understand why you told Joe Fukuda about it." Daniel made a face. "Why, Mom?"

Keiko sighed and took a long sip of tea. "He came over one day, wanting to ask Ray about how Hiro had died. He knew Ray was in the same battle, and that they stuck together wherever they went. I told him not to ask Ray, that this was a very bad idea, but Joe wouldn't listen to me and said he was going to wait for Ray to come home and ask him anyway. I started to get really nervous. I was afraid Ray would lose his temper. I was also afraid Joe might lose his, so I begged him to leave. He stared at me with a funny look and asked me why I was behaving so strangely, and I said talking about it would make Ray really upset and there would be trouble. Joe said, 'Not from me. I just need some answers. I have a right to know.' He pressed me pretty hard and finally I told him that Ray felt responsible for Hiro's death. Joe wanted to know why . . . I didn't want to tell him . . . but finally, I told him that Ray said he thought he could have saved Hiro, and that he was the reason Hiro got killed."

Keiko paused. She sipped from her tea cup.

"That night Joe confronted your dad. They had an awful argument and they fought, right out there." Keiko pointed to the backyard where Ray had crashed into the glass table. "It was terrible. Joe was younger, faster, and he knocked your dad down several times, hurting him pretty badly. There were cuts all over his face. When Joe was done swinging, he left."

Keiko drank the last of her tea and set the cup onto the saucer unsteadily. "I should never have said anything to Joe because after that, those two hated each other and I always worried they would have another one of those awful fights—"

"—Mom?" Daniel cut in.

"Yes, dear?"

"Was it true . . . about Dad? I have to know."

"I already told you, I don't know myself."

Daniel was surprised at his mother's calm eyes. She had said what needed to be said.

Could it possibly be true? he wondered.

Was Dad responsible for getting my real father killed? Why would he say it if it hadn't happened that way? Is this what haunted him the rest of his life? Could it explain why he acted like he did?

Daniel looked into his own teacup now. The tea was cold, but he drank it down in one convulsive gulp. He gripped the cup hard, and suddenly felt like throwing it against the wall.

All those years he tortured me. Tried to make me into something I wasn't. Called me a coward when, in truth, *he* was the real coward. Joe Fukuda was right. Joe smelled a rat and then he found out that rat stole his brother's wife.

My dad. The rat.

TWENTY-FOUR

PHILADELPHIA, PENNSYLVANIA
Hospital of the University of Pennsylvania
October 1998

"There's definitely a surprising amount of fat," Niraj commented, standing on the opposite side of the operating table.

Shut the hell up, Daniel thought to himself. Niraj was a good CT fellow and a nice guy too—not all cardiac surgeons were—but he should have known that such *nice guy* comments were irksome to Daniel. Who cares whether the fat is *surprising* or not? It's there, that's all.

Niraj said it because Daniel was having trouble finding the LAD. He tried again to carefully dissect the yellow fat away from the location where he thought it should be. The left anterior descending coronary artery supplied blood to the anterior half of the left ventricle. When a patient's LAD became occluded and a heart attack ensued, a significant part of the left ventricle would start to die in minutes, and so might the patient. This patient, a seventy-seven-year-old World War Two veteran, had a ninety-eight percent blockage of his LAD. The blockage needed to be bypassed or he could die of a heart attack at any time.

But where was it?

Daniel blinked a drop of sweat out of his eye and again used his pick-ups to grasp at the slippery yellow fat. With his other hand, he gently stroked at the heart tissue with a 15-blade scalpel.

It should be right here.

But it wasn't.

Daniel wanted to rage at his failure, which now owned him. He'd lost his edge. Everyone in the room knew it.

He glanced at the clock. Close to two hours already and he still hadn't finished a single bypass graft.

He was accustomed to finishing a triple bypass in three hours, three-and-a-half at the most. Now he'd hardly begun and every step was maddeningly difficult. A clumsy error at the start, when he dissected the LIMA—the left internal mammary artery—from the chest wall. This all-important artery would be sewn into the LAD distal to the blockage and provide a healthy new supply of blood to the heart. But Daniel was too cavalier with the bovie and cauterized too aggressively and nicked the LIMA itself. That novice mistake led to a lot of bleeding—embarrassing enough—but then, to control the bleeding he threw a stitch that narrowed the artery, making it worthless as a bypass conduit. If a fellow had made the same error, Daniel would have rightly been furious and may have even thrown him out of the case as a punishment for not being careful. When Daniel did it, no one said a word.

He knew what the others were thinking. They were sympathetic. This was his first case since returning from his leave of absence. His mother had been in the hospital. His father had just died. He was not quite himself—yet. But Daniel didn't want their pity. It made him angry, and angrier still because he knew anger always made a surgeon's performance worse. The plain truth was: if he wasn't in top form, he had no business being in a patient's chest. The stakes were too high.

"Damn," Daniel muttered under his breath. He went back to a

small diagonal branch to begin tracing it proximally to where it connected with the LAD. Unfortunately, in this case, the LAD dove into the yellow fat and muscle on the front of the heart. Intramyocardial LAD? he wondered. That might explain the difficulty he was having.

He tried to feel for the artery. In this overweight man with high cholesterol, hypertension, and a five-decade history of smoking, it wasn't surprising that he could feel hard nuggets of calcification within the artery. But then he lost it as the surrounding fat grew denser. He'd already pared off a dozen slivers of fat, but he hesitated to do more for fear of blindly entering the ventricular cavity and causing widespread bleeding.

"Suction, Niraj. Suction," Daniel said.

Niraj dutifully cleared the field.

"How's it going in here?"

Daniel looked up. It was Steve Feinberg, his colleague who'd been operating in the adjacent room.

"Hi Steve. Already done?" They had both started their first cases of the day at 7 am.

"Yeah. A double. Really bad vessels. But should do the lady some good." Steve leaned over the table to peer into the chest cavity. Daniel was annoyed and embarrassed by his unusually slow progress, but Steve didn't say a word.

"I'm having some trouble finding my LAD target," Daniel admitted. When Steve said nothing, Daniel added, "There's a lot of fat."

Steve nodded metronomically. "Definitely a lot of fat. I can see why it's tough to find."

Daniel's gaze dropped down into the operating field, hoping to hide his frustration.

"I'm between cases now," Steve said. "Do you want me to scrub in and give a look?"

Daniel shrugged. "If you want," he replied, trying to sound casual.

But as he waited for his friend to scrub, Daniel burned with embarrassment. *He* was usually the one people called on for help. *He* had a reputation for being the fastest, for getting the best results. He put down his instruments and used his hands to gently inspect the heart, but this gesture was merely an excuse not to look at anyone while he fumed inside. He knew his problem wasn't physical. It was mental. After thousands of cases, his hands and fingers could perform the surgery from muscle memory alone. But he'd lost his spark. His mind was dulled. Lethargy. Apathy. These were words no one would ever use to describe Daniel Tokunaga, but they were how he felt at the moment. And it had been like this ever since the revelations in California had shaken his sense of self, his identity. He was off. He knew it all too well. But what could he do about it?

Steve came back into the room, hands dripping water. The surgical assistant handed him a sterile towel, then held out a gown for him to step into. Niraj moved to the side to make room for him across the table from Daniel.

Steve held out his hands, a request for instruments. "Shall we take a look?"

"Be my guest," Daniel said. The assistant handed Steve forceps and a small scalpel.

Steve followed the visible portion of the artery proximally beginning at the apex of the heart. When it dove into fat, he carefully delaminated around it: gently scraping away surrounding tissues while remaining on top of the blood vessel. He worked slowly, methodically, and the course of the artery gradually began to emerge.

"It sure is calcified," Steve commented.

Daniel didn't respond. This dissection was difficult, for sure, but Steve was doing what *he* should have known to do when presented with a challenging situation: remain calm and patient. Proceed with a next step you know is in the right direction. Good things are more likely to happen to surgeons who are calm and methodical. He often said this to trainees. Yet this time, he'd done the opposite.

After several minutes, Steve made a few centimeters of the LAD visible. He looked up and squinted at the angiogram films that hung on a light box near the foot of the bed. He identified the area of narrowing, then looked down at the LAD and felt it between his fingers.

"What do you think of here? Where it's soft, just past the calcifications." He lifted his fingers so Daniel could see.

Daniel viewed the angiogram. He looked back to the heart and felt the vessel. He nodded. "Yes, I think we've got it."

The door to the operating room swung open and a nurse poked her head in. "Dr. Feinberg, we're ready for you next door."

Steve looked at Daniel.

"I've got it from here," Daniel said. "Go. Thanks a lot."

Steve stepped back and pulled off his gown. "Great. Good luck." He left the room.

It took Daniel two more hours to finish suturing all three bypass grafts. When he finished, he scrubbed out and left Niraj to close the chest and finish the case. In the men's locker room, Daniel sat on a bench and stared at the bank of lockers. He closed his right hand into a fist and clenched his jaw.

What's wrong with me?

—

Back in the office that afternoon, Daniel tried to refocus. He had hours of work strewn across his desk—letters to dictate, charts to review, research papers to write—but he couldn't concentrate. When he stared at a patient's lab results on his computer monitor, his vision went fuzzy. A nurse knocked, opened the door and said something to him, then asked if he was listening. He wasn't. It seemed ludicrous, but there was this unsettling feeling residing inside him: that he was somehow living someone else's life, one removed from his own. He couldn't shake the feeling.

He decided to hit the wards. He saw patients his partners had operated on, a couple of new patients admitted for angina, one elderly man with esophageal cancer and a woman suffering from a diseased heart valve. He tried almost desperately to listen to them: their complaints of intermittent chest pain, difficulty swallowing, and ways they'd tried to start exercising. He forced himself to concentrate when he touched his stethoscope to their chests. But when he did this, the elderly men and women only reminded him of his father, and the anger and resentment rose each time this happened. It was so weird that he sometimes imagined Ray's ghost was in the room whispering, "Big shot, eh?"

Near the end of the day, he returned to his office and decided to call Beth.

"Hello," she answered.

"It's me."

"Hi. How's work going?"

"Not so great."

"Well, it's just your first week back. Give it a little time."

Daniel glanced at the door to make sure it was closed. Then he lowered his voice and said, "I'm off, hon. My surgery this morning was terrible . . ."

"It couldn't have been that bad . . . you're always too hard on yourself."

"Well, it wasn't good. I'm in a funk and I don't know how to get out of it."

"What's on your mind?"

He closed his eyes and exhaled deeply. "I still can't wrap my head around the stuff with my dad. It's just so bizarre."

"That makes sense. It's not every day you learn your father wasn't who you thought he was."

"But why didn't he or my mom tell me the truth? I can understand why they wouldn't when I was young, but after I'd grown up? I mean, he lived a lie. That's not honorable. Yet, he was so big on honor. And what was my real father like? Where are his parents—my grand-parents? Are they alive? So many questions . . ."

"Maybe we can try and find out."

"I should have asked Joe Fukuda while I was out there."

"Why didn't you?"

"I don't know. He's kind of ornery and I didn't much like him. But I should have at least gotten his address or his phone number."

"I'm sure we can get them. Would you like me to try? I can start with your mom."

"Maybe."

"What else is bothering you?" Beth asked.

Daniel rocked back in his chair and put his feet up on the desk. "It's that medal. What could Dad have possibly done in the war to earn it?" He tried to picture his father leading men into battle, or rescuing someone in a tight situation, or surprising an enemy battalion and holding them off single-handedly—all the things he'd seen in movies and thought would be necessary to win an important medal came to him in comic book flashes. But in none of these images could he place his father in the imaginary role as hero.

"I don't know," Beth replied, "But whatever that medal was for, it had to be something good, right?"

"Yes, I'm sure that's true," Daniel said, remembering that he'd learned things about the man that defied everything he thought he knew. His father had helped Anne's family when they were in desperate straits. He'd married Keiko. Out of obligation? Out of friendship? Who knew? But when Daniel thought about that momentous act—it baffled him. Part of him wanted to believe his father was simply a tyrant. Stern. Implacable. Narrow-minded and prejudiced. He wanted to believe Ray was a coward who'd failed his friends in war. That simple picture made sense, and neatly fit the image of the man Daniel had scorned for decades.

Could he have been wrong? It seemed impossible. And yet—it was just as impossible to reconcile the conflict between the father he knew, and the man who would perform such selfless acts.

"Are you still there?" Beth asked.

"Yes."

"Daniel, these are problems we're not going to solve overnight. And sometimes it just takes time for things to feel normal again after a shock like this. For now, let's just commit to trying to learn as much as we can, and take it from there. What do you think?"

Daniel nodded. "Yeah, you're right. Thanks."

"Here's an idea. It's four-thirty now and I know you've probably still got some work to do. Why don't I come downtown and we can catch dinner in the city tonight? Then we can continue the conversation."

"That sounds great."

"Want to meet at Rittenhouse at six?"

"Yes. See you then."

Daniel hung up the phone. He pondered what Beth had said. Then he stood, put on his jacket and grabbed his briefcase on the way out the door.

His secretary, Melissa, looked up from her desk. "You're leaving?" she said, surprised.

"Not yet. One more stop before I go."

"Where?" she asked.

"The flower shop. Is that still on Founders Two?

"No," she chuckled at her boss. "It hasn't been there for at least five years, maybe six. Now it's on Ravdin One."

Daniel shrugged his shoulders, and grinned.

Melissa smiled broadly. "You *go*, Dr. Tokunaga."

———

Two days later, Daniel was close to completing his rounds at the hospital; he had only one post-operative patient left to see: Harold Simpkins—the man in whom Steve Feinberg had helped him find the LAD.

Daniel liked Harold, a farmer from Lancaster, Pennsylvania, a quiet sufferer who'd had unstable angina for years but had never complained about it. Stoic. That was the word doctors used for the men of his generation, the ones who'd grown up during the Depression, many of whom had fought in the Second World War. Harold Simpkins was originally from San Antonio, a place he and Daniel talked about because Beth's parents lived there. He had moved to Pennsylvania after he got married.

The day of his heart attack, he was splitting wood, swinging an ax for half an hour when suddenly it happened. His wife heard him cry out and found him lying on his side, fist over his chest, face tight with pain. She called 911 and he was taken to a local hospital. He got morphine, oxygen, nitroglycerin to dilate his coronary arteries, and aspirin. His pain lessened. But a cardiac catheterization revealed three-vessel disease—the LAD almost completely occluded.

Daniel felt guilty for the way Harold Simpkins' surgery had gone. It should have been routine. Instead it had been a five-hour ordeal with a botched LIMA graft.

Now, checking to see how his patient was doing, Daniel looked at the large white dressing that ran in a vertical line down the man's chest.

"How do you feel today, Mr. Simpkins?"

"Doing fine, thanks to you, Doc."

Daniel pulled a hospital chair closer to the bed.

"You're looking really good for two days out. Pain okay?"

"It's sore." Mr. Simpkins nodded at an IV bag hanging from a pole next to his bed. "But the meds are taking the edge off. When do you think I'll be able to go home?"

Daniel was mildly surprised. "You've just had major surgery, Mr. Simpkins. Let's not be in any hurry to get home."

Harold Simpkins let out a loud sigh. "Okay, Doc. I just know the sooner I'm back on the farm, the faster I'll recover."

Daniel shook his head. "Well, you've been though a lot with this surgery and you can't expect to spring back so quickly. You'll regain your health, but you've got to give yourself more time." Daniel gave him a reassuring smile.

Mr. Simpkins did not seem to take this well. "Doc, I think health is a state of mind. I'm healthy. It's going to take more than a little surgery to get me off my game."

"We'll see," Daniel said dubiously. "Some people do recover more quickly than others, and some go home a little sooner than expected."

"I know I'm a fast healer, Doc, and you know, I'm going to quit smoking, and I'm going to stay fit—I get plenty of exercise working on the farm—"

"—You'll have to lighten up on the physical work, Mr. Simpkins. Don't overdo it. When you get home—you shouldn't be doing anything too strenuous for a while."

"I won't do anything I can't handle."

"Well, let me take a listen to you." Daniel put the buds of his stethoscope into his ears and placed the bell on Mr. Simpkins' chest. The heart had a good, regular rhythm and sounded normal. He moved his stethoscope to either side and listened to the lungs, then he leaned Mr. Simpkins forward and moved the stethoscope to his back. "Now take a few deeper breaths, please."

As Daniel listened, he saw something he hadn't noticed before. There was a long, curving scar on Mr. Simpkins' back. The scar was dark, and a little raised, so that it looked like a scythe-shaped keloid. An old surgical scar? Daniel knew surgeons had made incisions like that in the old days for kidney operations. He took off his stethoscope.

"You sound very good. What was this long scar from? Did you have surgery previously? I don't remember that being in your record."

"That raised scar? A splinter did that."

"A splinter?" Daniel was astonished.

"It was during a German bombardment during the war."

"How'd it happen? The splinter . . . I've not heard of anything quite like that."

"We were in France, my battalion was trapped behind enemy lines. We'd gotten ourselves into some danger, you know, getting too far ahead of the rest of our troops. We're Texans, so we always have to rush out and be first, you know." He said this with a glint in his eye and he chuckled, but then grimaced and tried to stop because the laughing hurt his chest.

"Take it easy," Daniel said.

Mr. Simpkins took a deep breath, then went on, "We were surrounded. Stranded for . . . what was it now . . . five or six days . . . the whole time under bombardment. They called us the 'Lost Battalion.'"

"Wow," Daniel remarked, truly impressed. "That's incredible. And the splinter?"

"The Germans shelled us good, let me tell you. Cracked trees like matchsticks, splinters big as broomsticks and sharp as swords went flying everywhere. Went on like that for *days*."

"But you made it out in one piece, didn't you?"

"Rescued in the nick of time. Our guys finally got to us."

"Thank goodness. You were lucky."

"That I was," Mr. Simpkins said.

"And thank you for serving. We all owe you a lot. Every one of us."

"Well, Doc. You've saved my life. So that makes us even!" They both smiled. "Where's your family from, Doc? If you don't mind me asking."

"Me? Oh, my parents are Japanese, but I was born in California."

"Japanese," Mr. Simpkins said. "Wonderful people. Just wonderful."

The soft, reverent way he said this made Daniel pause. "You think so? I mean, I'm kind of surprised because you fought in the war, and Japan was our enemy."

Mr. Simpkins shook his head. "Japan had a bad government. Bad leaders. Not much they could do about that. It had been in place a long time. But the Japanese *people*—God don't make 'em any better. I told you we got rescued? It was Japanese soldiers who saved us."

Again, Daniel showed his surprise. "How did they do that?"

"Japanese-*American* soldiers. Their unit fought like hell to get us out of there. They came through when no one else would or could. There were 211 of us left when they got to us, and we'd have been dead if they hadn't come. I found out later they took 800 casualties trying to save us."

"You're not by any chance talking about the 442nd regiment?"

"Yes, that's right. How did you know?"

"The 442nd was an all Japanese unit. My father was in it."

Mr. Simpkins' face changed. "Your father? Really?"

"Yes."

"The 442nd saved us, pure and simple. Got wounded the day before they reached us, and I lost a lot of blood. Two Japanese fellows lugged me on a canvas stretcher three miles back to an aid station. *Three miles.*"

Mr. Simpkins' eyes were lost in memory for a moment. "I would love to meet your father. Where does he live?"

"Unfortunately, he just passed away, in California."

The old man's face fell. "Sorry to hear that. I'm sure he was some kind of man. They all were."

"Well, I must admit I don't know much about what he did in the war, or even where he was exactly."

"If he was in the 442nd, he was definitely one of them that saved our butts in France. They freed a bunch of towns. Did you know that? The Frenchies are so grateful they host reunions for the veterans."

"Have you ever been to one?"

"Maybe I didn't explain that just right. Not for just any veterans. It's for those Japanese Americans of the 442nd."

Daniel nodded. "I get it. But do you think many of the 442nd veterans go?"

"Well, sure enough, it's quite a big deal for them. But I bet there's fewer and fewer who make the trip these days. Didn't your dad talk about this?"

Daniel didn't reply.

Mr. Simpkins reached out to touch Daniel's hand. "Doc, you're a smart fellow. But I've lived a lot longer than you so pardon me if I offer a little piece of advice. If you don't know anything about your father and the job they did over yonder, you owe it to yourself to find out about it. You oughta go to France, if you can spare the time. See the places. Go to the reunion; see for yourself. I bet you might meet someone who fought alongside your dad."

"You know what, Mr. Simpkins? I might just do that."

TWENTY-FIVE

ÉPINAL, EASTERN FRANCE
Near Bruyères
October 1999

As they entered the grounds of the American military cemetery at Épinal, Beth suddenly stood completely still, stunned by the beauty of the place. It was just as she imagined it should be, and a lot like the magazine pictures she'd seen of the cemetery near Omaha Beach in Normandy. The field was covered by five thousand white marble crosses, the tombstones of Americans lost in the fight for the Vosges Mountains, all of them upright and clean, arranged in perfect rows on an unbroken blanket of pure green.

She watched Daniel stroll ahead, and wondered what thoughts might be going through his mind. Being here, with him, after all the tumultuous events of the past year, seemed surreal. When she thought about how they'd come to be in this place, and how her husband had changed—she could scarcely believe it had actually happened.

One day last fall, not long after Daniel's father had passed away, he'd asked his mother if she'd ever heard of the 442nd's reunions in France.

Reunion? she said. Sometimes we would hear about those, but Ray was never interested in going.

Then over the winter, Keiko received an invitation in the mail. There was also a hand-written note from the head of the reunion committee, addressed to her: *We were so sorry to hear of your husband's recent passing. We are overjoyed that he is under consideration for an upgrade to the Medal of Honor. We would like to extend a special invitation to you to attend our reunion in Bruyères. It is an event that you will never forget. We would all love to meet you and hope you can make it.*

Keiko called Daniel to say: *Why don't you go, Danny? And ask Beth to go too.*

By that time, they'd settled back into their routines at home. Daniel was back to his full surgical caseload at work, though Beth sensed something had changed because he no longer stayed so late and didn't seem to take calls from his partners or the hospital so often. She could see he was still reeling from the loss of his father and from his mother's revelations. She couldn't help noticing his lack of energy and poor appetite at times, or his lack of interest in traveling to give an honorary lecture. Her only thought was to support him in any way she could, though much of the time, she wasn't sure how to help.

Then, around Veteran's Day, he surprised her by suggesting they spend a long weekend in the Poconos. On a crisp, autumn day, he brought her to a trailhead for a hike in the woods. They climbed a small mountain and admired the breathtaking foliage. When Daniel asked another hiker to take a picture of them next to a sign near the top, she realized where they were. It was Hawk Mountain, a wild bird sanctuary they'd discovered twenty years ago, before the twins were born. They used to come here once or twice each fall, to watch the migrating hawks, eagles, and falcons. That day, they sat together on a boulder, passing the binoculars back and forth, watching the birds and the clouds, and talking.

The next week, Daniel surprised Beth again by cooking her dinner: spaghetti carbonara, a dish he'd last made in the weeks after the twins' birth, when Beth was overwhelmed with nursing and trying to catch sleep when she could. Beth laughed at the memory of Daniel making carbonara every few days, again and again—and his pride at mastering the simple recipe. Gradually, she found herself becoming more relaxed in Daniel's presence, and enjoying his company. She still worried about him spending too much time alone, so she stayed up late to watch SportsCenter and action movies with him. She started keeping track of his case schedule in order to meet him for lunch at the hospital in the doctor's dining room. Because his operating schedule was often unpredictable, she sometimes waited for over an hour to spend just ten or fifteen minutes with him, watching him inhale a sandwich. Over these lunch dates their conversations became more natural, and Daniel began to smile more. Their meetings grew longer, for Daniel would sometimes linger and lament having to leave to begin his next case.

In January, Beth finally decided to tell Daniel the plans she'd been contemplating ever since the kids left home. Looking back, it embarrassed her to recall how worried she'd initially felt about telling him. She'd decided to join an overseas medical mission. She would take a surgical technologist refresher course and join her church's medical team that traveled regularly to Laos and Cambodia. Fifteen years ago, a group of American churches had formed a group called Mercy Abroad that had built full-service hospitals in Vientiane and Phnom Penh with the goal of teaching local doctors modern, Western medicine. These hospitals were staffed by volunteer doctors, nurses, and staff from America on a rotating basis—most committed to going two or three weeks per year, but some stayed much longer, up to four to six months. Beth's friends who had gone called the experience life-changing.

When the thought first came to her, she worried that Daniel would call it a stupid idea and ask why he couldn't just make a big donation which would be sure to help far more people than she could single-handedly as a neophyte worker bee.

But then, when she asked him what he thought, he said he loved the idea.

And that had been a turning point of sorts. It gave Beth new purpose, a goal to strive for. She completed the refresher course in the summer and signed up for her first two-week stint in early January of the following year—in Laos. Daniel spent evenings with her at the kitchen table going over various operations she was likely to assist with, from cleft lip repair to cataract surgery to amputations.

But before her big trip, they'd agreed to make this journey to France for the 442nd's reunion in Bruyères. They'd stayed four nights in Paris before driving out to the eastern border of France and it was like a second honeymoon. They spent hours walking back and forth along the Seine. They marveled at the stained glass windows of Notre Dame and Sainte-Chapelle, and sipped cappuccinos at a café watching passersby in the idling afternoon on the Boulevard Saint-Michel. A year ago Daniel would have called it all a waste of time. But the events of the past year seemed to have forced a change in his perspective, his mind and heart.

In some ways, however, Beth sensed her husband's sense of self remained adrift. He rarely talked about Ray and the past. There were still secrets she knew he hid deep and might never share. But he'd also already changed in ways she'd never thought possible. She believed things would get better, and she hoped this trip to France would help him find some of the answers he'd been searching for.

"There it is." Beth pointed. Daniel crunched to a stop on the wide gravel path. He moved left, stepping onto a carpet of soft green grass, closer to the white marble cross at the end of a row. Beth was already reading the tombstone.

HIRO FUKUDA
PFC 442 INF REGT
CALIFORNIA OCT 19 1944

My father. Here.

Daniel knelt and ran his fingers across the sharply engraved letters.

Has anyone ever visited you before, Hiro Fukuda? After fifty-five years, am I the first?

He read the words again and waited to feel some emotion. Sadness. Grief or sorrow. But there was no feeling. He shed no tears. There was only . . . a deep and unfathomable regret.

He looked away, upward, at the puffy clouds dotting the clear blue sky. Beth touched him on the shoulder.

"Are you all right, honey?"

"Me? Sure, I'm fine."

"How do you *feel*?"

Daniel shrugged. "I didn't know this man. It's hard to feel sad about a person you don't know." He looked again across the sea of crosses. "He had friends out there, people buried here who died, like him. Those guys knew him. I didn't."

Beth wrapped her arms around him from behind and squeezed.

"You know some things about him. You know he was fun-loving and liked to laugh, your mom told us that. And you know he died fighting for something good. Not everyone does that, right? Your father was a good man."

When Beth said "father," Ray's face, not Hiro's, flashed before Daniel's mind. He made a mental shift and pictured Hiro's image from the old photo.

"Yes. I think he probably was a good man. And I want to find out more about him, if I can . . . but this . . . this is impersonal. It's a little hard to relate to in any kind of personal way. It's just . . . commemorative, I guess. At least for me." He turned around to face Beth, his face

214

oddly apologetic.

"We'll find someone who knows," she said reassuringly.

Daniel buried his face in her hair and inhaled—her scent of lilacs mingled with the aroma of roses planted at the site. He was glad they had come.

"It's bizarre, isn't it? Meeting my real father here, at a place like this, for the first time?"

"At least now you know the truth," she affirmed.

Daniel smiled a bit teasingly. "And you finally got that trip to France you always wanted." A ticklish breeze ran through his black, gray-tinged hair. He still had his hands on Beth's shoulders. She tapped him on the chest with her fingers and he drew her in close.

He'd still not regained his focus in the operating room and this bothered him. But he knew the nature of his problem and had finally concluded that, simply put, being a surgeon was no longer the first, second and third most important things in his life. At one point, late at night while watching Beth sleep, Daniel had the strange but wonderful feeling that he'd just emerged from a twenty-year dream and could now—for the first time—really see his wife, himself, and their lives together. And the more he listened to Beth talk about her life, her friends at church, her pride in their children, her hopes for the future—their future—the more he realized how lucky he was that he had such a woman to guide him.

⁓

"Easy on the clutch!" Daniel pleaded. Beth was driving again. She exited the N57 highway, into yet another traffic circle. France seemed filled with traffic circles.

"Quiet! I'll do the driving. You're the navigator. Read the signs," she ordered. A black four-door Renault trying to enter the circle swerved away and honked.

"Sorry," Beth mumbled. "Was I supposed to yield?"

Daniel, ignoring the question, strained to read an approaching road sign.

"There, it says Bruyères, take that, here. Now!"

She made an abrupt right onto the turn off; a cloud of dust enveloped them and three cars passed them in the left lane. A couple of the drivers shouted in French and glared at them.

Now on the straightaway Beth gunned it. "Actually, I kinda like the feeling of stick again, feels like I'm really driving."

Daniel forced himself to rest back in his seat. He didn't like how a gust of wind could rock the two-door Peugeot from side to side, and being unable to drive was frustrating—as was being yelled at in French and not knowing exactly what was being said, though the intent was quite clear.

"Well, no one ever taught me how to use a stick-shift," he said. "Not that I ever needed to learn."

"It's a good life skill, you know. Maybe I could teach you, using this car," Beth replied.

"No, thanks."

"Because I wouldn't teach you with a car of someone we knew, you'd probably screw up the engine. This is a rental, you know."

"Very funny," he said, catching her smile. "Eyes on the road, Mrs. Tokunaga."

The road snaked between foothills whose verdant slopes were patterned by small cottages and barns and fenced pastures. They passed herds of penned-up goats and sheep, and a picturesque lake. The French knew how to make bucolic even more beautiful and at the same time fairytale-like.

"Did you get to call your mom before we left?" Beth asked.

"Yes. She sounds on board with selling the house and moving to a senior living community soon. She's even called a realtor to ask what she might get for the house. And there are definitely some nice senior places nearby with good restaurants and lots of activities."

"That's good. As long as it isn't like a nursing home."

"No. These are places for people who just don't want to take care of a house or cook for themselves anymore."

"Sounds perfect."

"I still can't believe she agreed to it, but I'm glad she did."

Daniel hadn't returned to California since Ray had died a year ago, but now he called his mother more often, at least twice a week, to check up on her.

"How are the kids?" he asked. "You've talked to them more recently than I have, I think."

"James said he took the first big organic chemistry test of the year, and did well. That's a big deal, right?"

"Yeah. I guess sophomore year is the first real year of college. Freshman year you're just getting your feet wet."

"Well, anyway, he's really happy to be back with his friends. He said his roommate invited him to their house for Thanksgiving. They live outside Boston. He asked if that would be okay, instead of coming home."

"Is that a good idea?" Daniel asked. He'd never done stay-overs much when he was in college. It was all work and no play, plus he just wasn't comfortable staying at other people's houses. In his mind, James was just like him.

"I could call him again," Beth said. "See how badly he wants to go. But you know, I think we might be a bit provincial about this whole thing."

"You mean overly protective?"

"Yes, that's exactly what I mean. He's not a baby."

Daniel sighed. "My dad would never have let me stay over at some friend's house."

"Terrible, right? Because you had so many invites," Beth quipped.

"Very funny," Daniel said. "No, that's true, I didn't have friends to visit even if I wanted to—Dad saw to that as well. Ah, well. What's passed is past . . ."

"—And not necessary to repeat . . . right?"

"True."

A light rain began to fall. Beth switched on the windshield wipers. The swish-swish sound became a sort of road melody for a few moments, and both of them went with it, letting the conversation fall silent.

Then Beth said, "There's one more thing I should tell you. This one's a bigger deal, I'm afraid."

"Oh?"

"Julia called and says she loves being back at school."

"No surprise."

"She told me she has a boyfriend."

"What?"

"I know, I was surprised too. But it isn't really sudden. Apparently, she was friends with this boy all last year. I guess our little girl is really growing up."

"Go on, tell me what she said."

"His name is Allen. He's a junior."

"Older guy, huh?"

"Yes. He's studying computer science."

"Lemme guess, is he Asian?"

"Actually, yes, he is."

Daniel pictured a nerdy Asian kid with thick glasses.

"He's also on the swim team. He apparently got a full ride at Stanford. Was a state champion in a half-dozen events."

"Really?" Daniel's eyebrows lifted. Okay, maybe this Asian kid's buff and cool. He'd have to be to get Julia to like him. "What state?"

"What?"

"What state does he come from? Where was he a state champ?"

"Oh. Illinois."

"What else did she say about him?"

"Not much else. But she seems very happy."

"Of course she does. She's in love, probably. They better not be having sex."

"They are definitely *not* having sex, Daniel! Why would you even say that? You know Julia. You raised her."

"Did you ask her?"

"Of course not. But I think I know my own daughter."

Daniel shook his head and laughed. "Think of all the things we thought we knew just one year ago. I had a father I didn't know and the father I thought I did know, I didn't know at all. And now our daughter is a grown woman and she's with a man we don't know at all."

Now Beth laughed. "That's called *life,* Daniel."

"And one more thing," Daniel added.

"What?"

"I love you."

Beth glanced at him in surprise, and then smiled.

"I know."

As Beth drove through the rain, Daniel's thoughts turned to the day he'd brought Beth home to meet his parents for the first time. As a fellow, he only got one week of vacation per year, and he'd used it to bring her to California. His mother was ecstatic when he told her he was bringing home his new girlfriend. In her excitement, however, she'd quickly passed the phone to Ray.

"You have a girlfriend?" Ray had stated gruffly. When Daniel answered affirmatively, his father's only comment was: "You're training to be a surgeon. I don't think you have time for distractions."

On the way to the house from the airport, Daniel assured Beth that his mother would love her, but told her not to be discouraged if his father was a bit stand-offish.

That had made Beth even more nervous.

Then they arrived, and found that Daniel had been totally wrong.

At the house, Keiko opened the door with a huge smile on her face. But when she saw Beth, her surprise was evident. Afterwards,

Beth asked Daniel, "Why didn't you tell her I was white ahead of time?"

"I don't know," he said. "I never said you'd be Japanese—I guess she just assumed it."

Later that night, in his old bedroom, Beth had been so unhappy that she'd cried. Daniel held her, comforting her, realizing how badly she wanted his mother to like her and knowing there wasn't anything he could do about it.

Luckily, it seemed the opposite with Ray. Ray asked Beth about her parents, and she mentioned her father owned a small farm in Minnesota, and that her mother was a midwife. Watching her mother help women through their pregnancies was what had first gotten Beth interested in medicine. She explained that she'd been working toward earning enough to go to medical school herself someday, and Daniel watched his father perk up in a way he'd never seen before. He was actually . . . charming. He made polite small talk. He asked about her interest in theater and dance. He smiled at her a lot.

It was a wonderful, bizarre evening, Daniel remembered. He'd expected his father to be the one who cared about him marrying someone Japanese. Ray was always stressing Japanese customs, honor, and duty; and he definitely expected *his* wife to stay home and play a traditional role.

But he disliked Anne Mikado. Practically gave her the silent treatment. Once, he said Anne was too passive, too reserved. Daniel had always thought those would be traits he would want in a spouse, but instead he was drawn to Beth.

Go figure, Daniel thought. Just another example of how I never understood the man.

"See that sign? Bruyères, two kilometers," Daniel said.

"I see it," Beth said.

The view opened up into a lovely, expansive valley. The light rain stopped and a patch of bright sunshine illuminated the surrounding fields of harvested wheat. The town lay ahead. It was a cluster of many buildings on the valley floor; most were beige stucco or grey stone, with red-tiled roofs. Beth caught up to a small delivery truck and slowed down as they entered the town. A roadside sign read: "Bruyères. Population 3,000."

The road narrowed. A thin sidewalk provided only a little space from the sides of buildings that seemed to close in as they drove closer to the center of town. Beth drove carefully and pulled right to stop and let a car pass going in the opposite direction. Behind her, a horn tooted.

"I'm going, I'm going," she said as she shifted into gear and pulled away from the curb.

They were so close to pedestrians that Daniel could reach out his window and touch the arm of an old woman carrying a bag of groceries if he wanted to. He smelled a delightfully warm and embracing aroma that wafted through the open doors of a bakery. In the doorway, a little French girl, perhaps seven years old, with brown hair and some flour on her cheeks, waved at him. He waved back.

The truck ahead of them turned off to the right, and they came to a roundabout. The road wound around a shallow pool with a simple fountain shooting water lazily in the air. Off to one side they saw a greenish, bronze statue of a French soldier set upon a large stone pedestal.

"This must be the center of town. Joe Fukuda said to head northeast from here . . . that way," Daniel said, pointing.

Beth drove around the fountain and turned. The paved road narrowed even more and became cobblestone. After another minute, they were clear of the town and driving up into the hills.

"Now which way?" Beth asked. There was a confusing fork in the road up ahead.

"I don't know. We know it's up a hill, so try that one, go right."

"This is really all we have to go on? Joe Fukuda's memory from fifty years ago?"

Daniel said, "Joe's got a pretty good memory, I'll give him that."

"Why don't we ask that guy on the bike?" Beth suggested.

They pulled up beside an old man in a battered fedora from an earlier time; his face was creased like his hat. He was moving slow, huffing up the incline. His black bicycle was an antique; two baguettes in a cloth bag were strapped down in a basket behind his seat.

"Honey, we don't speak French, remember?"

"C'mon, we both took a couple years in high school. Besides, most of these people speak Frenchified English. You just don't like asking for directions."

The bicyclist saw them and stopped, his right foot connecting quickly with the roadside.

"Pardon me, *parlez-vous anglais?*" Daniel asked.

If the old man was surprised to see a Japanese tourist asking if he could speak English, he didn't show it.

"*Oui! Bien sûr!*" he said with pronounced self-assurance, and it was like Daniel had offended him by asking.

"Oh . . . good. I wonder, can help me find a place? We're looking for a hilltop where some men might have fought during World War Two. You know of any place like that right around here?"

The man broke into a smile for the first time, his face a myriad of wrinkles. He waved at the surrounding hills. "*Mais oui, Monsieur!* Battles fight on every hill *vous voyez.*"

Daniel smiled politely. There were half a dozen hilltops in sight.

"I see. This hill would have a road to the top—an uncle of mine who was here during the war told me. He said there also a farmhouse—"

"*Votre oncle? He was Japonais?*"

"Yes."

"*quatre-quatre-deux?*"

"442? Actually, yes."

The old man's crow's feet crinkled as he grinned and patted Daniel on the arm. "*Mon Dieu! Monsieur,* you are welcome here! Happy

222

to meet you, *mon ami*. Now . . ." He seemed to think hard about something as he looked up the road. "This hill, this road," he pointed, *"le top de cette* hill. Is good place to go, famous *vue de la ville*. This road is good. The other hills—no roads to top."

"And is there a house at the top of this one?"

"Non, but once, *oui*. In the war, *oui*. Now *le cimetière."*

"A cemetery?"

The man gave a nod.

"Okay, thanks."

"Bonne chance! You are . . . most welcome here!"

They waved goodbye and Beth took the right fork and the road turned to loose gravel. There was a rustic building on the right that looked abandoned. The road wrapped itself around the hill and steepened and shafts of sunlight gleamed down between the gaps in the trees that overspread the white dusty road. They drove for what seemed like a long time and then, near the top, the road leveled out, and a broad view of the whole valley opened up. Beth braked gently so they could admire the scenery. From five hundred feet up, the maroon roofs of Bruyères nestled among the valley's verdant leaf trees and neatly laid out fields. The scene was something out of an ancient tapestry.

The road ended at a small parking lot. There were spaces for five cars, and Daniel noticed a faded grey two-door Renault occupied the spot closest to the opening in a low stone wall that was the entrance to the cemetery.

"This is it?" Beth asked.

"Must be."

A sudden breeze blew autumn leaves of orange and red across their windshield. Beth shut off the car, and they walked into the cemetery, which was small, only about an acre. The gravestones were damp from recent rain; most were spotted with lichen, and some were festooned with rich green moss.

"This must be the place," Daniel repeated, but neither he nor Beth were sure because the enchantment of the countryside had put a mild spell on them, and they walked now with a diffidence that was dreamlike. Daniel began to stroll around the periphery. There was a blonde-haired young woman in a beige raincoat kneeling by a set of graves near the center of the cemetery.

Beth seemed content to study some of the headstones up close. Daniel moved on, feeling in some strange way that he'd visited this place before, perhaps in old pictures of the war, perhaps just in his imagination.

What happened here, fifty-five years ago? he pondered. Is this the spot I traveled halfway around the world to see? Maybe Joe Fukuda's memory is off.

He admitted this was possible. Joe's description was scant on details and landmarks. Weeks after the battle, after the Americans had pushed well beyond the Vosges and into Germany, his unit had come through this area. He'd gone AWOL for half a day to find the spot where his brother had died. *There was a road, and a small house*, he'd said. *Abandoned. The ground was rutted and muddy from the tires of many trucks.* That was all he'd seen. His brother's body had long since been removed and processed for burial.

But what if this *was* the spot? Was it a skirmish or a large engagement? Did the Germans or Americans hold the house? Daniel shook his head. It was no use trying to imagine something about which he knew virtually nothing.

Maybe I'll meet someone at the reunion tomorrow who remembers the way it was, he hoped.

The sound of Beth speaking French made him look up. She was talking to the Frenchwoman at the center of the cemetery. He smiled and thought, her French is way better than mine.

Daniel walked the entire perimeter of the graveyard and returned to the stone wall at the entrance. The tree-shaded hilltop was heavy with memory, stillness, the polite chirp of a bird now and then, but otherwise the wind was about all that spoke . . . yet now Beth's voice rose above the wind and she and the other woman were laughing and the Frenchwoman was speaking English, clearly and well. The grave-yard was now alive. The two were deep into an animated discussion about movies and Hollywood, of all things.

"Does he know any movie stars?" the Frenchwoman asked. She was slim, with light blue eyes and a pair of dimples when she smiled. Beneath her open raincoat she wore a hunter green Patagonia fleece and blue jeans.

Beth laughed. "No, none personally. Los Angeles is a very large city. And my husband's family didn't live in Hollywood, they lived in a modest working class neighborhood."

The woman was not the least bit interested in that, and she went on with her own little track: "When I was little, my mother watched films with Audrey Hepburn and Katherine Hepburn over and over. I think she thought they were sisters! I asked her why she loved them so much and she said that, after the war, these beautiful actresses gave them such hope. They needed that then."

"I understand; it must have been so hard after the war. But now look how beautiful this part of the country is."

"Yes, I thought of moving away from this region, for a better job, more opportunity, but I cannot seem to do it. Most of the people around here just stay and stay."

Daniel walked up to them.

"Oh, this is my husband, Daniel."

"Hello," Daniel said, holding out his hand to the woman.

"Hello, sir. I am Sophie and I have been having a most wonder-ful *tête-a-tête* with your charming wife." They shook hands.

"So you like all things American—or just our films?" Daniel asked.

Sophie smiled. "American movies *are* the best, but sometimes too much violence, don't you think?"

"I agree," Daniel replied. "And it's getting worse."

"With ours as well," Sophie said.

"So . . . do you come here often?" Daniel asked.

"I do. I like to visit my grandparents." She looked at the two nearby gravestones. "Besides, I don't live very far, just down the road at the bottom of the hill."

Overhead a small black squirrel leaped from one beech tree to another. Daniel followed the squirrel as it threw itself acrobatically from branch to branch toward the open view of the hills. "If I lived here," he said, "I'd come up here often just for the calming wind and the amazing view."

Sophie said, "This is a rare clear day for this time of year. Often there is rain and fog. I am glad you have a nice weather day. But why, may I ask, did you choose to spend your afternoon here? Was it the view, as you say, or did you know someone who was buried here?"

"We're here for the World War Two reunion . . . in Bruyères. Do you know about that?"

"Certainly. We remember. All of us do." Sophie grinned—her teeth bright white. "Even youngsters like me who are too young to remember, remember, if you know what I mean."

"Daniel's father served here," Beth explained. "But we have never come to a reunion. Truthfully, we don't know what to expect, but we're here and I'm sure it's going to be interesting."

"It is very moving to see the old soldiers, I can tell you that. And for the townspeople, those ones who lived through it and are still alive, it is a yearly rite of passage. A very important thing. Tomorrow you will see a lot more and then you will realize how much we honor the Americans who helped us. So . . . did your father come as well?"

"He died in the war."

"I'm sorry," Sophie replied. "So many families lost their loved ones . . . did he . . . did he perish near Bruyères? If you don't mind me asking."

Daniel cleared his throat and ran his hand through his hair. "Actually, I think he may have died right here."

"Here?" Sophie asked, confused.

"Where we are now standing. Would you know anything about a small battle that took place here? I even know the date: October 19, 1944. I think some Germans and Americans fought over this very hilltop."

Daniel noticed Sophie's eyes widen, a look of surprise. For several seconds, she said nothing, and seemed to drift off for a moment. Her eyes roved the cemetery, then looked off down the road that climbed the mountain, then came back ever so slowly to Daniel and Beth. She tried to smile but failed at that and instead nodded several times, but still said nothing.

"Do you know the battle I'm talking about?" Daniel asked.

She nodded again.

"Really? How?"

"Please excuse me," Sophie finally said. "I do not mean to be impolite. I must do something. Now. I must . . . go tell a friend about this. Would you please stay here a moment? It will only take me a few minutes—" She took a step toward her car.

"—What are you talking about?" Daniel said.

"There is someone I think you might like to meet. She only lives down this road a little way. In fact . . . perhaps it would be better if you came with me. To meet her."

"But why?"

"Because she lived here during the war. And her family's home was right on this spot, before it was taken down for the cemetery. She has been a friend of my parents for decades, and her family still owns all the land around this hilltop. I am sure she will want to meet you and talk to you about this."

Daniel and Beth looked at one another. "Yes," Daniel said, "I think we would like to meet her, too."

They followed Sophie's car halfway down the mountain, then turned left onto a narrow dirt lane that Beth hadn't noticed on the way up to the top. In another minute, they emerged into a small clearing in the center of which was a small stone cottage. The cottage's wood door was darkly stained and looked sleek from heavy coats of varnish. Two green-shuttered windows straddled the door, and these were matched above by two gables that broke the slope of the steeply pitched slate-shingle roof. A trail of smoke emanated from the chimney. Someone was home.

Sophie, Daniel, and Beth got out of their cars and went to the front door. Sophie knocked.

"Tata? It's me, Sophie. Are you there?" she said in French.

Inside the house there was the sound of footsteps padding closer. The door swung open. A white-haired woman with a kind, weathered face stood in the doorway wearing a red, cable-knit sweater, corduroy pants, and a pair of slippers. Her light green eyes traveled across the faces of her visitors.

"Sophie? How nice to see you. And who are your friends?"

"I'm sorry to surprise you like this, Tata, but I met this nice American couple from California in the cemetery and I thought you'd like to meet them."

"Oh, but of course. Hello," she said, switching to English as she shook Daniel's and then Beth's hand. "My name is Juliette." Daniel and Beth introduced themselves.

"Tata, Daniel says his father was in a battle around your old home. They would like to know more about it."

"Your father was here?" Juliette asked.

"Yes. In October, 1944."

Juliette nodded. "Yes, that was the time it happened. Did he tell you to come visit this spot?"

"Actually, no. The truth is, he died here."

Juliette frowned. "I'm so sorry."

"Thank you. I'm sure it was very difficult for your family to be living in a war zone."

"Yes, it was. I lost my parents, too. In the battle."

Beth gasped. "Really? But weren't they civilians? How did that happen?"

"The Germans . . . they came to our house one morning. We thought they had come to arrest us. I think they thought my father was part of the Resistance and there were plenty of stories of families being dragged off and never coming back. We knew the Americans were very close, so we were desperate not to be taken away. My father fought them. When he did, I ran and got away . . . but, both my parents died."

"I'm very sorry," Daniel said.

Juliette's eyes reddened, moist from the memory, but she gave Daniel a sweet, little smile. "Don't be. The Americans helped us, and— maybe you did not know this—they were all Japanese. This battle around my home was only a handful of men—could your father really have been one of those soldiers?"

Daniel reached into his back pocket and brought out his wallet. He found the small photo of Hiro and Ray and held it up. "This was my father," he said, pointing at Hiro.

Juliette took the photo and looked at it for what seemed to be a long time. Then, still holding it with the tips of her fingers, she studied Daniel's face.

"Which one did you say was your father?"

Daniel hesitated, then pointed to Hiro: "This one."

Juliette reached out and grabbed Daniel's forearm. Her grip was surprisingly strong. "You may not believe me, but I remember these men. Your father, he tried to save us. All by himself."

"He did?"

"Yes."

"And you saw this man as well?" He pointed to Ray.

Juliette pursed her lips. Then she raised and lowered her head once.

"What else do you remember about him? Please, tell me everything." Daniel's voice was pleading and it had an urgency in it, as if time were fleeting and would soon be lost.

"That man was here, too," Juliette said in a monotone. "But he ran away . . . to save . . . *himself*."

TWENTY-SIX

D aniel felt a hollowness grip his stomach, then the clench that followed made him feel a small stab of pain. The sky turned overcast; thin scudding clouds drifted low over the clearing and hung there like old, tattered rags. A front was coming in. All four felt the chill.

"Please," Juliette said. "You must all come inside."

Beth and Sophie entered the small cottage. Daniel followed them in a daze. They were in one large room with a sitting area to the left in front of a fireplace. There was a rectangular trestle table with chairs in the middle of the room, and a small kitchenette against the right wall.

"Make yourselves at home," Juliette said, gesturing to an antique, clawfoot sofa situated in front of the hearth where a small fire crackled. Beth and Daniel walked over—ancient pine floorboards creaked as they went—and sat down. Sophie took a seat in a corner rocking chair, beside a small table with a record player. Above this were three shelves jammed full of LPs.

Juliette switched on a nearby table lamp, then came to rest on a simple wooden stool next to the sofa.

"What do you mean that man ran away?" Daniel finally blurted out.

Juliette reached over and took the photo from Daniel's hand.

Pointing at the picture, she said, "That one ran away. He left this man, your father, to be captured by the Germans." She looked at Daniel with a featureless expression. He felt his stomach turning, then quieting, then turning. "You must be upset to hear this about your father's death and I am now sorry I was the one to bear such awful news, but so it was, so it is."

"Are you sure about what happened?"

"I will never forget this man's face as long as I live." She pointed at Ray. "He left your father and ran away when your father tried to save my family." She stared into the glowing embers of the fire. "My parents died that day, but I did not know your father died also. I thought he might have merely been taken prisoner."

"Did he say anything? The runaway man?"

"I did not know English. Therefore, I do not know." Her mouth twisted a little and she touched her lips with her right hand. "He was . . . afraid. That is all I seem to remember."

Daniel pressed her for a little more. "How old were you at that time?"

"I was ten. For the last fifty years, I have tried to forget what happened, but I still remember all of it. It was a cloudy day, and there was rain, and it was cold. There had been shooting in the town, and a lot of cannon fire. My little brother, Michael, and I wanted to run out and watch the town, but Papa would not let us leave the house." Juliette paused as rain began to patter on the roof. A gust of wind blew a flurry of leaves against the front windows. Juliette breathed deeply, and continued.

"When the Germans came into our house, I knew Papa wanted me to get away. He gave me a look that told me he was going to try something, and when he did, I knew I should run. The Germans were yelling. Mama was very frightened. And Michael was crying. They tried to arrest my father, but before they could get their hands on him, he punched one of them in the stomach. That is when I ran. I ran out the door and into the woods."

"Just you?"

"Yes, that is correct. They all stayed behind. I think Papa knew that only I had a chance to get out. Mama would never leave Michael, and Michael was too little to know anything. Papa must have thought they were taking us away for good, or to kill us. He hated the Germans. Other French people collaborated or looked the other way, but my father never hid his disgust. This made our lives very difficult. I think the Germans always suspected my father was part of the Resistance, and perhaps he was, I don't know." A single tear slid down Juliette's cheek. She wiped it away with the back of her hand. "When I reached the woods, I saw your father," she pointed at Hiro in the photo, "and, this other man. I admit I was quite shocked; I had never seen a Japanese before. I had heard about the Japanese fighting the Americans, but I did not know what one looked like. At first, I thought I was looking at, how do you say? A native American Indian. They looked strange wearing American uniforms, so I was very confused."

She paused and frowned. Daniel didn't dare speak or interrupt; he didn't want her to stop.

"Then I heard the gun. They shot my father."

Beth made a pained face. Sophie drew a short breath. Juliette's eyes were distant and Daniel thought it might be too difficult for her to go on. The flame flickered in the hearth, threatening to go out. Nobody moved.

"What happened next?" Daniel questioned. He pointed at Hiro and Ray in the photo, which Juliette was still holding and protecting. She finally spoke in a low voice.

"These soldiers talked to each other. I knew they were speaking English; it sounded strange. I didn't understand them, and I was probably hysterical because my father had just been murdered. I saw them go to the house."

"Both of them?"

"Yes. I watched them, praying that they would kill all the Germans. Your father tried to fight them. He tried to save my mama and brother. But not this other man. He just left."

"How?"

"He didn't fight. He ran back to the woods. I watched him run. He left his friend and I never saw him again."

Daniel closed his eyes and remembered the hilltop cemetery. He tried to imagine Hiro and Ray running across the open space. It was hard to erase the gravestones, and harder still to imagine a farmhouse where the gravestones now commanded so large a space.

So what Joe Fukuda said was true, Daniel thought. Ray left. Hiro died. End of story. No wonder his father hadn't wanted the government to investigate his medal. Because he hadn't earned it . . . worse, he'd lied and somehow grabbed credit for Hiro's heroism. If his false father hadn't been such a coward, his real father might still be alive today, and both of his parents would have been together for fifty years. His whole life would have been a different story altogether.

He was still reasoning in his head when the rain outside intensified, pounding the roof, the noise filling the cottage.

Juliette stood up. "I can see this is a lot to take in and all new to you. Let us take a moment and I will make some tea. I also have some photos of our old house on the hilltop that you might like to see."

Juliette walked across to the tiny kitchenette on the other side of the room.

Beth, getting up to help their host, asked, "Who took care of you and your brother after the war?"

"My aunt took us in. Her husband was a leather worker in the countryside. Times were very tough after the war."

"But you survived," Sophie added affirmingly.

Juliette smiled at her. "Yes, we did manage to survive." She began to prepare the tea set, which, like everything else, came from another time.

"Well, this is a beautiful place to have a home," Beth complimented. "It's so wonderfully peaceful here."

"I used to live in town with my husband," Juliette replied. "I never thought I'd live back here, even though my family has owned the land for generations, but when François died ten years ago, it just seemed right to return here. And it's fine, as long as I can still get around and have friends like Sophie to look in on me."

"Did you have children?" Daniel asked, as he came closer to where the women were.

"We had two: a boy and a girl. They both moved to Paris, and they want me to go live near them, but I won't. My friends are here, and I don't want to go to the big city. I only wish I could see my grandchildren more often; I have five of them."

"Five? That's wonderful!" Beth said.

"There are many family pictures on the mantelpiece. You can look at them if you'd like."

Beth admired the salt-glazed teacups and the silver tray the pretty cups adorned. "May I carry these out now?"

"Please do," Juliette said. "Just put the tray on the low table there and I'll bring the tea in a moment." She turned toward the stove and turned up the gas where she'd set a copper kettle of water to boil. "There are many families that wouldn't exist today if your soldiers had not helped us. My brother lives on a farm a few hours from here. His wife died last year, so he is alone, too. Maybe I will be able to introduce you to him if he comes to town before you leave."

Daniel watched Juliette as she picked up the kettle and removed it from the little two-burner stove. The way she moved her hands, purposefully, yet gracefully, was indicative of the way she was. There was a sureness about her and everything she did. Her pale fingers were slender and fine, and the way she used them was meticulous. Juliette brought the tea kettle into the living room and poured the water into the blue and grey floral teapot.

"Now, while we wait for the tea to steep," she said, "I want to show you some old photos."

Juliette went to the bookshelf with the records, and from the top shelf, she brought down a large, old, industrial-taped shoebox. She sat

next to Beth on the sofa and set the box on the table next to the teapot.
"My father loved to take photos. He took many of our town, and
of us as children, and . . ." Juliette uncovered the box, which was filled
to the brim with old black-and-whites, "our home."

She removed a stack and thumbed through a dozen before
pulling one out and handing it to Beth. Daniel and Sophie looked over
her shoulder. It was a farmhouse made of stone, one level, one
chimney, set in a large clearing.

"This is where the cemetery is today?" Daniel asked.

Juliette nodded. "The whole hillside is now covered. The
cemetery is even larger than our original plot because many more trees
were cleared around the edges. Here, I think I have some photos from
the day the town gathered to dedicate the cemetery."

She pulled out the remaining photos in one large stack and began
to look through them one by one, passing them slowly to Beth and
Sophie who studied each with interest. Daniel watched over Juliette's
shoulder. There were photos of windmills and horses, their family and
other gatherings of relatives. Daniel's eyes drifted to the open shoebox
on the table. There was a collection of letters at the bottom.

Daniel gasped, and almost fell over from shock. He gripped the
sofa hard enough to shake it, and the women, startled, looked up at
him.

It couldn't be.

"Daniel, what's wrong?" Beth said.

He walked around the sofa and knelt at the table, in front of the
box. Fingers trembling, he reached inside and took out the topmost
envelope.

He ran his fingers over the faded ink that spelled out Juliette's
name and address. There was no mistaking Ray's handwriting—
slanted and precise. It was postmarked July 1, 1946, Los Angeles,
California.

"Juliette," Daniel said, his voice quavering as he held up the
envelope, "What is this?"

Juliette wore a look of surprise, but then her expression changed. She took the envelope and held it carefully, with a look of solemnity, as if it were an heirloom. Beth and Sophie watched in rapt attention. "This, my dear, is one of many anonymous letters I have received throughout my life." She pointed to the box and Daniel looked—there were at least a dozen envelopes. He took them out and shuffled through them—all with Ray's handwriting.

"I really shouldn't call them letters. All I received were these empty envelopes, and I didn't keep them all, just these early ones. This will sound very strange, but for at least forty years, someone from America sent money to my bank account twice a year. The first time I got a check in the mail, but after that it was always straight to my bank; and later the money came by wire. At the beginning, I was just a child and my aunt handled things for me. There was never a return address, and it was just a bank check, so there was no name on it. Whenever the bank received a check by mail, they wrote me to tell me and included these empty envelopes for me to see them. Of course, I asked the bank to tell me who was sending the money, but they said there was no name, just a bank in California. I asked my bank to write the California bank to find out if it was a mistake. They wrote us back to say that it was no mistake, but that they were instructed to keep the source of the money anonymous."

Juliette paused to look at Beth and Daniel. Beth still wore a surprised expression, but Daniel did not.

He was still seeking missing information. Why had the old man done this? And how had he done it when the family was so tight with money at that time? There were many questions still to be answered.

"How much money was sent?" he asked. "If you don't mind saying."

"It was always the same amount. One hundred U.S. dollars, twice a year."

Two hundred in 1946 would be way more than a thousand today, Daniel thought. Why didn't I register how much money that really was when I discovered the box at home?

Juliette watched Daniel's eyes as he sifted through the information. Then she added, "The truth is that Michael and I badly needed money after the war. Times were difficult for many years. The money kept us clothed and fed and so much more. It seemed to me that it was a gift from God, and I eventually stopped worrying about where it was coming from . . . the only worry we had was that, someday, maybe, the United States government might ask us to pay it all back. But that dark, unhelpful thought eventually went away as well as the fear that inspired it. You can't imagine how crazy it was in France at that time. People were starving. Many were sick. Homeless. It was terrible. We were orphans, Michael and I, but we were the luckiest people on earth, and we knew it."

Daniel smiled, and said, "I don't think you need to worry about the government, or anyone else, coming after you, Juliette."

"How can you say that? Does this happen often in America? Do people send money to strangers?"

Daniel took one of the envelopes and passed it to Beth.

"Look carefully," he said.

Beth examined the writing, and a dawn of recognition crossed her face.

"Oh my God."

The handwriting—she'd seen it each year on James and Julia's birthday checks.

"You *know* something," Juliette declared.

Daniel's eyes met hers. "You're right, I do have something to say about this."

Steam emanating from the spout of the teapot on the table curled upward, but the tea service had been forgotten. All eyes were on Daniel.

"This is going to sound strange, but I know this money came from my dad."

The three women waited for further words. When they didn't

come quickly, Juliette said, "But you said your father was killed."

Daniel nodded. "Yes, my father was killed; it's complicated, but let me explain it to you . . ."

TWENTY-SEVEN

The entire population of Bruyères, or so it seemed, turned out for the celebration. The town square was bathed in sunlight, a crisp autumn day, not a cloud in the sky. Hundreds of people filled the square—aged veterans in thick wool uniforms, young parents chasing their children, tourists from afar wearing pastel fanny packs, reporters, cameramen, and others.

A temporary stage, adorned with red, white, and blue bunting, had been erected at one end of the square. Above it hung a banner that read, "55^{ieme} *Anniversaire de la Libération*." Below this were the names of the three towns the 442nd had liberated in the region: Belmont, Bruyères, and Biffontaine.

Beth and Daniel held hands, waded into the crowd, and headed for the last rows of chairs that weren't quite full yet.

"American?" a voice spoke, close by.

A middle-aged man with an old fashioned-twirled mustache tapped Beth on the shoulder. He sported a tattoo of an eagle on the side of his neck and had a tri-color ribbon over his brow and around the back of his head. That, and his weathered, black leather jacket gave him the look of a 70's motorcycle enthusiast. But then came his sweet-sounding, gentlemanly French accent.

"You are American? Yes?"

Beth turned and smiled politely. "*Oui*." The man nudged his pretty wife, who was wearing a necklace of red, white, and blue beads. "*Les Américains*," the man crowed and slapped Daniel on the back. He said it again more loudly, like he wanted everyone around him to hear . . . "*Américains bienvenue*," he exclaimed. Sure enough, heads turned and stared, but from their pleased looks Daniel saw that they were warm-hearted, friendly townspeople.

"Go there, go there," the happy Frenchman said, pointing. There was a table set up near the fountain. The space in front of it was clear, and there was a path through the crowd lined by red velvet ropes.

Beth thanked him, and they headed to the table. Behind it were two elderly women who rose as they approached. Both wore sweatshirts displaying crossed French and American flags.

The woman on the left, who bore a remarkable resemblance to Betty White, asked, "Are you American?"

"Yes," Daniel answered.

"Are you a family member of a 442 veteran?"

"Um, yes."

The white-haired woman on the right clapped her hands together in delight. "Welcome!" she said. "We are so glad you are here." She offered Daniel a clipboard. "Please write your names and the name of your family member." He wrote their names and then, hesitantly at first, printed "Ray Tokunaga."

"Please, wear these," the woman said. She gave Daniel and Beth a set of military-looking sashes. Daniel stooped so she could drape it over his head and onto his shoulder. "I hope you can join us for the festivities." She handed him a schedule. Among other things, there was a guided walking tour of the town, which would pass the monument to the 442nd, and *Rue du 442 ᵉᵐᵉ Régiment Américain d'Infanterie*, the street named in its honor. The residents of Belmont would host all veterans and their families for lunch. Afterwards—a hiking tour of Hill

B, where some of the heaviest fighting had happened.

"Now please, follow me," the celebration guide said.

They went down the central aisle, between rows of folding chairs. Daniel saw a television crew on a platform by the fountain, which was turned off. They approached the reserved area, and Beth and Daniel were shown to their seats. There were already at least forty people in this section, which was directly in front of the stage. Daniel counted at least fifteen Nisei veterans. His gaze lingered on some of the old Japanese men, their thinning hair and weather-beaten faces, and found that they reminded him of Ray. I can see Dad fitting right in with them, he mused.

A band of young musicians—probably a high school orchestra— began to play *The Star Spangled Banner*. Everyone rose for the anthem and The Stars and Stripes fluttered slowly up a flagpole off to the right. Next, *La Marseillaise*, and the French tricolor flapped away on the left. A group of French school kids emerged from behind the stage; they fanned out and flowed down the aisles, passing out little French and American flags.

A moment later there was complete silence. Then all heads turned to the four dignitaries who were seated on the stage. One of them, an elderly Frenchwoman, rose and walked to the podium. There were French and American flag pins on the shoulder of her blue blouse.

"*Bonjour, mes amis* and welcome friends from afar. I am, as some of you already know, Madame Therrien, mayor of Bruyères. I speak English in honor of our guests." She looked at their section and smiled warmly. "We are so glad that you have joined us on this wonderful anniversary. Thank you for traveling far to be here today. Fifty-five years ago, my family and I spent three days and nights in the cellar of our apartment building. That building was destroyed . . . and it was right over there," she pointed toward the southwestern corner of the square. "I was never more terrified in my life. I was a young nurse, and my parents grudgingly let me out whenever the shelling stopped so that I could help the wounded. We set up a hospital in the hotel, which was only two blocks from here. I remember the first American soldier I met. He was shorter than me, and very tan. He spoke English in a way that was hard to understand—but I learned that he was from the Hawaiian Islands. Everywhere I looked, I saw Japanese American soldiers. This was a shock, but you know, nothing was normal in those days. The Japanese were our enemies but our enemies were also our friends. And soon, all that mattered to me was the valiant, wounded men who came to our hospital.

"And the men were brave. Some with horrible wounds who, no doubt, knew they were going to die. I did what I could to help our doctors but it did not feel like much. My memories are snapshots now. Just flashes in my mind . . . a boy who asked me to write a letter to his parents but did not want to tell them that he had lost his right arm . . . a man who fought back tears when his friend died in the cot next to him . . . the long midnight hours I spent holding a soldier's hand as he mumbled in his sleep and kept trying to cover his head.

"After the shelling ended and we no longer needed to stay underground, I spent all of my time at the hospital, and I personally witnessed the cost of liberating our town, almost one thousand killed or wounded. This is a debt we can never repay. To those men who were there—" suddenly she looked down, removed her wire-rimmed glasses and quickly touched the tears from her eyes. ". . . We will never forget what you did here. Thank you from the bottoms of our hearts."

The crowd began to applaud and then, still clapping, everyone stood up. The mayor smiled, eyes glistening, and nodded solemnly to the veterans seated in Daniel's section.

—

"Are you really Ray Tokunaga's son?"

The ceremony was over and a distinguished Nisei veteran had stopped Daniel at the end of their row. He leaned on a cane and held a clipboard in his hand—the one Daniel had used to sign in at the welcome table. The old man looked at Daniel, then at Beth, and back to Daniel. His eyes seemed to dance with excitement.

"Yes, I am," Daniel replied, curious to know who this person was.

The straight-backed man offered his hand. "I'm Frank Masato. It's a real honor to meet you."

"The honor is mine, sir. How did you—"

Frank turned and called to two friends. "Ed! Charlie! Do you know who this is? Ray Tokunaga's boy!"

"What did you say?" said a hunchbacked man in the row behind them. A younger man led him by the arm closer to where they were standing.

"I said this is Ray Tokunaga's son, Ed!"

"Ray Tokunaga?" The man managed to stand up a little straighter. His wan face lit up. "Really? Could it be?"

"Is it really him?" asked another uniformed veteran who was sitting in a wheelchair and was wheeled forward by a young girl. "I'm Charlie," he said, offering his hand.

They did a round of handshaking. Daniel introduced Beth, and in a moment, they were surrounded by a dozen or more people—wives, sons, daughters, grandchildren.

"You all knew my dad?"

"Knew him?" Frank said, grinning. "Course we knew him. When I saw your name on the list I couldn't wait to talk to you."

"Where's your father?" Charlie asked. "We haven't seen him in over fifty years."

"Unfortunately, my dad passed away last year."

Charlie's face fell. All three of the old veterans looked crestfallen. For several seconds no one said anything.

"Real sorry to hear that, Daniel. Real sorry," Frank said softly.

For a minute they were a morose bunch: two dozen people watching three sad old warriors, working through their distant memories. The scene began to draw a few others. Then more. Daniel looked over at Beth; both of them were at a loss for words.

"What can you tell us about Ray?" Ed asked. "What did he do after the war?"

"Well, we lived in Los Angeles—"

"You did?" Frank and Ed exclaimed in unison. "Why didn't he ever contact us?" Frank said. "We both live there, too. The 442nd Association had an address for him but there was never any reply, and we assumed he must have moved away. It was like he just disappeared. We didn't know if he was alive or dead."

Daniel wasn't sure what to say. All eyes were on him, including Beth's.

"The thing about my dad . . . he didn't like talking about the war. He got married. Had two kids. Worked at the McDonnell Douglas plant for forty years."

"He was so close to us, all this time," Charlie mumbled, shaking his head. He looked up at Daniel. "I really wish we'd gotten to see him again." Charlie's eyes were red and moist. His granddaughter handed him a handkerchief and he dabbed his eyes. "But hey, we're glad you're here! What made you come to our reunion after all this time?"

"Me? Well, I guess I wanted to learn more about what my dad did in the war. After he died, I found out about these reunions, and here I am."

The larger crowd was beginning to disperse. Half the chairs were empty, and Daniel saw a lady waving a small American flag, beckoning to people interested in taking a tour of the town.

"You know," Frank said. "I named my first son after your dad. He's Ryoji Masato, but he goes by Ray, too."

"You did?" Daniel was shocked. "Why'd you do that?"

"Why? Well, because your dad saved my life." Frank looked at Ed and Charlie, who added, "He saved all our lives. And a lot of people in this town, too."

"He did?"

Frank's expression changed. He looked suspicious. "He didn't tell you?"

"No."

"You're definitely Ray Tokunaga's son?"

There was a lump in Daniel's throat. He said with conviction, "No mistake about that . . . he was my dad."

"You know about his medal?" Ed asked.

"Yes, I do. But I don't know why he got it."

Frank slapped his forehead, thunderstruck. "You don't know? How could you not know?"

Daniel shrugged. "I'm embarrassed that I don't. But if you'd tell me, I'd really appreciate it."

The three vets looked at each other again. Then Frank touched Daniel's shoulder and said, "Why don't you sit down? This might take a little while."

Daniel got a chair for Beth and one for himself, and the four made a small circle, leaving room for Charlie in the wheelchair, and Frank began his tale.

———

October 19, 1944

The sound of the cheerful brook reminded Ray of home, of the stream near Manoa Falls where he'd hike on Sunday afternoons. His friends and cousins always headed to Waikiki, to surf and score a few dimes from the *haole* tourists, but Ray liked to be alone. Sundays were his day off. He didn't mind working in the pineapple fields, even though the chalky red dirt got everywhere: under fingernails, in his ears, hair, and nostrils. He'd worked at the Dole Plantation every summer since he'd turned thirteen. The pay was fifteen dollars a week, and there was no prouder moment than the first time he'd handed his earnings over to his father, and the old man looked at him approvingly.

Would he ever see home again? It was half a world away.

He couldn't guess how long he sat there, next to the brook in the dark forest. Ten minutes or two hours? A terrible feeling in his gut, equal parts anguish and shame, sapped his strength, and it seemed to take all his energy to draw another breath. This must be a dream, he thought. He just wanted to wake up.

Voices jolted him from his trance. They were Americans, no doubt, and he even recognized them, but with his foggy brain he could not remember the names of the men they belonged to.

The voices drew closer.

He could simply stay silent. He could cover himself with mud and leaves and hide. If he hid long enough, perhaps the Army would take him for dead and he could run away to somewhere he could be someone else, where no one knew him or what he had done. He gasped for air. Why so hard to breathe?

How desperately he wished for another chance, or for something he could do to redeem himself. He'd give his life, right now, without hesitation, if it would somehow save Hiro. But what could he do? Hiro was gone. Ray had betrayed him, and it was too late. He couldn't turn back time.

The shame was unbearable, worse than death. He remembered his fear—his paralyzing fear—but it paled in comparison to the shame of what he'd done and what he'd failed to do. How could he live with himself? He didn't want to. If he couldn't make amends, he'd just shoot himself. It wasn't a hard decision. The samurai did it all the time.

But then, he remembered he had no weapon.

A low-lying mist slithered between the birch and hemlock beside the stream, pushed by a chill breeze. Ray waited. Then he saw them, ten yards away.

"Quit griping, keep moving," the lead man said, a Nisei soldier Ray recognized as Frank, from another squad in his company. He was short and stocky, built like a fireplug. His backpack looked too big on him, but his stockiness was his strength and he plowed along on his thick legs.

"Shh! Not so loud. That shot we heard, there's definitely Krauts on this hill," Charlie said. He was a taller man with a lean, wolfish face. No matter how much he ate, he always looked like he was starving. A long-limbed, barrel-chested lobo wolf.

The last man in line was Ed, known for running a craps game in barracks. Ray knew all three of them, not well, but he knew them and liked them well enough.

They followed the stream and walked straight toward him. It was too late to hide or run away.

"Hey, guys," Ray rasped.

The three men froze and pointed their rifles at Ray.

"Hold on," Ray said. Slowly, he stood up.

"Ray Tokunaga? Is that you?" Frank asked, lowering his weapon.

"Yeah, it's me."

The three men came up closer. "Where's the rest of your squad?" Ed said.

"We got separated. Hard to see anything."

"We heard a gunshot a while back. Are we up there or what?"

Ray said, "Yeah, I think so. I think Hiro went up there."

"Just him?"

"I'm not sure. Like I said, we got separated." Ray turned his head and looked uphill. "I was just going up there myself to find out. We should see what's happening."

Charlie looked annoyed. He was breathing heavily. "We've climbed all over this damn hill for two hours. Lost our lieutenant right away, haven't seen the sarge either. Might be going in circles. Let's take a rest, and maybe find someone who knows the way."

"I know the way," Ray said.

"Let's wait for the fog to lift," Charlie advised. "In this soup we're liable to shoot our own guys."

A loud roar split the air like a freight train zooming overhead. The ground shook. All four soldiers dropped to the ground.

There followed an eerie silence. Ray's ears continued to ring.

"Howitzer," he said, matter-of-factly. His voice sounded oddly far off to him. "They're shelling the town from the top of this hill, so we've got to go now."

Frank, Charlie, and Ed looked at each other uncertainly.

"We can't just sit here while they bomb our guys in town."

Ray held his breath, waiting for their response and hoping they might respect him for knowing the terrain better than they did.

Finally, Frank groaned and nodded and pointed a finger uphill without saying anything. Ray started to climb the slope. The three men followed.

It wasn't hard for Ray to retrace his steps—the same signs were there, the crooked stump, the occasional boot track.

"Hey Ray," Frank said. "Where's your M1?"

"Lost it," Ray said. He wondered if they believed him . . . no matter.

Ten minutes later, they were at the clearing.

To Ray's eyes, the site looked very different. A blanket of cloud hung low—a flat white ceiling barely higher than the roof of the house, but near the ground the air was clear, and the area seemed to be teeming with Germans. The back door of the house was wide open, hanging off broken hinges. Gray-white smoke leaked out of the chimney and melded with the low cloud bank. The truck was in the same place, and Ray saw Hiro—still alive! He was sitting in the truck with the mother and boy. A German infantryman paced the ground beside the truck, rifle slung over one shoulder, uniform a size too large. Cupping his hands close to his mouth, he breathed warm air into them.

An officer stood in the open. He gazed toward Bruyères with his binoculars, trying to penetrate the clouds and fog. Then he shouted a quick command to two men manning the cannon.

The howitzer stood in the backyard, halfway between the tree line and the house. Ray and the three other Nisei were hidden on a small rise where the beech trees grew. The huge gun pointed skyward. Two soldiers opened the breech, preparing to load a new shell.

The wind came up and a wreath of mist momentarily obscured them.

There were more Germans in the clearing: one leaned against the side of the house, smoking a cigarette, two pulled a wheeled cart to retrieve another shell, and two near a fenced enclosure off to Ray's right, at the eastern edge of the clearing. These soldiers amused themselves by throwing rocks at the milk cow inside.

Ray counted to himself—nine enemy soldiers. That made bad odds. This is suicide, he thought. He wanted to run away again, but he looked at Hiro and knew that if he did, his soul was as good as dead anyway. For him, there was only one choice.

Frank whispered, "Let's pull back."

Ray did that, and so did the others. Several yards back into the woods they huddled and conferred.

"I saw Hiro," Charlie said softly.

"Yes," Ray said, nodding.

"How'd he get himself captured?"

"And where are the rest of our guys?" Frank wondered.

"Doesn't matter," Ray said. "We've got to get Hiro before they take him away and torture or kill him."

A tremendous blast ripped the air and made all four men drop low.

They lay flat and covered their ears. More shelling. The ground rumbled and shivered; leaves showered down around them. Because of the fog, the Germans were shooting blind, but that didn't stop them from firing round after round. Bruyères was taking a terrible pounding.

"We're going to rescue Hiro," Ray said.

"How?" Ed asked. "They've got men, machine guns, and plenty of ammo. Not to mention the other truck . . . did you see the second one with the machine gun mounted and pointed this way? This is prime territory. They're gonna fight for it."

Ray tried a different tack. "Our orders are to seek out and destroy enemy artillery. Here we are, let's find a way to take it out."

No one said anything.

"We'll have surprise," Ray added. "That counts for a lot."

Frank coughed and quickly covered his mouth. "Wouldn't it be smarter to sit tight, or go find the rest of our guys? There must be at least twenty GIs roaming this hill, looking for this spot. Why not wait?"

Ray shook his head. "No telling how much time we have. They could drive Hiro out of here and then we'd never get him back." Ray remembered these men hardly knew Hiro. "And the longer we wait, the more time that cannon has to kill our guys in town, not to mention innocent civilians."

Ed and Charlie looked at Frank. "Not a good idea," Frank said.

"Damn you guys! I don't care what you think," Ray exclaimed. His voice was muffled, but his eyes were burning with rage.

"Now look here," Ed protested.

"No, *you* look here. I'm going in. I'm going to save my friend. You can back me up or you can leave. I don't care."

"Ray, you don't even have a weapon," Charlie said coolly. "You'll be going in there empty-handed and empty-headed, as far as I'm concerned."

"That's the best way," Ray said. "Can I borrow your bayonet?"

The other three men shared looks that said Ray was crazy. Still, Charlie unbuttoned the clasp that held his bayonet on his belt.

"You can't be serious—" Ed said. "Better think this over—"

"—I have." Ray wrapped his hand around the bayonet grip, testing its weight and feel. "If you guys want to back me up, I'd appreciate it."

Leaving them no chance to reply, Ray turned and moved, still crouching, along the left edge of the woods toward Hiro. He darted from tree to tree, eyes on the Germans in the clearing.

"Going to get himself killed," Ed whispered. "Us too."

"You're right," Frank said. "I'll go get him." Frank got up and ran in the direction Ray had taken. He ran low using the trees as cover, but when he got almost up to where Ray had stopped, he stumbled, made a grunting noise, and fell forward onto the mud-slick ground.

The two German soldiers smoking cigarettes out in the open looked up to see what had made the sound. Frank froze and flattened himself.

The nearest soldier walked toward the place where Frank was hiding. He was ten feet from Frank. Five feet. The German stepped over a fallen log and stared into the woods. Frank was close enough to touch his boot. The soldier scanned left, then right. A long moment passed, then the man seemed to relax. He put his rifle down, resting it against a tree. Next he unzipped his fly, lowered his pants, and began to piss in the dirt.

KA-BOOM!

The roar and bump of the howitzer caused the German to lose his balance. He did a sort of hop on one foot and his boot struck Frank's hip. Now the soldier totally lost his balance and went backwards. Frank froze. The soldier landed on his back. He looked at Frank and his eyes grew wide with comprehension. Pants down around his knees, he fumbled with his belt, going for a knife. Frank reached for his M-1, but the German was faster. He lunged at Frank, dagger aimed at Frank's chest.

A blur appeared on Frank's left. The shadowy form crashed into the German—Ray! Frank watched as Ray plunged his bayonet into the man's chest. Ray pulled it free and jammed it into the gagging man's neck. A rooster tail of red blood sprayed up and out, onto Ray's face.

The German kicked a few times and then lay still.

An angry, guttural cry from the clearing—the second German now saw what was happening and came forward, leveling his rifle at Ray.

This time Frank had the German in his sights. He fired. The German crumpled.

More firing began to hammer the clearing—Ed and Charlie—opening up on the other soldiers near the house and the howitzer.

One of the gunners dropped a heavy shell and fell over. The men by the cow pen ducked and ran for the house. Shots were being loosed in all directions. It was a moment of complete confusion. But the forest and the ground-hugging mist hid the Nisei snipers, and the Germans' shots flew wildly.

Ray ran along the tree line, toward Hiro. He pressed his back against the rough bark of an oak tree, only ten yards from the truck that held his friend. He wiped the sweat out of his eyes and peered around the tree. The guard was nowhere in sight. Hiro sat in the truck, watching the firefight. There were jagged slashes on his face. One eye was purpled, swollen shut. The mother and son were down low in the truck bed.

Hiro searched the nearby trees. His good eye fell upon Ray.

Hiro gave a weak smile.

Ray knew he had to be quick. Frank, Ed, and Charlie were making a terrific diversion. This was his only chance. He ran for the truck.

The truck was high off the ground. Ray stepped up on one of the rear tires and used both hands to pull himself up the truck's wood-slatted side.

The mother and boy were alive but unmoving. The corpse of the German Hiro had killed lay face down in a corner. Hiro's face was swollen, his lips cracked and bleeding. He held his right forearm, which was bent at a weird angle and obviously broken.

Their eyes met.

"Hiro!" Ray cried.

Hiro stared, his good eye opened wider.

"You came back," he rasped.

"Let me get you out of here," Ray said.

He reached down and tried to lift him, but Hiro groaned in pain when Ray pressed his side. Broken ribs? Ray tried again and this time managed to slide him toward the end of the truck. Hiro was heavy. Ray wanted to get him to the edge and take him in a fireman carry, but it was all he could do to inch him backward and try not to hurt him.

"Can you move at all?" Ray asked. He caught a glimpse of the boy, who clung to his mother.

Hiro tried to raise himself with his good arm.

"That's it. C'mon." Ray stood up a little straighter and gently put his arm around Hiro's back.

The mother screamed.

Ray looked at her, then felt someone punch him in the left shoulder. He dropped Hiro and spun around.

There was no one there.

The guard.

The German who had been watching over the truck was ten feet away, leveling his rifle at Ray for another shot. Ray dropped to the floor of the truck bed as the gun cracked. The shot rang against the side of the truck.

Ray vaulted off the end of the truck and rushed the soldier, who worked the bolt of his Mauser to chamber another round. Ray sidestepped and grabbed the barrel just as the man squeezed off a shot. The hot barrel seared his hands and he let go. The German stepped back and used the rifle butt to jab Ray hard in the face. Ray toppled backward, landing on his back.

His vision was blurred from the blow but he got to his feet in a hurry and drew Charlie's bayonet. He lunged forward. The blade struck the soldier in the chest and hit hard sternum. The stunned German made a guttering noise in his throat, but refused to go down. Ray slammed it home again and this time the bayonet struck a rib, then slipped into soft, spongy tissue where the blade sank deep.

Ray released his hold on the bayonet. For a moment, the two men stood near enough to touch. They wobbled. Then the heavy Mauser clattered to the stony ground. The man stared into Ray's eyes then dropped to his knees and fell to his side.

Ray breathed heavily. He felt pain, remembered his shoulder and reached in under his shirt. His hand came away wet.

I've been shot.

The wound made him lightheaded. He felt faint, but fought against it. His own M-1 was lying on the ground at the corner of the house where he'd dropped it. He ran to retrieve it. The ground next to the house was piled high with German weapons—a veritable arsenal of artillery shells, rifles, machine gun rounds, and even a half-dozen Panzerfaust anti-tank rockets. From this corner of the structure, Ray got a better view of the firefight. Two Germans fired from inside the house, one hid behind the howitzer, and there were more shots coming from the opposite side of the building—all together an impressive wall of fire directed at the south-side tree line. Ray couldn't see his friends; there was little shooting coming from the trees.

No one seemed to be watching the prisoners, so Ray turned back to the truck. Hiro was trying to drop off the back end and the woman was trying to help him.

Ray ran to them. As he neared his friend something caught his eye—it was at the mouth of the road that led down the hill.

And then he heard it.

An engine, rumbling, and a third, dark grey German army truck lumbered into view. It was identical to the other two, with an open truck bed and wood-slatted walls up the sides, but this one was loaded high in the rear with artillery shells. And then, yet another truck followed behind, this one carrying a half-dozen more soldiers.

Ray froze in his tracks. They were dead. It was over. If he ran for the woods he could get away. But he looked at Hiro and knew he couldn't do it. He spun around, searching for something . . . then, "Get down!" he shouted at Hiro and the woman.

Ray dropped his rifle and sprinted back toward the house. He grabbed a Panzerfaust and dropped to one knee. Aiming at the lead truck, he fired, startled by the rocket blast. The missile smashed into the back of the truck. A split-second later, the artillery shells detonated and the vehicle erupted in a giant orange fireball.

An instant flash of intense heat made Ray raise his arms to shield his face. He turned away. The ground shook; the air filled with shrapnel. Ray dove for cover behind the truck holding Hiro, putting it between him and the explosions that kept coming—incessant, deafening, concussive slams.

Thirty seconds later, when he opened his eyes, the smell of cordite hung thick. Ray spat the bitter, metal-tasting dirt out of his mouth and got to his feet. The blasted German truck was a mangled heap of twisted black metal, now blocking the road. The truck that had closely followed it was on fire, the windshield blown out, the driver's body unrecognizable, and the rear full of bodies. Some soldiers had been thrown clear; one was blown far up into a tree, where he hung like a limp, grey, sooty rag. Ray didn't see anyone moving. The air smelled of burnt rubber, incinerated metal, and flaming octane.

Ray climbed into the truck where Hiro was lying.

Hiro was face down, not moving. Ray turned him over. His friend's face was pale and contorted. He put his hand over Hiro's mouth and felt . . . nothing. He bent down, put his ear near the mouth. He waited. A small, thin breath. Hiro's chest rose and fell ever so slightly.

Ray now saw the mother—her body was cut up by shrapnel that had shredded the back of the truck. Her neck was almost completely severed.

Ray turned away from this nightmare. But then—

The body moved!

Ray shuddered. It wasn't possible.

The ruined body moved again, then turned. From underneath, a little hand poked out. The boy! Ray seized the tiny hand, and gently but forcefully brought the boy out from under his dead mother. He was unconscious, his arms and legs working as if in a dream.

A bullet whistled past Ray's ear. It hit the cab and ricocheted away. Ray twisted toward the house where he thought the shot had come from. A soldier standing in the doorway raised his rifle for a second shot.

Ray slipped over the side of the truck—putting the vehicle between him and the house. He got his M-1 off the ground and lay flat, under the truck, placing the rifle over his damaged left arm. The German was in view from the waist down. Ray took aim, fired. A spurt of blood at the soldier's thigh. The German hollered and dropped back into the house.

Ray unclipped a grenade, pulled the pin, and ran at the house, tossing it through the open door. The explosion racked and nearly raised the one-room building. A belch of thick, black smoke coiled out of the doorway.

Ray waited for the smoke to disperse. Then, peeking through the door, he quickly went in. The room was roiling with smoke and small incendiary fires. He coughed, squinted. The German he'd shot was dead, body contorted from the blast.

As the smoke began to clear, Ray saw the room more clearly. There was a large table, and to its right, a cast iron stove. Straight ahead, an open back door and a square window to the right of it. Underneath this window, another body. Ray saw from the insignia on the man's collar that he was an officer.

Ray stepped over the body and glanced out the window. The woods where his companions should be looked somehow deserted. Had they pulled back and left him? A few German soldiers were still firing steadily into the woods, but there seemed to be no return fire.

Then—movement? Yes, two men. Charlie and Ed. They were going to their right, toward the cow enclosure. One German was still behind the howitzer in the middle of the rear yard.

The sputtering sound of an engine outside the house, to Ray's left, on the east side. The final infantry truck was slowly grinding around the house.

Ray worked his rifle up on the shattered window sill. Using only his right arm, he aimed at the soldier who was at the howitzer. The gunsight trembled. He couldn't hold the M-1 steady, but it wasn't for lack of his hurt arm, it was his whole body that was shaking. A couple of deep breaths—he squeezed the trigger.

And missed! The German raised his head, peered around, confused.

Ray fired again. The bullet struck the howitzer next to the man, but the bullet whined away into the pine woods. Or did it? Now the soldier clutched his chest and leaned awkwardly, but he had no idea where the shots had come from.

Ray fired again. This time the bullet slammed the German square in the back, and the impact righted him for a moment. He stood straight, then drifted to the side and pitched, face forward, into the dirt.

Ray looked left. A new sound: the dreaded *ack-ack* of a truck-mounted machine gun. He couldn't see the vehicle, but the woods near Ed and Charlie erupted in a cloud of smoke and splintering pine.

Ray's left shoulder was worsening, his arm nearly paralyzed. He reached up to feel the exit wound, a divot in his shoulder. It wasn't bleeding, but he might have touched a nerve because a hot wire of pain shot down his arm. The pain began to increase as if on command. Ray leaned back against the wall. His head spun and the room narrowed, darkened into a tunnel. The machine gun paused for a moment. Then a fresh burst of deadly ack-ack beats.

Ray struggled to make his mind work. Come out of the darkness, he told it. Gradually, the light returned—like a puncture hole in the black that grew larger and larger.

His buddies were no match for a mounted machine gun. Ray willed himself to move, and very unsteadily, he staggered toward the front door, banging his hip against the corner of the large oak table as he did so. He lurched out the doorway and went along the front wall of the house.

The last truck had stopped no more than ten yards away. The gunner crouched behind the cab, pivoting the gun on a swivel, spraying the woods left and right. He was the very image of a German war-youth, blonde and lean with a uniform that was too big for him. The driver's side door opened, and another boy, no older than seventeen, climbed down and then up into the back of the truck. He fumbled with a rectangular can and dropped it. Coils of ammo belts spilled onto the floor of the truck bed.

Ray saw Charlie dart out of the woods and run for the stack of firewood next to the cow pen.

German bullets chased him—chewing at the fence rail. More bullets chomped across the cow's body, successive hammerings that tore into the animal's flesh. The cow dropped mechanically, one knee at a time, moaning low in its throat.

Charlie was almost safe when a bullet bit him in the right leg. He tumbled, got up, and somehow managed to fling himself behind the woodpile.

From the woods, Ed fired a shot at the truck. Then another. Both shots made a ringing noise against the steel-reinforced sides of the vehicle.

Ray hesitated at the corner of the house.

I have to get Hiro out of danger.

But that machine gun would keep Charlie pinned down. Ed too, for that matter. Ray was the odd-man out, the only one, at that moment, who was not in German gunsights.

Ray tightened his grip on his M-1 and stepped out from behind the house. He raised the rifle with his right hand, but with nothing to prop it on, he couldn't hold it steady enough to aim. The Germans still faced away from him, but then—

"*Achtung!*"

Ray locked eyes with the boy who was feeding a new belt of bullets into the machine gun. The gunner turned. Ray dropped back behind the corner of the house. A second later, the house's stone wall seemed to explode outward. Bullets pulverized stone. Ray hit the ground, scrabbled crab-like, dragging his useless arm through the open front door and into the safety of the house.

The building shook as it took more rounds of machine gun fire. Ray lay on the plank floor while plaster dust enveloped the room. His eyes burned, but he scanned the room for a weapon he could use with one hand, hoping for a German grenade, but there was nothing. The machine gun stopped. Far away in the pine woods a crow cawed. The dust settled.

Ray looked at his blood-soaked left arm. A wave of helplessness overtook him. He was exhausted. His mind drifted and flashed on the verdant Ko'olau Mountains that ran down Oahu's spine. He imagined a soft breeze coming in off the water at Hanauma Bay, and the fleeting beauty of cherry blossoms that graced the grounds of a Buddhist temple near his home. A bitter smile crossed his lips. He was thinking of these things now, as his life ebbed away, as blood filled the arm of his jacket, as the room swirled in a gyre of smoky plaster dust. He would never see the Ko'olau again. He would never again taste the salt wind of Hanauma Bay, or glimpse a cherry blossom drift gracefully to the ground. Worse—his parents might never know that he died on the pine plank floor of an insufferable one-room house in a distant country as the enemy pounded lead at him and ground the building he was in down to atoms of dust. In truth, he was afraid to die. To close his eyes on the end of all things he'd known. A cold calm now claimed the upper left half of his body. He stared at the dead German officer who looked quite peaceful. Merely asleep. Sleeping merely. Another, longer kind of sleep. Ray envied him. He wanted it over with.

The shooting outside was intermittent. Any second, the Germans would come inside to finish him off. Surely they were just outside the door.

His gaze fell to something in the officer's hand, something partly hidden under the body. It was black and metal. It was a Luger.

Ray dragged himself to the hand.

The pistol seemed to give him strength. He got to his knees and then wobbled to his feet. Out the window he saw Ed throw a grenade—a bullet caught him in the arm mid-throw and his grenade went flying off to the left. Ed dropped out of sight behind the woodpile.

Ray ran out the front door and wheeled right. He charged the truck. The loader turned. Ray fired on the run: two, three, four shots. The cab's rear windshield shattered, another hit the chassis, but two chuffed into the German's chest, and the boy folded.

The gunner turned. Ray slid to a stop at the foot of the truck. He leveled the pistol and pulled the trigger.

Nothing happened.

He pulled again, and again. Nothing.

The gunner realized Ray was seriously wounded and had only an empty gun. He jumped over the side of the truck and came at Ray full speed. They collided.

Ray jerked the helmet off the man's head and banged him across the nose. Twice the enemy soldier jabbed at Ray with a knife, and twice it struck home—piercing Ray's forearm. The world spun out of control. Ray felt like a ragdoll, and the young German was merely a grey blur that jabbed at him. Ray tried to get away, but now the point of the blade pierced his left shoulder, near the bullet wound. The German twisted the blade. Ray let out an agonizing cry and his right elbow shot up, almost involuntarily, and caught the man's chin so hard he let go of the knife and fell backward. He was out cold. Ray pulled the knife free and prepared to plunge it into his enemy's chest. But the German boy was still, eyes closed, a crumpled body lying in the dirt.

Ray lowered the knife.

It was over.

The clearing was quiet. There was only the sound of the wind, and high above in the leaden sky a flock of black ravens cawing a few times before disappearing into the trees. The smell of cordite and melted metal filled Ray's nostrils. He glimpsed the woodpile and opened his mouth to shout to Charlie and Ed, but then—there was movement out of the corner of his eye.

Through the haze of his narrowing eyesight, he saw another man. Then, oddly, a lot of men in dark green uniforms. What was happening? All along the tree line, men were coming into the clearing, but it took him more than a moment to realize they were *his* men. U.S. soldiers. Nisei.

Fresh rain drops began to fall from the sky. Ray heard Charlie talking to one of the soldiers. Shouts of recognition, word being passed from man to man. Ray staggered across the front yard to where Hiro lay in the truck bed. The little boy was there, crying. Hiro was doubled up in a fetal crouch.

Ray climbed up in the truck next to Hiro, whose one eye was half-open. It seemed to search the sky, and finally came to rest on Ray.

Ray shouted, "Medic!" The rain came down harder, drumming on the truck's metal.

Ray leaned close to his friend. "You're gonna be okay, Hiro. Our guys are here. Help is coming."

Hiro shook his head. His lips moved. Ray leaned closer. Hiro whispered, "No need . . . *kodomo no tameni.*"

Ray knew: *For the sake of the children.*

"Don't try to speak." Tears welled in Ray's eyes. "Hiro, I'm sorry. I'm so sorry."

Hiro smiled faintly. "*Shikata ga nai.*"

It can't be helped.

"Don't go!" He searched Hiro's face for a response. "Please, forgive me."

Hiro's eye closed.

Ray looked to the sky, and his tears mixed with the rain.

TWENTY-EIGHT

"I saw it all from the woods," Frank said. "He jumped that German who was about to kill me. I tried to follow him, but I got hit in the gut with a bullet. He fought hand to hand with the guard, and then—that huge truck explosion. I can still feel the heat . . ." Frank touched the side of his face. "That explosion is what killed Hiro; no one could have survived it, close as they were. Your dad went into the house and Ed and Charlie ran in, but they wouldn't have made it if he hadn't taken out that machine gun."

"He was nominated for the Medal of Honor," Charlie added. "And he should've gotten it, too. But they gave him the Distinguished Service Cross instead."

Frank looked away, like he was studying the rooflines around the square, but it was clear he was really holding back tears. A little girl wearing a bright blue skirt and beret skipped down the aisle, her toddler brother chasing her; she giggled and broke into a run. Not a care in the world.

"Were *all* of you wounded?" Daniel asked.

Ed nodded. "Charlie and me made quick recoveries. A couple days in the hospital, then back home. Frank and your Dad . . . well, they had it worse."

Frank said, "Your dad and I spent a few weeks in beds next to each other at the hospital. We both had surgery; I had two, to patch up my gut inside. Your dad's shoulder was hurt pretty bad. Was he able to use it later on?"

"There was a big scar, and he favored his right arm, but he could use it."

"And I guess it never worked out with Celeste, huh? They never got married, did they?"

"Excuse me?" Daniel said.

Frank looked confused. He made a face and scratched his head. "Maybe you don't know about that—"

"—About what?"

Frank stared at the pavement, lost in thought.

"Who's Celeste?" Daniel asked.

"I am," said a soft voice behind him.

Daniel turned. The mayor was standing in front of him. She had kind eyes, and when she touched Daniel's hand, he felt a warmth that traveled right to his heart.

"Allow me to introduce myself. I am Celeste Therrien. And you are Mr. Tokunaga, isn't that right?"

"Yes, Daniel Tokunaga, and this is my wife, Beth."

"How do you do?" Beth said. She and Celeste smiled and shook hands.

"I am fine, thank you for asking." Then Celeste looked at Daniel. It was a searching look. "And you are Ray Tokunaga's son?"

"That's right."

Daniel watched Celeste's eyes travel up and down his face. She made a humming sound, as if only partially satisfied. "My friend from the welcome table came to tell me. I didn't believe her until now. Your father, is he well?"

"He passed away last year."

"Oh." Celeste's hand flew to her lips. She closed her eyes and inhaled sharply. "So he's gone," she said, not quite believing.

"I'm sorry, can you please explain how you knew him?"

She drew a handkerchief out of her purse and dabbed at her eyes, though she wasn't crying. She took another long breath, sighed, then managed to smile. "Of course, but I think this will take some time. Perhaps you would like to join me at my home for lunch? It's not far, only two blocks away. There is so much I would like to ask you."

Beth and Daniel, equally baffled, agreed to go, and they bid farewell to Frank, Charlie, and Ed, promising to meet up again that afternoon to talk some more.

Then, Daniel and Beth followed the mayor of Bruyères to her house.

—

The home was a two-story row house squeezed between two larger buildings. The façades of the buildings on both sides of the street matched: grey sandstone blocks with large windows and green shutters. Cobblestones in the street were well worn and a little shiny from the previous day's rain. A man delivering packages doffed his cap to them and made a little bow to Celeste.

"Hello, Renaud," she said to him in a cheery voice.

Celeste opened her door—it wasn't locked—and said, "Please, come in. I will prepare sandwiches."

The inside was decorated in a contemporary style. There were snow white, stylish leather sofas. She had a fifty-inch projection television and a galley kitchen with stainless steel appliances and marble counters.

"Make yourselves at home," she said, motioning them to the sofa. "I know you have many questions. Let me bring some coffee first, and then we can talk."

Daniel scanned the family photos on a bookshelf. There was a black and white picture of Celeste as a young woman in a nurse's

265

uniform. He felt a catch in his throat. She was beautiful, and he lingered awhile, fascinated with her youthful face. Strangely, it seemed he had known her before . . . when she was young like this . . . but how could that be?

In another photograph he saw her with a sporty-looking, well-tanned young man. They were in bathing suits on a beach somewhere. Other snapshots showed their wedding, and one was a family portrait with two blonde-haired, blue-eyed boys. What could a woman like this have to do with his dad?

"We were married in 1950," Celeste said, seeing Daniel was studying the photos. "But my husband passed away two years ago."

"We're very sorry to hear that," Beth said.

Celeste brought three cups of coffee on a tray, along with sugar and cream. "Thank you. It's alright, really. He was . . ." she paused, remembering, ". . . a good man. He was a good father. I'm glad we were married." She said this in an odd way, and Daniel thought it strange that she would need to say such things out loud. And stranger still that when he looked at Celeste, he found her staring at him. There were tears in her eyes.

"I'm sorry," Daniel said, "the memory of your husband—we've upset you."

She went to her pocketbook and took out another handkerchief to dry her eyes. "No, no. Please. You do not understand. I must explain it."

Beth and Daniel sat down on the sofa. Celeste sat in a chair opposite them. Sunlight through the window cast a rectangle of light across the purple heartwood coffee table between them, and now Daniel saw that Celeste had placed a wooden box on the table.

"Let me begin this way. Please let me tell the whole story; I do not think I have ever told all of it to anyone, and I don't know if I can make it, but I will try." She took a deep breath and dabbed her eyes again. Then she straightened up and began her story.

"During the battle for our town, I was a nurse. One day, they brought in a soldier who had been shot and stabbed in the shoulder. I was assigned to take care of him and several other men, but in time, the other men either died or got better. This soldier stayed for many weeks. After a while, it wasn't his wound that kept him from leaving. You see, from the very beginning, he was so despondent that he would not eat, and he could not sleep. We did not know why; he would not tell us. He had terrible dreams and would scream in his sleep and even fight if I tried to wake him. The doctors worried that he might try to hurt himself, so we watched him around the clock. By then the war had passed us by and the town was quiet, so I had plenty of time to do this.

"He was given his own room, and I would sit with him for hours. Sometimes I would read. Sometimes I would just watch him. He had a kind and gentle face. Without his uniform, I could not picture him as a soldier. I was specially assigned to him because my English was very good. My parents had taken me to live in England for two years during grade school. The doctors thought that it might help him if he talked to someone, and they hoped he would talk to me. He was very polite and kind to me. He always thanked me for bringing him things and for sitting with him, but he remained a little remote. He seemed like such a tender soul. Yet so isolated. Not from me so much—from everything going on around him.

"After a few weeks, he was able to get out of bed and I used to push him around the hospital garden in a wheelchair. That was when we started to talk. I told him everything about myself—that I liked to read and had been a debate champion in our school, but that, with the war on, it seemed that nursing was the best thing to be doing. He told me about his home in Hawaii. It was hard to imagine the beauty of the places he described. He was like an exile from paradise.

"One day I walked in on him getting dressed. I was mortified, but then—he started laughing. I had never seen him laugh before, and it was like he was a different person. That day a big change took place. He started eating again. He became interested in me, asking me about my likes and dislikes. Asking what I wanted to do after the war. We confided in each other—at least I confided in him. I became very attached to him, and I dreaded the day when he would be transferred to a hospital in Paris or back to America.

"One day, I asked him how he had been wounded. I knew he had done something heroic, because a general arrived once to pin a medal on him and a reporter came to interview him. He would not tell me. He just told me that, for the first time in a long time, he was beginning to feel good again, and he said it was because of me. I could tell he had tried very hard to put the bad memories behind him, so I did not press further. But I did have one clue about what he'd done. The other nurses found out he'd saved a young boy and girl whose parents had been killed. They were living in the orphanage not far from the hospital, and when I asked him if he would like to visit these children he was very eager to do it. So we went, but when we arrived, we learned the children had already gone to live with their aunt and uncle in the countryside. I could tell he was very sad to hear this, and he asked for the names and address of the relatives. I thought he wanted to find them, but he never got the chance. Even though he never told me why, I was very touched by how he cared about those two little French children.

"And I must admit that I fell in love with him before he did with me. I was young, and very naïve, but we were kindred souls, and I knew that I had found the man I wanted to marry, and that he loved me, too.

"Our last week together was the happiest of my life. He was healing well and was able to walk a good distance on his own. We made plans. He would have to go back to the United States, of course. But Germany was losing the war, and soon it would all be over. He would come back for me as soon as he could. He didn't ask me to marry him, but in some ways, we talked as if we were already husband and wife. He said he was willing to live in France, but he told me that he would like me to see Hawaii before we made our decision.

"I didn't tell my parents about him. They thought I was a very dedicated nurse because of all the extra hours I spent at the hospital. I suppose I was a little worried they might not accept him because he was Japanese. For me, I never cared at all about race. After all, most of the American soldiers I'd seen were Japanese! Our love went beyond anything as confining as race. I knew he would be the love of my life—it was that simple.

"He went back to America, but I was happy, because I knew the sooner he left and finished his rehabilitation, the sooner he would be back. The war ended. I waited for his letter. Nothing came for a long time. I didn't worry, the mail was slow in those days. I knew he would come back for me. I would wait as long as it took."

Now Celeste opened the small wooden box and took out a thin folded aerogram. She carefully unfolded it. The thin, fragile paper was nearly translucent.

"The day I received this was the worst day of my life." She passed it to Daniel. He handled it carefully and began to read Ray's familiar slanted script. The letter was short.

Dear Celeste,

I am very sorry that I have not written to you before now. It has been difficult for me to write because I must tell you that my family circumstances have changed. I am very sorry, but I cannot return to France, and we cannot be together now. Please forgive me. I know you will have many questions and I am sorry that I cannot answer them. My reasons are very difficult and would be impossible to explain. Please just know that you're the only girl I've ever loved. I would not do this if I could find another way,

269

but I feel like I have no other choice. I will never forget you.

Always, Ray

"Your father sent it to me after the war was over. I never saw him again. I never understood why he did not come back. I wondered if he had met another woman, or if he had told his parents about me, and they didn't like that I was French. I was devastated. I became depressed. Emotionally, I was little better off than he was when he first came to our hospital. And I had no way of reaching him. Even if I had the money to go to America, where would I look?"

Celeste stopped to dry her eyes. Even now, Daniel noticed, in the way she spoke and in her movements, she was graceful, dignified.

"Eventually, I married. We had children, whom I love. But I will never forget your father. I have never forgotten." She sighed heavily. "That is my long, sad story about a very short time in my life. Now, God has seen fit to bring you here, today. Please tell me about yourselves, and what happened to your father after the war. I would like to understand, after all these years."

As Daniel listened to Celeste's story, he was troubled over this quixotic man that she loved, this mysterious man that he'd called Dad for fifty-four years. He didn't know the man she described, a person capable of great happiness and passionate love. Then it hit him—finally—the photo of the woman in Ray's shoebox. It was Celeste.

He really did love her.

And Daniel suddenly felt very sad that all through his life, his dad was never as happy as when he'd been in France with Celeste. He wished he could have made Ray happier, or that his mother could have; but perhaps, he realized, it had never been in their power to do so.

And the knowledge that Ray gave up true love to marry Keiko, and to be Daniel's father, floored Daniel. What a choice to have to make, he thought. He squeezed Beth's hand. She looked at him and understood completely.

"Madame Therrien—"

"Please, call me Celeste."

"Celeste, I would love to tell you about my dad. I'm very proud of him."

TWENTY-NINE

LOS ANGELES, CALIFORNIA
December 1999

The 5 was a parking lot. Daniel watched the layer of low-hanging smog and brown hills surrounding the valley and remembered what he most disliked about southern California. He loved the green, seasons, snow, streams, and rivers of the northeast. When California would get a heat advisory or drought, he used to think that God did not intend for people to inhabit this desert. His mother once told him that the Owens Valley, where Manzanar was located, used to be lush and green, filled with apple and pear orchards. "Manzanar" was Spanish for "apple orchard." But then the L.A. aqueduct was built between 1908 and 1913, to siphon all the water down to L.A. so the population could grow, and the land around Manzanar became desert.

Daniel had been back in California for two days to visit his mother. He told her that he'd learned in France that Ray was a hero, a true hero. He did not mention Celeste, but he told her all about Frank, Ed and Charlie. They all planned to get together later in the week.

272

I miss my dad, Daniel thought as the traffic inched along. How he wished he had known these things about him before he died. He wished Ray had gotten to see Celeste again, and that he and Keiko had learned to love each other more than they had.

When Daniel thought of how close he'd been to never learning the truth, he shuddered. How many families have secrets that never get told? His dad and his father were both heroes. He knew that now.

He wondered if he could ever sacrifice what they had, for the sake of their country, their honor, and most of all, their friendship. He suddenly wanted to have a long talk with James. He wanted to tell him about his grandfather, his real one and the one he might have known but barely had. He wanted their examples to encourage him to live a life of honor, duty, and sacrifice.

I won't say it, but I hope he finds true love as well, Daniel thought. He realized how rare this was, to find and fall in love with a woman so deeply that there was no question in your mind that you must share the rest of your life with her or else you will be incomplete.

Crawling along on the highway, Daniel looked to the east, to the San Gabriel Mountains. There was snow up on the caps, enticing and beautiful. The last time he'd gone into the mountains was on a Boy Scout camping trip. Ray had taken him; Daniel was about nine. Ray was very military about the whole excursion. Other fathers looked at him funny when he insisted they take care to pitch their tents on the high ground, and when he said, "We'll take point," he meant he'd hike up front and lead the group to the next destination.

Daniel remembered fishing at a little stream with all the other kids. It was crowded, and Ray said, "Let's get out of here. We'll find a better place." They were supposed to stay together as a group, but Ray and Daniel slipped away and hiked a ways into the thin forest and up into the hills above the campground. They came to a much wider stream, a river, really. Daniel thought this would satisfy his dad, and they could get down to fishing, but then Ray pointed and Daniel saw a small island in the middle of the river. "Let's go," Ray said. "It'll be our island for the day." And his dad's face *had* lit up at that moment, with child-like delight. The water was deep and moving faster than Daniel anticipated. He couldn't touch bottom, so Ray brought him up on his back, piggy-back, and waded out toward the island. The water reached Ray's chest, but he didn't turn back. Daniel was frightened, and wanted to turn around. Ray said, "Sometimes, Danny, you have to do the hard thing. To know your worth." He was always saying things like that, axioms about building strength or character or perseverance. And now Daniel knew why.

They spent all afternoon on that little island, fishing and napping and watching the clouds float by. Daniel loved it.

When Daniel arrived at his mother's house, he found a note on the kitchen table in Beth's handwriting. It said: "I am dropping your mom off at church. Be back soon." Next to the note was a thick manila folder with a yellow post-it note stuck on it. The message was also from Beth: "Your mom found this in your dad's desk drawer."

Daniel opened the folder. There were over a dozen newspaper clippings, faded and crisp from age. It took a few seconds for Daniel to realize they were articles he had written for the high school newspaper. He'd written feature articles on the civil rights movement, the Cuban Missile Crisis, JFK's assassination, and the escalating war in Vietnam. The folder also held Daniel's high school graduation program and a certificate he'd won for placing first in the Los Angeles County science fair. Beneath these, Daniel found programs from his graduations at Columbia and Harvard Medical School, and he realized his mother must have given Ray these. There were articles announcing Daniel's appointment on the staff of the hospital at Penn, and another one announcing his appointment to chairman of his department. Beneath these there were photos of Julia and James growing up, from infancy to high school. Some were taken by Daniel's mom, others were ones Beth had sent with their Christmas card each year.

As Daniel perused his dad's archive of his life, he felt a deep sense of regret. *Was it my fault for keeping us apart all those years? Was it me who robbed both him and my children of a relationship they could have shared?* And Daniel realized, it was.

"Daniel, what's wrong, honey?"

He looked up from the table and saw Beth standing in front of him. He realized his eyes were wet and wiped them with his sleeve.

Beth came closer, knelt down and hugged him.

"I thought you might like to see everything in here. It's amazing. He kept everything about you."

Daniel nodded.

"Beth?"

"Yes, dear."

"Am I a good man?"

"Of course you are. Why would you think anything else?" She gave him a hug, after which they looked into each other's eyes without saying anything. A moment or two passed in silence and then Daniel said, "Was I wrong to keep my dad out of our life?"

"You're asking me? Don't you know what I'm going to say?"

He shook his head. "I get confused sometimes. I have these memories about the past . . . about Dad and me."

"Of course you're a good man, Daniel. You've dedicated your life to saving lives; you're a wonderful father, and a good husband, thoughtful and reasonable. But—the thing with your father—it's complicated. What he did to you, what you did to him, what happened to him in the war, it's a big ball of yarn. All I can say is that it must've been hard on both of you. Don't forget, you have secrets too, Daniel. Your father wasn't the only one. Maybe you learned it from him. I realized a long time ago there were just going to be things you would never tell me. And it took me a while, but I learned to ignore those things."

"That must have been very hard for you."

"Yes, it was."

"I'm sorry, baby. I know I haven't been good about expressing my feelings, and I know this is why we grew apart. Now I see, in a lot of ways, I'm not all that different from my dad—I shut out you and the kids. James and Julia could've easily resented me for not being around when they needed me. You helped me change and gave me a second chance. But with my dad . . . I'll never get a second chance. I just wish I could go back and do it differently."

Beth sat down in the chair across the table from him. "You *can* do it differently. Start right now. Just start by being a person who's not carrying a burden. Now that we know where that burden came from, why don't you put it down and leave it there?"

Daniel's gaze drifted to the clippings and photos spread across the kitchen table. Then his eyes met Beth's, and in them saw her love—tender, constant, and forgiving. He hugged his wife and closed his eyes and saw the green island shimmering in the summer sunlight. He saw his father as he always wanted him to be: free as a cloud, a bee, a butterfly. Free as an island in the sun. Free as a father and child with nothing but love for one another. Free as a man who had never gone to war, never left the woman he loved for the woman he had to marry to make things right.

Daniel saw himself on that island now. He was with Beth.

THIRTY

"Are you nervous?"

Beth was driving. They had one more day in LA and were stopping by Keiko's house to pick her up on the way to meet Julia and her boyfriend Allen at LAX. It was Stanford's winter break. Keiko had insisted on being present for the momentous introduction to this boy who had apparently captured her granddaughter's heart. Tonight they were all having dinner with Allen's parents, who had flown to LA to meet them.

"Nervous?" Daniel said. "Why should I be? Because of your driving?"

Beth laughed. "I know you. You're probably thinking about when she was a little girl and used to run at you for a big hug whenever you walked through the door, or when you used to give her baths, or the first time we got her to ride that bike . . ."

"All right, all right," Daniel said, smiling. "Guilty. And I'm not embarrassed."

"All we're doing is meeting Allen's parents. It's not like they're getting married."

"Yet."

Daniel had had some reservations when Julia started dating. This was her first real boyfriend. But they'd met Allen when he and Julia had flown home for Thanksgiving, and Daniel had to admit, he did seem like a nice kid. Beth liked him right away. Still, it would take Daniel more time to become used to the whole idea.

"I mean, isn't this all happening a little fast? His parents are flying all the way out here just to meet us—where did they say they were from?"

"Illinois."

"Right. Are they from Chicago?"

"No." Beth rolled her eyes. "Don't you pay attention? They're from somewhere in the middle of Illinois."

"Like . . .?"

"Okay, I don't remember exactly, but I know it's not Chicago." They both cracked up. "Why?" Beth giggled. "Are you holding that against them?"

"Me? No. To be honest, I think it's a positive. If Allen grew up in the middle of nowhere, he was probably one of the only Asian kids there. That can be tough, and yet, it looks like he turned out to be a great kid, mature and well-adjusted. If anything, it's a point in his favor."

"I've met some very nice people from the Midwest."

"Right. By the way, are *you* nervous?"

Beth tucked her hair behind her ear, and Daniel smiled at her classic tell.

"Only because I don't want to make a bad impression. They're Korean, right?"

"Yes."

"Well, I suppose after marrying into *your* family I should be ready for anything. I'll just smile and nod a lot."

"You got a gift for them? For sure they'll have something for us," Daniel said.

"Of course. This is our daughter's happiness we're talking about."

"And you're sure it's a good idea to bring my mom?"

"Why not? She's great with people. Plus, there's no way she'd let this pass without being there."

"That's true."

Daniel was glad to see his mom doing well in the year after Ray had passed; she had a lot of friends and remained remarkably fit for her age. But, Daniel had to admit, at seventy-three, no one could know how many years might be left.

Beth seemed to read his mind, because she said, "You know, at some point we should think about where she's going to live when she needs extra care."

Daniel had wondered the same thing more than once. But rather than admit it, he said, "Well, what do *you* think?"

"Why don't we invite her to come live with us? When the time comes. It'll be a lot better than a nursing home. We can't put her in a home."

"Really? You'd be okay with her living with us?"

"We have the space and I know we'd enjoy having her around. It's what you do for family. Or haven't you learned that yet?"

Daniel stared out the windshield. He thought of their long talk the day before, in which he'd told her how he'd loved Anne Mikado and planned to marry her. About how he'd blamed his father for his brother's death in Vietnam. Beth had listened patiently. And when he'd finished, Daniel was surprised to find that instead of being angry, or resentful, or sad, she was happy. Happy to finally know her husband had no more secrets. Daniel marveled at Beth's ability to forgive. He had truly married a remarkable woman.

"Yes, dear," he said. "I've learned that. Thank you. Thanks for being willing to do this for my mom."

It struck Daniel how great an impact his children's choice of a spouse would have on *his* life. In twenty years, I'll be the old, decrepit geezer in need of being taken care of, he thought. If Beth thinks Allen is a good kid, probably he is. I should go easy on him.

"Has your mom decided whether to move your dad yet?" Beth asked.

"I don't know."

"To be offered a spot at Arlington National Cemetery, that's a real honor."

"I know. It's because of his Distinguished Service Cross. But I was thinking, if they're willing to bury him in Arlington, I'd bet they'd let us move him to the Punchbowl, too."

"The National Cemetery in Hawaii? Isn't that for soldiers who died in the Pacific?"

"Mostly. But it's where Dad's from. I think that's where he'd like to be."

"Then you should ask."

The car crested a rise, and for a few seconds they could see the Pacific Ocean far to the west. It was a beautiful day with a clear, blue sky. Since it was a Sunday, the traffic was light, and they were almost at Keiko's exit.

"James will sure be happy to have an extra excuse to visit Hawaii on a regular basis," Beth said.

"You're right about that."

"Are you disappointed that he isn't coming home for Christmas?"

"James? Sure. He just told you he's visiting this new girl's family?"

"She lives in New Hampshire. She's studying English, and she sounds very nice."

"I hope they aren't too serious already. He needs to study for his MCATs. He doesn't need distractions."

"Now you sound like your father. Is that what I was to you? A distraction?"

"Oh, yes, a very nice distraction." Daniel grinned as Beth elbowed him.

"It's good for him to have someone to rely on," Beth said. "It'll help get him through medical school."

Daniel stared at his wife's profile. Her flaxen hair glowed in the light. She's as beautiful as she's ever been, he thought. No one on Earth knows me or understands me better.

A short time later they pulled up to Keiko's house and saw her standing on the porch. When she saw their car, she ran across the yard toward them.

Daniel jumped out of the car.

"Mom, what's wrong?"

There were tears in her eyes. She held a large yellow envelope in her hands.

"What's the matter?"

"Danny, oh Danny, look! Look!"

He took the envelope and removed the papers inside. The letterhead said "United States Department of Defense."

Dear Mrs. Ryoji Tokunaga,

It was with great sadness that we learned of your husband's recent passing. He was a great American and patriot. Our nation owes him a debt that can never be repaid.

As you know, our department has conducted an extensive review of servicemen who were originally recommended for the Medal of Honor but who were awarded a lesser decoration. Our review was initiated out of concern that racial bias may have influenced decision-making at the time.

Our review of your husband's service record is complete. Our commission has voted unanimously to upgrade your husband's Distinguished Service Cross to the Medal of Honor. You will henceforth receive all honors and rewards commensurate with this great honor.

In addition, we would be honored if you or a family member would be present to accept your husband's Medal of Honor at a ceremony at the White House on June 21, 2000. On that date, the President will award twenty Medals of Honor to former members of the 442nd Regimental Combat Team. For your reference, a list of the other recipients is enclosed with this mailing. We thank you for your husband's service to our country. His actions reflected the best traditions of our armed forces.

Respectfully,
William Cohen
Secretary of Defense

Daniel handed the letter to Beth and folded his mother into his arms. Her body felt small and frail, but she was trembling with excitement.

"Oh Danny, isn't it wonderful?"

"Yes, Mom. It truly is."

"And look what else . . ." She showed him the paper listing the twenty honorees. The names were listed, as well as next of kin. Daniel saw that only six of the twenty recipients were still alive.

"Look, here." She pointed. Daniel read: "Hiro Fukuda. For actions near Bruyères, France, October 17, 1944. Posthumous. Next of kin: Joseph Fukuda."

"Hiro won it, too."

"Yes, he did, Mom. Yes, he did."

And for the first time in Daniel's life, he felt at peace. No stress. No anger. No secrets. Everything was as it should be.

As he held his mother his thoughts drifted back to Ray, and all he had done for him, for his mother, and for his father. It was too late for Daniel to atone for all he'd done, all he'd failed to do.

But somehow he was certain that Ray, more than anyone, would have understood.

HISTORICAL NOTES

In 1996, Congress directed the Secretary of the Army to review the records of Asian Americans who had won the Distinguished Service Cross during World War II, but who may have been denied the Medal of Honor due to racial discrimination. A team of researchers spent two years reviewing these cases and determined that the heroic acts of twenty-two soldiers merited the Medal of Honor. Twenty of the honorees had fought with the 442nd Regimental Combat Team.

Prior to this, only one member of the 442nd had won the Medal of Honor: Private Sadao Munemori, who was honored posthumously in 1945, for single-handedly destroying two enemy machine gun nests and smothering a grenade blast with his own body to save two nearby comrades.

On June 21, 2000, in a ceremony at the White House, President William Jefferson Clinton awarded the Medal of Honor to seven Asian Americans, six of them 442nd veterans. The additional fifteen Medals of Honor were awarded posthumously. In honoring these heroes, President Clinton said, "As sons set off to war, so many mothers and fathers told them, live if you can, die if you must, but fight always with honor, and never, ever bring shame upon your family or your country.

Rarely has a nation been so well-served by a people it so ill-treated."

442nd Regimental Combat Team

The 442nd was a segregated U.S. Army unit comprised of Japanese American Nisei that fought with uncommon valor in Italy, France, and Germany. The unit was preceded by the all-Nisei 100th Infantry Battalion, formed from 1,400 volunteers of the Hawaii National Guard. The soldiers of the 100th were sent to train at Camp Shelby, Mississippi, and first saw combat in Italy in September 1943. They were later folded into the 442nd Regimental Combat Team, which was initially comprised of 3,000 more volunteers from Hawaii and 800 from the mainland internment camps.

The 442nd sailed for Italy on May 1, 1944. Throughout the summer of 1944, they distinguished themselves in fierce fighting at Belvedere, Castellina, and around the Arno River. In September, the 442nd was transferred to France, and in October, fought ferociously in the Vosges Mountains, close to the German border. They liberated Bruyères, Biffontaine, and Belmont. In their most famous engagement, they rescued the Texans of the "Lost Battalion," which had been cut off behind enemy lines. Over four days, the 442nd suffered 800 casualties in brutal fighting to rescue 211 surviving Texan soldiers. In the spring of 1945, the 442nd again fought with distinction in northern Italy where their offensives finally helped to break the German Gothic line near the end of the war.

The 14,000 men who ultimately served in the 442nd were awarded 9,486 Purple Hearts. The regiment won an unprecedented seven Presidential Unit Citations. Its members won 21 Medals of Honor, 52 Distinguished Service Crosses, 560 Silver Stars, and 4,000 Bronze Stars. Per capita, the 442nd is recognized as the most decorated unit in U.S. military history.

Legacy of the 442nd and Hawaii Statehood

In July 1946, during a ceremony to present the 442nd with yet another Presidential Unit Citation, President Harry Truman said, "You fought not only the enemy, but you fought prejudice—and you have won." The 442nd's impressive wartime record helped to calm anti-Japanese American sentiment at home and helped to ease restrictions in the mainland internment camps. In the late 1950s, opponents of Hawaii statehood feared admission of a state whose population was majority non-white, but the 442nd's exemplary record and display of Asian American loyalty diminished such opposition in Congress. Statehood was ultimately approved in 1959.

Some veterans of the 442nd went on to distinguished political service, including Senator Spark Matsunaga, and Senator Daniel Inouye, recipient of the Congressional Medal of Honor and second longest-serving member in the history of the U.S. Senate.

Manzanar and the Internment of Japanese Americans

On February 19, 1942, President Franklin D. Roosevelt signed Executive Order 9066, authorizing regional military commanders to designate "military areas" as exclusion zones from which "any or all persons may be excluded." This order enabled Lieutenant General John L. DeWitt, Commander of the Western Defense Command, to forcibly relocate approximately 110,000 persons of Japanese ancestry from the west coast (California, Oregon, Washington, and Arizona) to ten isolated inland camps. The ten camps were:

Manzanar, California
Tule Lake, California
Poston, Arizona
Gila River, Arizona
Granada, Colorado

Heart Mountain, Wyoming
Minidoka, Idaho
Topaz, Utah
Rohwer, Arkansas
Jerome, Arkansas

In many cases, evacuees were given less than a week's notice to relocate, forcing many to leave their property behind or sell to predatory secondhand merchants at rock-bottom prices. Before relocation to the camps, most evacuees spent several weeks or months held in temporary staging facilities—usually set up at horse racing tracks or fairgrounds.

In 1976, President Gerald Ford stated that internment was "wrong," and a "national mistake" which "shall never again be repeated." President Ronald Reagan signed the Civil Liberties Act of 1988, which allocated $20,000 in reparations to each surviving detainee. Approximately 82,000 individuals qualified for redress payments, and about $1.6 billion was ultimately disbursed.

At no point during World War II was there even one act of sabotage or espionage committed by a Japanese American person.

ACKNOWLEDGMENTS

I owe deep thanks to several friends and colleagues who generously gave of their time and talent to help me bring *Repentance* to completion. Special thanks go to Katherine Lu Hsu, for helping me envision the central characters and plot the course of the novel, and to Gerald Hausman, master writer, editor, and friend who has a gift for making any writing even better.

Thank you to Mink Choi, Fletcher & Company literary agent, who believed in this book, took it on, and provided tremendous encouragement through the strength of her conviction that this was an important and timely tale to tell.

For selflessly sharing their advice and expertise, I am indebted to: Scott Kim, Chris Min Park, Alice Tasman, Dan Engelman, Elbert Kuo, Alex Lin, Irene Rideout, James McIlwain, Susumu Ito, and Wilfred & Esther Lam.

Thank you to the fabulous team at Tiny Fox Press, including editor Galen Surlak-Ramsey, for believing so strongly in this novel; Jen Henderson, for sharing her design talents; Jenn Wallace, an incredibly talented editor; Mary Beth Surlak-Ramsey, for meticulous copy editing; Joshua Cohen, for his support of the project; and Kristyn Shannon, for helping to bring *Repentance* to readers all over the world.

And my deepest thanks go to my wife, Christina, to whom this book is dedicated, for being my counselor and partner, always.

ABOUT THE AUTHOR

Andrew Lam, M.D., was born in Philadelphia and raised in central Illinois. He graduated *summa cum laude* in history from Yale University and subsequently went to medical school at the University of Pennsylvania, followed by specialty training to become a retinal surgeon. He currently practices with New England Retina Consultants, P.C., in western Massachusetts, and is an Assistant Professor of Ophthalmology at the University of Massachusetts Medical School.

Repentance is Dr. Lam's third book. His previous, award-winning works include: *Saving Sight* and *Two Sons of China*. His writing has appeared in *The New York Times* and *The Washington Post*. He resides with his wife and four children in Longmeadow, Massachusetts. Learn more at www.AndrewLamMD.com.

ABOUT THE PUBLISHER

Tiny Fox Press LLC
5020 Kingsley Road
North Port, FL 34287

www.tinyfoxpress.com

CPSIA information can be obtained
at www.ICGtesting.com
Printed in the USA
FFHW021824020319
50664540-56095FF

9 781946 501127